THE ADVENTURERS

BRYCE OAKLEY

Edited by Amanda Laufhutte

CHAPTER ONE

JOEY

"Wait, are you calling off the wedding?" Joey stared at Raina, horrified.

Raina rolled her eyes. "Please don't be dramatic," she said, sighing.

"An engagement kind of translates to the promise of a wedding," Joey said, her throat tightening with emotion. She hated it when that happened. It made her squeaky, and no one took a squeaking person seriously.

"That's not what I said. I just don't want to talk about it anymore. There's no wedding yet." Raina's grip tightened on the steering wheel.

They were parked outside of their favorite pizza place, about to have dinner with friends.

Joey took a breath, trying to calm her racing heart. "Then, what *are* you saying?" She asked, trying to speak slowly and in a non-squeaky, even tone.

"I'm saying that the wedding is already kind of over-whelming," Raina said, exhaling slowly. "We've only been engaged for a month. I need you to slow down."

It was true that Joey had approached wedding planning, much like she did all things in life, with about as much grace and subtlety as a stampeding crowd on Black Friday. She was just *so* excited to be able to finally be getting married.

They had been dating for two years, and she was ready to move into their next phase of life — marriage. So, she had started nearly the moment the ring had gone on her finger. Well, the proverbial ring. Raina hadn't picked it out yet. Sure, it had only officially been a month into their engagement, but her Pinterest boards had been quietly filling up for years.

"Let's just pump the brakes," Raina said, reaching across the center console to squeeze Joey's hand.

Translation: This is going to be a very long engagement.

Joey felt as though something inside of her had deflated like Raina had taken a pin to the balloon of excitement, and the air had come out not with a pop but a sad, slow whooshing sound. Still, she wanted to marry Raina, and if approaching the subject with a bit of care was what her fiancée needed, then that's what she would do.

She nodded, swallowing her pride. "Alright. We can take it a little slower." Like the past two years?

"Let's try to get through dinner without mentioning it at all," Raina said, pushing her carefully coiffed hair off of her forehead in the rearview mirror. She was always so put-together. She was tall, athletic, and gorgeous, with dark hair, sun-kissed skin, and swagger. Joey always felt like she had to step up her game in order to look like she belonged beside her.

"Uh, sure," Joey said, furrowing her brow as she opened the car door. They were about to have a meal with friends they hadn't seen since the engagement announcement — was Raina really expecting none of them to talk about the wedding at all?

"Just pizza," Joey added.

She let Raina lead the way to the door and as they each

opened a door to walk in, loud, screams of "Surprise!" stopped Joey in her tracks.

Fuck, Raina hated surprises.

Her eyes adjusted to the lighting to see that the pizza parlor was packed with all of their friends and families. A large banner that read, "Happy Engagement!" was strung up across the large room.

She laughed, still startled, but excited to see all of her loved ones. Her dad was holding a bouquet of flowers and her mom was wiping at the corners of her eyes.

She reached for Raina's hand, ready to walk in and celebrate, but Raina stuffed her hands in her pockets.

"I can't do this," Raina said, and Joey turned to see that her face was ghostly white.

Joey stepped closer to Raina, the only woman in the room that mattered to her at that moment. "It's okay, I know it isn't ideal timing, but let's remember why we're doing this. Look at everyone we love here to celebrate *our* love," Joey said, reaching again for Raina.

Raina blinked, then narrowed her eyes. "I mean it, J. I can't do this."

"Uh, *this*? Like the party?" Joey asked, and she could feel the blood draining from her face.

"No, I mean this." She gestured widely. "The party. The engagement. Us. I can't. It's not going to work." She turned on her heel and walked back out of the front doors.

Joey felt frozen in place, watching Raina storm out of the building and get into her car.

"What's going on?" Sunny, Joey's sister, asked, stepping beside her. She had Joey's nephew, Elliott, on her hip. "What's wrong? Is Raina in one of her moods? Your friend thought this would be a fun surprise."

"Raina go bye-bye?" Elliott asked.

"Uh," Joey said, unable to form words. She looked back at

the pizza parlor full of her friends and family, then to Raina, who was getting in the car. "Which friend?"

Sunny pointed at Nikki, one of the friends they had come to meet, as she ran outside in a blur of purple hair. She waved her arms at Raina as she began to back out of the parking spot at an alarming speed. Raina stopped and Nikki hopped in the passenger seat.

What the fuck just happened?

Joey held up her arms in a *What's going on?* gesture towards the two of them, and Nikki gave her a wave and a *Call You Later* gesture.

Would Nikki be able to smooth it over? She had always been a close friend, but Raina looked pissed as she sped out of the parking lot.

Shouldn't she be the one running out and getting in the car? On a shallow level, she wanted to. But on a deeper level she dared not investigate just yet, she felt... relieved.

"What's going on?" Joey's parents asked, approaching her.

"She left?" Joey asked more than said, staring at the open front door in confusion.

"Left? Like to go get something?" Joey's dad asked.

"No, I don't think she's coming back," Joey said. And as she said the words, she knew what they meant.

Raina was gone, along with all of her dreams of their life together.

———

Joey loaded the last of the boxes into the back of her sensible station wagon. Beside her, her trusty pup Ozzy sniffed at the boxes he could reach, his ears back.

"Don't worry, you're coming with me," Joey said, reaching to scratch Ozzy behind the ears.

It had been one month since Raina had stormed out of their engagement party and approximately twenty-nine-and-a-half days since they had spoken. Not that she was counting. She was done – done with putting up with someone else's timeline.

Had she spent the last month wallowing and crying and generally feeling as though her world was ending? Of course.

Even Nikki hadn't been able to convince Raina to give Joey a chance. Raina had put her walls up immediately — she didn't answer Joey's calls, she didn't respond to emails or texts, and she didn't answer the door when Joey showed up at her apartment.

That was the worst part. The lack of closure. It made Joey feel like maybe if she just gave Raina some space, she'd come around.

Nikki had brought Joey's belongings over to her house for her and had picked up Raina's things at Joey's.

The blessing in disguise was that they hadn't even moved in together officially — Raina had always preferred to have her own separate space. She had said it was healthy to maintain their own places.

How had Sunny put it? Joey had "traipsed through the fields of red flags as though they were flowers lining her path for two years."

It wasn't until the friendly cashier at the tortilleria near her house questioned why she wasn't getting any food for her girlfriend that she realized what she needed.

And more than needed, what she wanted.

Space. For herself, not just for Raina.

A fresh start. A new life. A life where people didn't grimace or flinch when they saw her. A life where The Worst Pizza Party Ever wasn't a title. A life where she wasn't an ex. A life that did not hinge on her relationship to anyone else, be it ex-fiancee, sister, or daughter.

Her family, of course, had been overly kind about the entire breakup ordeal. They had cooked her meals, let her sleep on the couch, and gave her time to generally mourn the loss of the life she thought she knew.

But they had panicked the moment she had floated the idea of moving away — an idea so absurd to her close-knit family that she hadn't even left town to go to college, but had instead gone to the state school just five blocks from home. She'd studied abroad for six months in France and they'd video chatted with her for hours every weekend.

Her mother was concerned that she wouldn't be okay on her own — how would she be able to find the nearest grocery store?

It was as though moving one hour — one hour! Sixty miles! — south was an estrangement.

She had always thought she might move to Denver, but the actual concrete decision came to her a tad hastily, even she could admit.

Still, her job was remote, and she could translate hair dye instructions into French from any surface on which she could set her laptop.

"Is that it?" Sunny asked, holding a throw pillow in her arms. Her parents had opted to pretend the move wasn't happening. She came from a long legacy of very mature humans who were very good at dealing with their feelings.

Joey studied her sister's face, the frown at the edge of her mouth. She looked so much like Joey in some ways — freckles, hazel eyes, but she had curly dark hair instead of the golden brown that the rest of the Moores shared.

"That's it," Joey said, looking at her car, packed to the brim. And that wasn't even including any furniture — she had opted to just sell most of it rather than try to imagine it in her new place. She didn't want to look at the table they shared or think about what they had done together on the couch.

She'd have to spend a small fortune at IKEA to replace her things, but she'd be fine.

She'd be *fine*.

A fresh start.

Where the delivery drivers didn't tell her to say hello to Raina for them.

"It's only an hour away," Joey said.

"Feels like too far already," Sunny said, her brow furrowing as though she might burst into tears.

"It'll all be alright," Joey said, pulling Sunny into her arms. "Isn't it your duty as an older sibling to reassure *me*?"

"Yeah, whatever," Sunny said, squeezing Joey so hard she thought her ribs might pop. "You're sure you don't need help unloading? Aren't there a lot of stairs to your new place?"

"No, it's fine. I know you have Elliott," Joey said.

Sunny was a single mom to Joey's favorite little kid in the world, and Joey didn't want to put pressure on her to find a babysitter. Or worse, bring a toddler to help move in.

"Okay, okay," Joey said, pushing Sunny away. "I'll call when I get there. In one hour. Because it's only an hour away. And not like, in Australia or something." She was anxious to get settled before nightfall. Evenings were the worst without Raina. She could distract herself during the day, but when everything slowed down and she just sat, thinking about her...

"Take good care of my nephew," Sunny said, interrupting her sour mood as she scratched Ozzy behind the ears as he licked her arm.

"Nah, he's on his own," Joey teased, opening the door for Ozzy to jump in the passenger seat. "You take good care of *my* nephew."

Sunny saluted her with a wink. "Yes ma'am. But only because you demanded so kindly."

Joey swallowed the lump of emotion forming in her throat. She wouldn't cry in front of Sunny.

"It's only an hour!" She repeated, jumping in her car and waving out the window.

Three hours later, she was all moved into her new place. It

was a third-floor studio walkup in an old house and it was just as gorgeous as she remembered when she'd toured it. Smaller than she remembered, but she could deal with something small if it had stunning crown molding accents, right? Right.

She stood in her living room, staring at her boxes.

"Yeah, she definitely would have hated that millwork around the windows," she said to Ozzy. "But I like it even more for that very reason."

Ozzy tilted his head to the side in question. He was a fuzzy little mutt, some mix of Australian Shepherd, Spaniel, Retriever... mashup. When people asked her what breed he was, she shrugged. She had rescued him two years before from a friend who had fostered him, and he had quickly become her dog. Raina had never even mentioned who would keep Oz. It was just understood.

And thank God for that.

She took a swig of her beer, sitting down on the floor next to a cardboard box that she had designated as a table. Ozzy moved to the windowsill, watching squirrels out the open window. The late spring breeze made the long hair on his ears wave with elegance, and she laughed, watching concerned wrinkles appear on his forehead, feeling lighter than she had in years.

She opened her phone, scrolling through her texts. She had sent a "Made it!" text to the family group chat with Sunny and her parents when she had pulled up to the new apartment, but that wasn't the text she was looking for.

She opened the thread, knowing she shouldn't.

She scrolled up. Raina hadn't answered a single text in the last month, but that hadn't stopped Joey from sending them.

Joey: Are you okay?
Joey: Can we talk? Where are you?
Joey: Can you open your door?

She paused, finishing her beer. She contemplated getting another — beer was the only thing in her fridge so far.

She scrolled down, past the denial texts and into the angry texts, then into the begging texts.

Finally, the texts she had sent that morning.

Joey: I'm moving today if you want to say bye to Ozzy.

Okay, so that had been a little manipulative — even she was self-aware enough to realize that.

Joey: Just moving to Denver, not super far.
Joey: Looks like I'll be heading out around noon, so come by before then if you are going to.
Joey: But no pressure, I'm sure you're busy.

She scowled at the texts. One month before, Raina had wanted to marry her, and now she couldn't even be bothered to say goodbye? Not even to Ozzy?

Ozzy nudged her face under Joey's arm, slurping her cheek.

She wrapped an arm around him, pulling him close.

"Just you and me, buddy. That's all we need, huh?" She said, trying her hardest not to cry into the soft fur of his neck, but he didn't seem to mind. He stayed still, resting his head on her shoulder, and let her hold him for as long as she needed.

CHAPTER TWO

KENDALL

"He barked funny," the woman said, her eyes wide with panic. She was a small woman with bleached blonde hair and a startling amount of eyeliner and mascara.

Kendall kneeled on the floor in front of Brutus, a tiny, fluffy pomeranian. She blinked at the explanation, trying not to reveal her true thoughts with her expression. She nodded, checking Brutus' gum color.

"Can you describe what was strange about it?" Kendall asked, examining his teeth while she had his mouth open.

"It was just... funny. It was weird. Usually it's like," the woman began, then let out a sharp bark that startled Kendall.

Even Brutus jumped at the sound.

"Mmhmm," Kendall said. "And today?" She knew the woman would bark again. She'd have bet money on it.

"And then today, it was more like," the woman added, barking just slightly lower.

How she wished she could communicate telepathically with Brutus to apologize to him for getting such a strange owner.

With twenty years of experience in her field, she had seen it all. This woman hadn't been the first barking owner and wouldn't be the last.

Sure, owners like this lady were weird, but they loved their pets. Kendall had seen enough bad in the world to make her recognize the good owners, even when it didn't match her own particular brand of normal.

"Interesting," Kendall said, putting in the eartips of her stethoscope. She checked lung function on both sides, then the heart. Everything sounded normal. She wrapped the device back around her neck, checking the dog's eyes and ears.

"Is he on a heartworm preventative?" Kendall asked, sizing up his kidneys and liver.

The woman nodded.

"Any other difference in demeanor? Eating, drinking, bowel movements, all okay?" She asked as she manipulated Brutus' legs to check his reflexes. Without much to go on, all she could do was a regular wellness check.

Dogs were funny creatures — crybabies about certain things, of course, but stoic about most pain. She had to take the owner's word that something was wrong. Kendall enjoyed that part of it — like solving a riddle. Although she had sincere doubts about Brutus having an illness, she was always grateful for the opportunity to check over a pup to ensure they were in good health otherwise.

"Well, his poop yesterday was a little runny," the owner conceded.

"Okay, is he still eating and drinking normally?" Kendall repeated.

The woman nodded. "So, what do you think is wrong with him?" Brutus jumped back into his owner's lap.

"Everything sounds good. Lungs, heart... as far as I can tell, he's perfectly healthy," she said. "For the loose bowel movements..." She turned, opening a cabinet of samples she had. She pulled out a few packs of dog probiotic powder. "Try these with his food for a few days and see if that helps."

"Monitor his eating and drinking, and if he stops drinking water, give us a call and we'll do some blood work," Kendall said. "I don't think you have to worry about that yet, though. I think he's going to be just fine." Because nothing was wrong with him.

The woman nodded.

"Do you have any more questions?" Kendall asked, leaning against the counter. Her stomach rumbled. She tried to casually glance at the clock, seeing it was already 3 p.m.

"If it's not too much trouble, could I get his... uh," the woman motioned towards the dog's back end.

"Does he need his anal glands expressed?" Kendall asked. She never knew why people were so afraid of using technical terms, even when they sounded gross. It was biology, not something disgusting.

The woman grimaced, but nodded.

"No problem," Kendall said, reaching in her pocket to offer Brutus a treat as a reward for behaving so well.

"And his nails trimmed," the woman added.

"Of course. I'll send in a tech," Kendall said, reaching out to shake the woman's hand. "Please let us know if Brutus isn't feeling better in a few days. Gotta get that barker back to normal, buddy." She scratched Brutus' chin and walked out of the room.

She paused by Taylor's desk in the back. "Glands and nails in two, pretty please," she said, picking up the paperwork that the tech had on their desk.

"Anal nails, got it," Taylor said, typing a few notes into the laptop in front of them. Their thick eyebrows furrowed as they concentrated.

Kendall raised an eyebrow. "Ah, Anal Nails, my favorite Swedish death metal band," she joked. She opened the fridge, grabbing out a container of yogurt for lunch.

Taylor laughed, standing to wash their hands. She always forgot how tall Taylor was until they were standing beside her, towering over her own 5'8" frame. "I heard they're coming to town next month to tour their new album, what was that called again?" They asked, soft-balling Kendall a joke.

Kendall popped the plastic top off of her yogurt container. "You mean *My Sad, Epistaxis Lifestyle*?" Epistaxis was one of her favorite weirdly intense medical terms. It just meant nose bleed, but what a metal way to describe one.

"You nerd." Taylor laughed, shaking their head as they walked out of the room.

A long sigh came from the other side of the back room. "You're eating in the lab again, Dr. O'Hara?"

Kendall turned, seeing the other vet of the clinic was sitting at a bench in the corner, writing notes in condolences cards for the week's euthanasia patients. Dr. Rothlisberger was an older man with gray hair who never smiled and never told dogs and cats and bunnies that they were the cutest thing he'd ever seen. That was just Veterinary Bedside Manner 101, in her opinion. In fact, he never even wrote a note in the cards. He just signed his name and made the receptionist write the rest.

"You're sighing in the lab again, Paul?" She said lightly. She never rose to the occasion with Dr. Rothlisberger, mainly because she liked her clinic and wanted to stay there. As the head vet, it was technically his decision. She dug around in her desk drawer for a spoon. She only had a few moments before her next patient to scarf down the yogurt.

"Do you really think it's appropriate to joke like that with the techs?" He asked.

She raised an eyebrow, but didn't answer... She hated very few things in life, but the top of the list would be men telling her how to act. The next one down was Dr. Rothlisberger's attitude. Those two things in combination were not going to work out very well for her sanity's sake. She stuffed a large bite of yogurt in her mouth to avoid saying anything that would make her lose her job.

Dr. Rothlisberger owned the clinic, but she was the name on all of the thank you cards. Her name was mentioned more on social media. She'd built up such a reputation at the practice that she was often questioned why she didn't just strike out on her own and open her own clinic. But that had never been her dream. That was way too far outside of her comfort zone. Way, way too far. When Dr. Rothlisberger retired in a few years, it was her hope that he'd let her take over the clinic as her own — that way she could avoid all of the hassle of starting a private practice and could simply inherit it. Win-win-win. She just had to hold her tongue for a few more years.

"We need you on call tonight," he said, turning back to his cards.

"Is everything okay?" She asked. Typically he did the on-call shifts Thursday through Monday, so she only had Monday evening through Thursday morning.

He frowned. "I don't know, is it?" He sighed, turning back to his work.

Okay, weirdo.

Kendall glanced at the clock. It was only late afternoon, but she had been there since 7 a.m. and she was exhausted. It was a patient-facing day, not a surgery day — surgeries were her favorite — so she'd been running around like a chicken with its head cut off since the moment she had stepped in the door.

Taylor walked back into the room with a clipboard that they handed to Kendall. "Patient in exam room three is ready. It's a tortie. Lotta drool. Lotta hissing. She ate a bee, apparently," they said.

Some days were just like that. Weird barks and bee-eating

days. Other days could get much worse, so she was happy with the small wins for now.

"Thanks for the heads up," Kendall said, scooping one last bite of yogurt into her mouth before popping it back in the fridge. Maybe she'd get a few more bites after. "Okay, brief me," she said, washing her hands in the sink and giving Taylor an expectant look.

Kendall unlocked her front door. Neither of her two cats, Bacon and Eggs, came to greet her. Typical. Jerks. They'd pretend to appreciate her existence as soon as she grabbed the cat food.

She walked through the living room and into the kitchen, setting her bags down on the floor. It took every ounce of her self-control to resist the urge to lie down across her countertop. She grabbed her cell phone, making sure it was on ring in case she was called in.

Emergencies were rare, but she was prepared, regardless.

She desperately wanted a glass of wine, but couldn't justify it, just in case she was called in.

She crossed the room to the fridge to grab the cat's canned food.

That's when she noticed that she was standing in a puddle of water.

"What the," she murmured, flipping on the light.

The entire kitchen was flooded in an inch or two of water. She rushed to pick up her bags, tossing them onto the dining table nearby. She checked under the sink and around the dishwasher, but it appeared that the water was coming from the laundry area towards her back door.

When she went to investigate, she saw that the washing machine was leaking water with the intensity of a spurting artery.

She grabbed her phone and searched for nearby emergency plumbers, calling the first one on the list. She explained the water and unplugged the washing machine and turned off the water as the man on the other end of the line instructed, then scheduled for them to come as soon as possible that night.

Her phone rang as she was throwing every towel she owned onto the ground to try to mop up some of the water and save her floors.

"Hi Kendall, we have a dog hit by a car coming in as soon as possible," Jenny, the evening receptionist said. "Possible amputation."

Kendall sighed. "No problem," she said. "I can be there in thirty. What techs are on tonight?"

"Taylor and Kat," Jenny answered.

Thank God. She knew she worked well with Taylor, and Kat was good at people — which would be important for the dog's owners. The other techs weren't terrible, but Taylor was the person she most trusted when things got dicey on the operating table and Kat was the person she trusted when the news was bad.

She glanced back to the washing machine.

It was only in moments of weakness like these that she wished she had a roommate or, worse, a partner.

Instead, she only had one reliable person who she knew could help on such short notice. She dialed her best friend's number from memory.

"Hey, whatcha up to?" She asked, taking off her wet shoes and socks to change into fresh ones.

"Just doing a bit of work," Imogen said.

Kendall could hear a metallic grinding noise in the background. She envisioned her best friend's woodworking shop and the sweet smell of sawdust.

"Finishing a new piece," Imogen added.

"That's great," Kendall said, feeling the guilt of asking for a favor almost immediately.

"Alright, out with it. Tell me what you need," Imogen said, and Kendall guessed she had recognized her tone almost immediately.

"Well, have I told you lately that you're the most beautiful woman in the world?" Kendall asked, walking into her bedroom to flip on the light. Her two cats lay snuggled on the bed in a cozy pile of white and orange fluff, blinking in the light as if to make her feel like she had disturbed them.

"Feel free to tell me that as often as possible, and then coach my wife on telling me more, too," Imogen joked.

She explained the situation and thankfully, Imogen agreed to be over soon — she had a key, and given that she lived less than ten minutes away, it wasn't too much of a hassle for her. Kendall still felt guilty, though, knowing that she was taking Imogen away from her work. She grabbed one of her nicer bottles of wine off of the shelf in her dining room and set it on the table as a thank you. Even if Imogen was pregnant, it would age well until she could drink again.

As she was hanging up, her phone rang again. She recognized the clinic's number again.

"Hey, I'm on my way," she said, annoyed that they were calling her again. It had been less than ten minutes, and it took her five minutes to get there.

"Sorry Kendall, I just wanted to give you a heads up that Dr. Rothlisberger wants you to bring home a pair of bottle babies," Jenny said. "I didn't want you to be surprised once you got here."

Bottle babies were, as the name suggested, young kittens that needed to be hand-fed every few hours. No offense to the babies, but they were the last thing she needed.

"Why can't one of the techs take them?" Kendall asked, finding a non-wet pair of clogs to wear.

"Taylor's roommate is allergic to cats and Kat is going out of town tomorrow, so," Jenny said.

Kendall sighed. "Convenient. But, alright," she conceded. "Any other surprises I should know before I leave my house?"

It was 1 a.m. when she walked back in her front door with a box containing two tiny, squeaking gray tabby kittens. They had been brought in after their mother had been killed. It wasn't their fault that they were a pain in the ass to keep alive and take care of. Their eyes weren't even open, so they were less than a week old.

Kendall knew that their chances of survival were slim, and although she was frustrated that the techs couldn't take them, she knew that the kittens were going to get their best chance with her.

The plumber had called earlier to let her know that a creature had chewed through the washing machine hose and that she'd need a replacement, but he didn't have any with him, and it would be a few days until he'd be able to order one in.

She found a book and a note on the table. She set the kittens down, and Eggs sauntered into the room with his orange ears perked up, poking his little pink nose around curiously for the source of the squeaks.

Loved this and thought you might like it, too! Love, Gen

She flipped the book over in her hands. "Tipping velvet, hmm?" She said to no one in particular, or perhaps the cats. "Wonder what the hell that means."

The kittens made squeaking noises and she rummaged through her bag to find the bottles and formula she had brought home. They were young enough that they'd have to be fed every two hours, which meant she was in for a very long night, on top of her already long night.

Better get started, then.

CHAPTER THREE

JOEY

Joey sat at the laundromat, scowling down at Instagram on her phone. Her friends back home were hanging out for a birthday and hadn't bothered to invite her. She didn't even like the bar they were at — it was definitely an undergrad bro hangout. Still, she would have very much liked the option of saying no.

"No thanks, I've got a big date," would have felt very good to say, even if the date in question was a laundromat.

A laundromat on a Saturday night. What a cool, happening place to be. She had only shown up that night because her mom had dropped laundry detergent and other Costco bulk goods by earlier that day, and then Joey couldn't get laundry out of her head.

She sighed and set her phone down in her lap, glancing around.

The place was entirely empty, save for herself and one other woman who was wearing scrubs and sitting across the aisle staring intently into her bag.

...Was she talking *to* her bag?

Uhh, super weird.

A vibration made her look back at her phone. It was her pet cam, alerting her that Ozzy was barking. She opened the app, watching him run around the living room like a wild animal with... was that her favorite bra in his mouth?

She pressed the talk button and forcefully said, "Ozzy, leave it." She watched as he paused, glancing towards the camera. He dropped the bra and walked over, waiting for a treat to be dispensed.

She grinned, tossing him a treat.

Ah, technology. Bless it.

Then, he turned and ran right back to the bra, shaking his head and the bra, as though he wanted to snap its bra-y neck. Or maybe just the underwire. Either way, not great.

"Ozzy, put the bra down. Ozzy!" She scolded. "That's my good bra, Oz."

Ozzy conveniently did not hear her over his bra-shaking escapades.

A woman in scrubs sitting across the aisle laughed, then covered her mouth.

"Oh, I'm so sorry," Joey said, turning the sound off. "Just incredible how dogs know exactly what you're saying until they choose not to," Joey said, shaking her head.

The woman laughed. "Ain't that the truth," she said, then glanced back down to her bag.

Joey noticed the woman had a book in her lap. She glanced at the cover and nearly gasped when she saw that it was a Sarah Waters novel.

Ah, a queer woman! Finding another queer woman in a new city was like accidentally crossing paths with a unicorn. But maybe she was just reading it for... the, uh... dialogue? Or maybe she picked it up on accident, not knowing what it was.

She looked the woman over more closely, seeing her short nails — but, she was also wearing scrubs, so that could be chalked up to her job. Her chin-length hair was just messy enough to pass for edgy instead of soccer mom, but she might just have had a very good stylist.

She was beautiful in an interesting way with high cheek-bones and a wide mouth. Joey would have bet money on the fact that she was the type of woman who was just casually gorgeous, like she just threw on her clothes and then reacted with a surprised but attractive laugh when you told her she looked wonderful.

Joey's gaydar was swinging back and forth between *Ehhhh* and *I Think Maybe Yes*!

Her scrubs didn't have any kind of indication of what doctor's office or hospital she worked at. Nurse? Doctor? She looked smart and capable. Maybe mid-forties?

Joey would be remiss not to take into account that the woman had been talking to her bag, though. So, queer novel or not, Joey thought she might want to keep her guard up.

The woman's light blue eyes flicked upwards as she looked at Joey, blinking. "Everything okay?"

Joey straightened, knowing that her more femme attire meant that she was basically invisible as a queer lady. "Yeah, sorry, just love that book," she said. Ah ha, the classic flag — mention something gay right off the bat.

The woman turned the book in her hands as though she had forgotten what she was reading. "Oh, yeah? I just started it. It's a little hard to get into, you know?" She said.

"Yeah, how many pages of oyster shucking do we *need*? We *get* it, it's a metaphor," Joey joked, rolling her eyes in exasperation.

The woman laughed. "Yeah, that's a little on the nose," she said. "Have you read anything else by her?"

Was the woman asking her if she was queer, too?

Joey nodded. "All of it."

Translation: I am super gay.

"My friend recommended it to me," the woman said.

Joey's gaydar twirled in a confused circle.

Joey tried to stifle a laugh. "It might be a little awkward knowing that your friend read it," she said.

"Oh? Why?" The woman asked.

"Just... uh, just wait. It gets..." Joey cleared her throat. "Descriptive."

The woman frowned in contemplation. "Yeah, that would make sense," she said. "She's one of those really *supportive* friends, you know?"

Joey's gaydar gave her a tentative high-five.

The woman looked slightly surprised, looking back down into her bag. Her bag... made a noise. Her bag *squeaked*?

"Oh no, what have you done?" The woman said, reaching into her bag and shuffling something around. "That doesn't look good."

Joey leaned forward, suddenly more curious than skeptical. What the hell was in that thing? And why was she referring to her bag as a baby?

"Hey, I... sorry. I've got a..." She gestured to her squeaking bag. "It's a long story. Really nice meeting you," the woman said, standing up quickly. She ran over to the attendant, clutching her bag to her chest, then walked quickly out of the laundromat and disappeared into the parking lot.

Joey turned in her chair, watching out the front windows to see where the woman was going.

She didn't strike Joey as a woman who would talk to a bag for no good reason.

Joey picked up her phone, reminded of the FOMO Birthday Party. She groaned, putting her phone back down. At least she had a few moments of ignorant bliss.

And what wasn't cool about hanging out at a laundromat on a Saturday night? She could be cool and fun. She just didn't know many people in the city yet, save for all of the people she went to high school with who got out of town before her. That wasn't her demographic.

She watched as the attendant walked over to the dryers

and opened one of the machines with a bag in hand, but her phone buzzed, drawing her attention.

It was a text from Nikki. Finally.

Nikki: Hey, miss you, girlie!

If she missed her so much, where was her invite, then?

Nikki: Wish you were here!
Joey: I could potentially make it later? What are the plans?

She stared down at her phone, willing Nikki to text her back. She could show up and everyone would be so excited and surprised to see her.

Joey: Where are you guys?

Nothing. Not even the dots.

She watched the minutes flick by on the clock as she stared at her phone, willing a text to come through.

In a moment of weakness, she checked her texts from Raina. Anything? Were the notifications on? Had she muted them in a moment of self-restraint? She triple checked. Nothing. Zero. Nada.

"Miss?" The attendant said, pointing to the dryer that had just buzzed. "That's yours."

Joey glanced around. She was the only one in the entire place — why was the attendant rushing her?

She stood, carrying her laundry bag over to the machines. Every machine in the place looked the same and there were dozens. She was thankful that she was the only one there, given she'd never have remembered what machine she had claimed earlier.

Her phone buzzed in her pocket. It was her dog camera, alerting her about barking again.

She sighed, opening the machine with one hand as she opened the app in the other.

Ozzy was rolling around in a *pile* of bras, barking happily on his back. And wait, was that... her underwear? It wasn't just a pile of bras. It was everything from the dresser, including but not limited to, bras, underwear, tights... but the cherry on top, was that in his mouth was her strap-on harness, in all its red leather glory. It had cost a small fortune to purchase, and she had used it so few times that she sincerely did not want it to die an untimely death before she really got her money's worth.

That was the last straw.

She pressed the button in a panic, scooping her clothes into her bag as fast as she could. "Ozzy, *stop* that," she said.

He continued barking happily, celebrating his victory.

She grabbed the last sock out of the tub and pulled her laundry bag shut as she rushed out the door to go rescue the last tiny shred of her dignity.

CHAPTER FOUR

KENDALL

Damn kittens.

The female had thrown up all over the male, a bad sign for both her digestive tract and also the bag.

She had just been talking to a cute queer-with-a-question-mark woman — way too young for her, but adorable, none-theless — when the kitten had thrown up her entire third dinner. Or was it her fifth lunch?

She was too tired to be able to tell these days. She hadn't known how long the laundromat would take, so she had brought the kittens with her, snuggled safely in a shoebox bed over a hot water bottle in her bag. At this age, they slept for nearly one hundred percent of the time they weren't eating, so she figured they'd snooze while she got her laundry done.

She was bitter about even having to be at the laundromat. Her own cats, those awful creatures, had either chewed through the washer hose themselves or allowed another animal, like a mouse, to chew through it. Either way, they were definitely on her shit list.

And now the kittens were, too.

Upon seeing the spit-up, which in itself wasn't terribly uncommon for bottle babies, she had reached into the bag to feel the kitten, she noticed how cold she was. And that's when panic set in.

She wasn't about to have a kitten die in her purse for laundry or a cute girl.

She had slipped the attendant $50 to get her laundry out for her and put it in a bag that she could pick up in a few hours, once she had stabilized the kitten.

They had been doing fine, but she should have known better.

She sped home, rushing inside to place the kittens back in the Kitten Jail, a tub with a warming bed where she kept the kittens wrangled. Though they were blind and tiny, they could sure get around when motivated by food.

She knew her chances of keeping both kittens alive wasn't entirely in her favor, but she had to try.

She held her hands around the kitten, trying to add any kind of warmth to her.

The kitten's temperature stabilized after a few minutes, and then her hungry cries kicked back in.

"Demanding little thing," she said, rolling her eyes. She grabbed the formula and mixed up a bottle, then held the kitten as she placed a drop of food on her tongue and felt her throat, waiting for her to swallow. Once she did, she held her in place to eat while still on the heated bed. "You're living the dream over here. I wish people brought me food while I was warm and cozy in bed."

Right on cue, Eggs came into the living room to see what all the fuss was about. Bacon lagged behind, standing in the hallway and watching from afar, wanting to stay out of whatever she deemed chaotic at any given moment, which was almost all moments around the babies.

Eggs probably just wanted to check out the formula. He had become overly attentive during food time, especially when the kittens missed a few drops. He was very helpful in terms of cleanup.

Bacon, on the other hand, preferred to cuddle the kittens, bathing them with whatever leftover maternal instinct she had left after being spayed early on in her life.

"You're all very, very lucky that you're cute," she said to the crew.

And then she realized she was talking to a bunch of cats, alone in her house on a Saturday night.

She managed to make it back to the laundromat before it closed, but only barely. She had to knock on the locked door until the attendant came to the front to tell her that she couldn't start a load of laundry past 9 p.m.

"Remember me? I left after my ca—" She stopped herself short before saying cat, given that having a kitten in a laundromat was probably against some sort of rule. "Car. Car had trouble."

The attendant rolled his eyes, but retrieved her laundry basket behind the desk where he had sat while Kendall was there earlier.

"Thank you so much," she said, trying her best to be overly nice as she took the basket and waved. The attendant locked the door before she had even stepped away.

Friendly.

She hurried back to her car. Not having a washing machine was such a pain in the ass, and she was completely out of clean scrubs.

She had arrived home, checked on the kittens, and sat down in bed with a glass of wine, ready to fold her clean clothes. She smirked, realizing the only thing cooler than talking to her cats on a Saturday night was drinking in bed while folding laundry. She sure knew how to get wild.

She opened the lid of her laundry basket and reached inside, pulling out a pair of ripped jeans.

What the... these weren't hers...

She kneeled, looking into the top of the basket. She sorted through skirts, flannel shirts, and thongs. Definitely not her clothes.

She murmured a curse under her breath and put the laundry back in the basket, sighing in frustration.

Was it karma for trying to pay the attendant to grab her things out of the dryer for her? What ancient deity had she pissed off so much in the past week that was now punishing her?

She opened the lid of the hamper again, digging through the offerings. Were these the clothes of the cute girl who had been sitting across from her? She held up the jeans. The younger woman had been kind of femme... Her long brown hair was tied back in two loose braids and she had a smattering of freckles across her nose, making her look even younger.

It didn't solve the issue of the lack of scrubs, unfortunately.

She took a drink from her wine glass and grabbed her phone. She dialed Imogen's number.

"Hey," Imogen said, picking up on the first ring.

"Hey, you busy?" She asked.

"Nah, just sitting in the bath," Imogen said.

"Ooh, the dream," Kendall teased.

"Oh, you bet it is. Especially these swollen feet. Did you know you can get stretch marks on your feet?" Imogen said, exasperated.

"You can?" Kendall said, considering the idea. "I mean, it makes sense, but I just never imagined."

"You're the fucking best, I love you so much," Imogen said, softer for a moment, as if she was holding the phone away from her ear.

"Somehow I don't think you're talking to me," Kendall joked.

"Sorry, Kenny. Gertie just brought me a turkey sandwich," Imogen said. Then, raising her voice. "And I love her for it."

"Wait, let me get this right. You're in the bathtub, eating a turkey sandwich," Kendall asked, laughing.

"Hell yes. Gertie is drinking that bottle of wine without me, but I'm fine because I have an oatmeal bath," Imogen said, crunching into her sandwich.

"Does the plate balance on your stomach in there?" Kendall teased.

"Of course. Making this baby earn his keep," Imogen laughed. "What's new with you?"

"Thanks for the book," she started.

"Oh yeah, it's like canonical lesbian fiction, figured you'd like it," Imogen said, chewing loudly.

Kendall caught her up on the laundromat mystery girl and her laundry.

"Thongs?" Imogen asked. "Like, sexy thongs or practical thongs?"

"Wait, what's the difference?" Kendall asked.

Imogen laughed. "Big difference. Like, lace?"

"I think there was lace on some I guess?" Kendall said, trying to recall.

"God, remember wearing thongs in our youth?" Imogen laughed.

"Thongs are a young woman's game, for sure. I don't think I've worn one since like... 'The Thong Song' was popular?" Kendall said, laughing.

"You mean college?" Imogen said. "Oh my God, those halcyon days we'd go out dancing and you knew all the words."

"You say that like you don't think I still know all the words," Kendall said. "I'm *very* hip, you know."

"I hate to burst your bubble, but I don't think 'The Thong

Song' has been hip since like... twenty minutes after it was released," Imogen said.

"How dare you insult Sisqo's artistic genius," Kendall joked. "You know that song samples 'Eleanor Rigby' And 'Flight of the Bumblebees'?"

"Wow, you're making single life sound very exciting. So glad you swore off relationships so you could eventually die alone with the knowledge of what samples are used in the fucking thong song," Imogen teased.

Kendall laughed, shaking her head. Imogen was one of her closest friends and had gotten her through the worst, darkest days after her divorce, so if anyone could get away with saying things like that, it was her.

"How are you going to track this girl down, though?" Imogen asked. "I'm living vicariously through you. I don't think I've had adventure since like... the first trimester. I don't even remember what my bush looks like. What if I don't even have toes anymore? I'd never know."

"I'm sure everything's fine below your waist, and I'm also sure Gertie would let you know if that were to change," Kendall said, grinning. "And I don't know how to find her. People don't write their phone numbers on the tags of their clothing after like... kindergarten."

"You could put up like a Lost and Found flyer? Lost scrubs. Found thongs," Imogen giggled. "Wait, I just had an idea. Do you have any of your scrubs embroidered with your name or Mountain View's logo?"

Kendall sighed. She had been meaning to get her scrubs embroidered with her clinic's logo for... years, honestly. It would save her the hassle of wearing a nametag, at least. "No, but good thinking," she said. "Wait, I think maybe one of the jackets they gave out for Christmas a few years ago might be in there. Maybe she'll come to the clinic and find me?"

"If she doesn't, she's an idiot," Imogen said.

"And a laundry thief," Kendall said.

"Seriously, who doesn't realize they've taken someone else's clothing?" Imogen said, scoffing. "Alright, I have to go, because I suddenly have to pee like a fucking racehorse right now, and if this kid keeps kicking my bladder, things are going to get gross in this bathtub really fast."

"Yikes, I can take a hint, you don't have to get all descriptive," Kendall joked.

They said their goodbyes and hung up.

As if summoned by the sudden quiet, the kittens began to mew from their Kitten Jail. Kendall checked her watch. Ah, fantastic, another feeding time.

CHAPTER FIVE

JOEY

Joey rubbed her eyes, glancing at the time on her phone. It was 10 p.m. — she hadn't yet found a routine since moving, and found that late-night translation suited her... until she was too tired to see clearly. She had spent the entire evening at a coffee shop in an effort to get out of her apartment and see the outside world.

She preferred working at night, given that the night was the hardest time to stop thinking about Raina. If she passed out in bed from exhaustion each night, she wouldn't lie awake thinking about all of the regrets she had.

She walked into her apartment, pushing a wiggling Ozzy back so she could fit through the door without him darting out in his haste to get outside to pee and then bark at squirrels. In that order, hopefully.

"I know, buddy, you've been holding it for a while," she cooed as she grabbed his leash. The air had a slight chill to it, but it was still late spring, so it wasn't freezing anymore, at least. She opened her tiny coat closet, peeking inside. Everything she had hung up was too warm.

Without even bothering to turn on the lights, She glanced at the laundry sack that she had brought home the night before. Of course she hadn't put it away yet. What kind of monster put away their laundry immediately after washing it? The only way she did laundry was to let it hang out for a few days — weeks, at times — picking through it piece-by-piece until the point it got too annoying *not* to put away.

She reached into the bag, feeling around until her fingers hit the fleece she was looking for.

She grabbed the jacket, throwing it over her arm as she hooked Ozzy's harness onto him, then clipped the leash to him.

It wasn't until outside that she put on the jacket, slightly surprised that it fit differently than she'd remembered — had it shrunk in the dryer? Maybe she had accidentally grabbed Sunny's jacket instead.

She walked Ozzy to a shrub that he had taken a shine to and let him sniff it excitedly to check for hints of other dogs. Seriously, the bush must have been some sort of message board, because Ozzy ran straight to it and sniffed for nearly five minutes before deciding what he was going to write with his own pee.

She walked him around the block, persuading him to go on a shorter walk for now given the time. He hadn't pooped yet, but she could take him on a long walk once she woke up around noon.

She was almost back to the front steps of her building when Ozzy stopped and started hunching his back and gagging as though he was about to vomit.

"Oh buddy, you okay?" She asked, kneeling down beside him to pet him. She contemplated holding back his ears, but thought that it might distract or bother him in the moment.

Better the front lawn than her rug, right?

Although he gagged and gagged, nothing came up.

Eventually, he looked up at her with what she read as a sad and tired expression.

"Something's really upsetting your tummy, huh?" She asked. "Come on, I have some pumpkin upstairs that we can try."

She walked him carefully and slowly up the stairs, then back into the apartment.

And that's when she noticed it.

Her favorite red leather harness.

In shreds.

All over her apartment.

D-rings, rivets... the whole lot of it.

"Oh, you *asshole*," she said to Ozzy, who was sniffing his handiwork.

And then the gagging continued.

She noticed that he hadn't touched his food from dinner — not a good sign.

Joey stared at him, trying to determine if he was simply trying to win an Oscar — it wouldn't have been the first time — or if he was truly so ill that he couldn't vomit properly.

It was only when he hunched the other way, trying to go to the bathroom and not succeeding, that she looked up the name of the nearest emergency vet.

Their full voicemail box advised her to call her local vet.

What if she didn't have a local vet yet?

She looked up the vet clinic closest to her new place — Mountain View something — relieved when a person answered. She explained that Ozzy had eaten something... he shouldn't have. The person, identifying themselves as a tech, said that they typically didn't take emergency patients they hadn't seen yet, but that she'd contact the vet on call. The tech called back shortly, saying the vet had apparently waived the stipulation, hearing that it was a possible foreign body.

Well, that sounded expensive.

She glanced back down at him as he began to pant.

Although it was the more frustrating and financially-difficult decision, it was the right decision. She hadn't gotten a dog because they were cost-effective, at least.

Her frustration had begun to wane, turning instead to rising panic.

She walked him back downstairs and loaded him into the car, praying he wouldn't vomit in her car, or if he did, that it would stay contained in the backseat dog sling.

She pulled up at the vet and hopped out, allowing Ozzy an extra moment to try pooping again on the grass outside. Surely the message board shrubs at this place would be exciting enough to encourage *some* kind of movement.

An employee in scrubs opened the door. "Hi, did you just call?" She asked.

Joey nodded. "Yeah, my dog ate... a thing, I think."

"Alright, come on in and we'll get you in the system, then check this little cutie out. I'm Kat, and I'll be one of your vet techs," the woman said.

Joey walked in the clinic, looking around. The waiting area was cozy but clean, and the walls were littered with pictures of dogs and cats and bunnies and... was that an iguana?

"Can I get a full name?" Kat asked from behind the desk. In the light, Joey could see that Kat was generically gorgeous, with tanned skin and highlighted blonde hair. It made Joey feel a bit silly for wearing yoga pants and a too-tight jacket.

Seriously, who looked that good in scrubs? Besides that woman at the laundromat…

Kat was looking at her, waiting for an answer. Shit, what was the question? Oh, right. His full name.

"Oh, sure. Ozzy Pawsbourne, Prince of Barkness," Joey said clearly.

Kat paused. "Oh, I mean *your* full name," she said with a grin.

"Oh, sorry, yeah, it's Josephine Moore," she said.

"Wow, that's a *fantastic* dog name," a woman said as she walked in from the back hallway in jeans and a t-shirt, drying her hands on a paper towel. The only reason she looked vaguely official was the stethoscope around her neck.

Joey stared in surprise as she recognized the woman. "Oh hey, you're the laundromat bag lady!" She said without thinking.

Without her scrubs on, she looked like a normal person. Her hair was pulled into a low ponytail, with a few strands falling around her face. It wasn't fair for her to look so cool and put together at 11 p.m. Was she really a vet?

"Bag lady?" The woman asked, recognition dawning on her. "Oh, laundry thief!"

"Excuse me?" Joey asked, her defenses rising immediately. Her grip tightened on Ozzy's leash.

"Our laundry got switched," Bag Lady said, gesturing to Joey's jacket. "That's mine."

Joey glanced down at the jacket she was wearing. Sure enough, it wasn't hers. It was blue, for one thing, and had Dr. Kendall O'Hara, Mountain View Vet Hospital embroidered on the side. "Huh," she said, conceding. "I guess... it is."

"You're telling me you didn't even realize you were wearing my jacket?" Bag Lady asked, looking at Joey like she was crazy.

"Wait, you're telling me you looked through my laundry?" Joey asked, feeling like that was a trespass on her privacy.

"How else was I supposed to know that it wasn't mine?" Bag Lady asked, shrugging.

Good point...

Kat cleared her throat.

"Anyway, we can exchange all that later," Bag Lady said, waving her back into an exam room. "I'm Dr. O'Hara, Kendall is fine. What seems to be the matter with the Prince of Barkness over here?"

Joey shifted her weight on her feet uneasily. "I'm Joey," she said, trying to delay the inevitable. "And, uh, well, he ate something," she said.

"Something he shouldn't have," Kendall said, nodding. "Wait, wasn't he eating your bras or something last night?"

Kat cleared her throat again.

"He sure was," Joey said, nodding as she recalled yelling at the pet cam.

Kendall sat on the floor beside Ozzy, gently feeling his stomach. Joey was surprised that she was just... sitting on the floor. Her last vet always struggled to make Ozzy stay still on a large metal table.

Kendall checked Ozzy's mouth and tongue. "Okay, well, then that makes me a bit nervous about underwires. Could have punctured something in there. If that's the case, there could be internal—"

"No, it wasn't a bra," Joey said quickly, cutting her off.

"Oh, okay. But, you *do* know what it was?" Kendall asked, unwinding the stethoscope from around her neck, listening for a moment.

"Uh, yes. But... it's..." Joey said, swallowing. She fidgeted with Ozzy's leash in her hands. Her cheeks were so hot that it was entirely possible they might burst into flames at any moment. She stole a sideways look at the tech, who was typing things into a computer.

Kendall fixed her with a stare, her blue eyes pinning Joey in place. "I've seen dogs eat all sorts of things. Nothing you are going to say will embarrass me. So, the faster you get it out, the faster we can know what we're dealing with in order to get Ozzy feeling better."

"A leather harness," Joey said as quickly as she could. There. It was out there. It was out in the world for all of the judgment.

Kendall gave her an uncertain look. "Harness?" She repeated. "Like for dogs?"

"Yeah, like... you know, for..." Joey said, dropping her

voice to a whisper as she stared a hole into the linoleum flooring. "Sex."

"Oh, like for a strap-on?" Kendall asked, and Joey glanced up to see recognition dawning on her face.

Joey nodded. She swallowed the last dredges of her pride. "And it was red," she added, but then immediately regretted the detail. Why did Kendall have to know it was red? Why did she say that?

"Red leather harness," Kendall repeated, feeling Ozzy's stomach again. "Sounds fancy." Her tone was light as she held Ozzy for the tech to get a temperature.

Was… was the vet grinning?

Joey laughed, feeling nervous suddenly. "Um, thanks," she murmured, and she thought she saw the edge of Kendall's mouth quirk up in a smile.

"Okay, temp is good," Kendall said, glancing over Kat's shoulder at the computer they typed in. "Let's get some x-rays."

The x-rays showed, in Kendall's exact words, "Upset and gassy insides." She was calm as she pointed out exactly where she thought most of the blockage was, and reassured Joey with confidence that although it sounded scary, it was a common procedure that she had done hundreds of times.

Kat had given her all of the cost proposals and Joey talked through the options with Kendall. In the end, she agreed to the surgery, even though it would take up all of her couch savings and then some. She could sit on the floor forever if it meant that Ozzy would be okay again.

Joey held Ozzy in her arms and kissed his fuzzy little face as Kendall explained the surgery she was about to do. They were going to cut him open from his sternum to his pelvic bone and feel around until they got all of the icky things out.

Kat unhooked Ozzy's collar and handed it to Joey to hold.

She sat with the collar in her hands, the tears coming in earnest now.

It was easier when she was mad at him. The idea of losing him was too much to consider.

"Hey, you did the right thing by bringing him in at the first sign of distress. You saved his life because you thought fast," Kendall said, squeezing Joey's shoulder.

"Thanks," Joey said, wiping at her face with the back of her hand. "He'll be okay, right?" She hated looking weak, but Ozzy was her Achilles Heel.

"Honestly, my professional opinion is that I think he's a great candidate for a quick recovery. He's healthy and you caught it fast. But I also don't want to lie to you. So, here's what I'll tell you," Kendall said, squatting down to Joey's eye level. Kendall fixed her with kind, blue eyes that made Joey trust her, like they were in it together. "I am going to try my hardest. I've been doing this a long time, and I'm pretty good at it if I do say so myself."

"Kendall, Taylor just got here," Kat said, glancing towards the back door.

"Okay. I called in the best, so the cards can be stacked in Ozzy's favor," Kendall said.

Joey felt a sense of calm come over her as she gave Ozzy one last kiss on the little dip between his eyes and watched the tech lead Ozzy from the room. She trusted Kendall. She hardly knew her and thought she talked to bags — okay, she wasn't entirely sure she *didn't* talk to bags yet — but she had a presence that made Joey feel like Ozzy was in good hands.

She texted the family group chat to keep them updated, then rested her head against the wall, tears slipping down her cheeks as she waited.

The next thing she knew, Kendall was shaking her shoulder. Joey opened her eyes to see that Kendall was sitting beside her.

"Ozzy is fine, but we've got some good news and some bad news," Kendall said.

"Bad news?" Joey said, sitting up straight.

"Well, the good news is that it was fairly straightforward to get that leather and O-ring out of Ozzy's stomach," Kendall said. "He's sewed up and resting on some really good drugs right now."

Joey burst into tears with relief. And tiredness. Mostly relief. Maybe even some hormonal tears, if she was being honest with herself.

Kendall patted her shoulder, as if she didn't know how to comfort her with the new wave of intensity.

"I'm sorry, it's just that he's everything to me," Joey said in between sobs. She felt foolish for crying at the good news, but she was unable to turn off the waterworks.

Kendall nodded, then finally relaxed and wrapped an arm around her, hugging her. "Hey, it's okay. He's going to be totally fine," she said.

Joey let herself be comforted for a moment, then sat up and sniffled, wiping her nose on her jacket arm without thinking twice about it.

Kendall cringed. "Hey," she said, pointing to the jacket.

"Oh my God," Joey said, staring down at her snot, clearly visible on the jacket sleeve. "I'm so sor– Wait, what was the bad news?" She sniffled again, but resisted the urge to wipe her nose on her sleeve.

"The bad news is that I was unable to repair your harness," Kendall said, handing her a tissue.

Was she… was she *grinning*?

"Oh, we've got jokes now? It's like 2 a.m. and we've got jokes?" Joey said, her eyes widening as she stared at Kendall in disbelief. She sniffled again, wiping her nose on the tissue.

"Bad joke, alright, I'm sorry. I owe you," Kendall said, holding up her palms in surrender. "The important thing is that he did great. He's resting. I want to monitor him throughout the day, but if he urinates, has a bowel movement, and drinks water, he can come home with you by tonight."

"Tonight? I have to leave him here all day?" Joey asked,

blinking in surprise. She hadn't spent an entire day without Ozzy since she had rescued him.

"He's in very capable hands. And on the bright side, you can bring my laundry back when you come to get him," Kendall said with a smirk.

"Sounds like a fair trade. As long as you have my laundry, too," Joey said, surprised by the laughter bubbling up. She must have been delirious from having all the feelings on zero sleep.

"Tell me the truth, it would have taken you many, many days to realize that wasn't your laundry," Kendall said with a laugh.

Joey nodded. "I mean, I am wearing your jacket without even realizing it," she said, shrugging. "But scrubs seem comfortable, too. Why aren't you wearing them? I think I'd just live in them."

"I mean, I *do* live in them. When they're clean. And with me," Kendall said with a pointed look.

"Yeah, that does make sense," Joey said, clearing her throat.

Kendall laughed. "So, we'll give you a call–"

They were interrupted by Joey's phone ringing. She glanced at the caller ID, expecting it to be her sister or mom. Her stomach fell when she saw it was Raina's name.

"I'm so sorry, it's uh, Ozzy's other mom," she said, then mentally kicked herself for calling Raina that. She didn't deserve that title anymore.

"No problem," Kendall said, her posture stiffening slightly. "We close at seven tonight, so come back around 6:30 and we'll go through instructions then. Take your time." She walked out of the room, giving a wave as she closed the door.

Joey nodded, standing up. She took a deep breath, then hit the green button.

"Hey," she said, trying to force herself to sound casual.

"What's going on?" Raina asked, sounding worried.

Good. She should be worried.

"I couldn't make out a word of your voicemail," Raina said. "You were just sobbing hysterically."

Ah, yes. The voicemail. Joey had left it in a moment of weakness after Ozzy had been taken to the back room. She didn't know who else to call. None of her friends would have cared and her family wasn't awake or answering texts. She craved comfort. Raina always used to be her comfort, but now... She wasn't so sure who to call in this situation anymore.

"Ozzy had to have surgery," Joey said, summoning all of her courage not to break down on the phone again. She took a deep, stilted breath.

"That's it? I thought someone fucking died," Raina said, sighing. She sounded sleepy, like she had just woken up.

"Excuse me? So sorry you think Ozzy having emergency surgery after nearly dying isn't a big deal," Joey snapped.

"Don't twist my words. I'm glad Ozzy's okay," Raina said. "Do you need money for it?"

Joey narrowed her eyes, glaring at a poster of dog teeth on the wall. "No," she said.

"Well, alright. I hope he gets better soon. Give me an update in like a week, I guess? Unless he takes a turn for the worse," Raina said.

"Jesus, Ray," Joey said, rubbing her eyes. "Not helpful. I'll call you if there's anything to report."

She hung up the phone feeling much worse. She wished she hadn't even answered it, or better yet, that she hadn't left that stupid voicemail.

She opened her contacts and deleted Raina's phone number before she could spare the idea a second thought.

Wow, that felt... surprisingly good.

She sniffled, wiping her nose with a tissue instead of the sleeve of Kendall's jacket, making a mental note to visit the laundromat again before returning said jacket, and walked out of the room.

———————

Later that night, she fidgeted with the lid of the cupcake box placed carefully on top of a laundry basket of Kendall's clothing as she walked back into the clinic. She had stopped to pick up a representation of her sincere gratitude, and what better way to say that than with baked goods? Thank You For Saving My Dog's Life cupcakes. A classic.

She had spent most of the day pacing around her apartment, finally dog-proofing a bit better. She had been used to her old apartment, where Ozzy was calm and comfortable and didn't find things to get into trouble.

She resolved to walk him three times a day and look into doggie daycare at least twice a week. She could be the parent he needed. She had let her good habits slip after the breakup, when her routine was thrown out the window.

Was Ozzy acting out? Maybe she'd ask Kendall about a dog trainer.

She walked up to the front desk where an older man was standing over the shoulder of another woman she didn't recognize. "Hi, I'm here to pick up my dog, Ozzy. He had surgery," she said, placing the cupcakes on the counter in front of her.

The older man looked up at her. "Marie, go get Ozzy," he said to the woman sitting at the desk.

Joey wanted to cringe at the tone of his voice. Wow, what a kind animal lover he must be.

"How is he?" Joey asked.

"Fine," the man said.

Joey glanced at his nametag, which said, Dr. Rothlisberger. That was a mouthful. He must be another vet at the practice.

"Is Dr. O'Hara here?" Joey asked. "I was hoping to talk to

her about his care and give her these cupcakes for performing an emergency surgery at 2 a.m."

Dr. Rothlisberger raised one of his hairy eyebrows at her. "She's in the back," he said, as if that was a helpful bit of information.

"Oh, okay, will you please see that these get to her, then? And also, this is random, but I have her laundry?" Joey said.

Taylor, one of the techs she recognized from the night before, popped in from the hallway. "Hey Ms. Moore, Kendall is busy but if you can wait two minutes, she wants to discuss Ozzy's discharge instructions with you."

Joey nodded.

"Oh, and uh, Dr. O'Hara is vegan," Taylor said in a loud whisper, pointing to the cupcakes.

"Oh, fuck," Joey said, looking down at her decidedly not-vegan cupcakes. She should have thought of that. "Well, then these are for the rest of you, then."

"Don't mind if I do," Taylor said, walking into the room. "Thank you. Ozzy's been adorable all day, you know. We've loved having him."

Joey smiled, and some of the guilt of having to leave Ozzy alone in a new place to start mending without her lessened. Some.

Kendall walked into the room with a smile on her face, completely ignoring Dr. Rothlisberger at the desk. She reached to shake Joey's hand in a gesture that was both hilariously formal and kind. "Good to see you again, Joey," she said. "Come on back, I'll let you see your little man and tell you all about what you should look out for in the next few days."

Joey looked down at the laundry basket at her feet. "Uh," she began with uncertainty. "And I brought this."

"Oh, perfect," Kendall said, reaching down to grab it, then she stopped with wide eyes. "Dammit, I forgot yours," she said.

"That's okay," Joey said automatically. "I brought you cupcakes that you can't eat, so we're even."

Kendall glanced at the box of cupcakes. "Ah, well, it's a kind gesture, regardless," she said with a surprised smile.

She led Joey to the back room where Ozzy was lying down in a kennel wearing a cone of shame. Upon seeing Joey, his tail began to beat against the metal wall rhythmically.

"Oh, you recognize your mama?" Kendall said with a smile, opening Ozzy's kennel to reach in and scratch his chin.

"Can I... pet him?" Joey asked, uncertain.

"Of course," Kendall said, stepping out of the way. "Just make sure he doesn't get too excited. If you can get him to roll onto his back, I'll show you his stitches."

"Oh, that's easy, you just pet him right here," Joey said, scratching the top of his chest until Ozzy gingerly rolled over. He didn't stick out his arms as he normally would, but Joey could see his shaved belly and the gnarly scar through it. "Damn, they did a number on you, huh?"

"Yeah, lotta leather in those guts," Kendall said lightly.

Joey laughed awkwardly, her cheeks burning in embarrassment.

Kendall talked her through the aftercare and Joey nodded, following along with what signs to look out for.

Kendall handed her a card with her personal cell phone number written on the back.

Joey watched as Kendall stepped closer to her, pointing to the number. Something about Kendall being so close to her was both exhilarating and unnerving. She could try to act cool.

She straightened, trying not to focus on how smooth Kendall's skin looked or how Kendall's foot was nearly touching hers.

"I still owe you your clothes," Kendall said. "Do you want me to drop them by and we can discuss—"

A loud animal cry interrupted her and startled Joey.

"Oh goodness gracious, you'd think they hadn't been fed in days," Kendall said, rolling her eyes. "Sorry, I have a pair of young kittens I have to nurse around the clock right now."

Joey nodded, then a realization hit her. "Wait, did you have kittens in your bag the other day at the laundromat?" She asked.

Kendall's eyes widened in surprise. "Of course not, that would be absolutely against the rules," she said, and even though she was saying no, she gave a quick nod and wink.

"Ah, so you're not a crazy lady who talks to her bag," Joey said.

"I mean, technically I am. There's just also the distinction that living animals are inside the bag," Kendall said with a laugh.

Joey grinned. "Anyway, you've already done enough, so I can stop by and grab my laundry from you," she said. "I owe you big time."

"It's fine, I'll come by this evening and maybe I can show you how to set up a comfortable bed for Ozzy? Do you have a crate?" Kendall asked.

Joey shook her head.

"Okay, I'll bring a crate you can borrow, too," Kendall said.

"You really don't have to do that," Joey said, surprised.

"You're really going to argue with a doctor?" Kendall said, giving her a pointed look.

Joey opened her mouth to continue arguing but stopped, rolling her eyes. "If you insist," she said.

Kendall smiled. "Good answer."

CHAPTER SIX

KENDALL

"Uh oh," Taylor said as they watched Joey walk out to her beat-up car and bend to pick up Ozzy.

"No, she's doing fine," Kendall said.

"That's not what I'm uh-ohing about," Taylor said. "I am instead expressing my concern that you might have a little... bias towards Ms. Moore."

Kendall turned, her brow furrowed. "I do *not*," she said firmly. "I simply care about my patients and prefer that they convalesce safely."

"Mmhmm," Taylor said, adjusting their glasses in a decidedly snarky way.

Kendall pointed a finger at them. "I only care about the dog," she said, raising her eyebrows.

Taylor widened their bright green eyes and put up both hands as if they were being held at gunpoint, but their wide smile still remained. "Whatever you say."

Kendall watched Joey drive away, then glanced over at the box of cupcakes. "I can't believe you told her I was vegan. Now she thinks I don't like them," she said.

"But, you... are vegan," Taylor said, confused, their head tilting to the side as their short dark hair fell over their eyes.

"But you didn't have to tell her that," Kendall said, sighing. "Imagine your friend comes in to bring you a gift and I'm like, 'Oh sorry, they hate the color red and therefore this thing you brought.'"

Taylor's eyes widened. "First of all, you just called one of our patients your friend," they said, grinning in a *Gotcha!* kind of way. "And second, I love the color red. I love all colors. Because I'm not Colorist."

"Colorist?" Kendall laughed, caught off-guard.

"But don't worry, I'll be better at reading your mind next time," Taylor said. "Sorry that I told the truth without your express permission."

Kendall gave them an exasperated look. "Keep making fun of me and I'm going to make sure you are *only* cleaning rooms for the rest of the week, buddy," she said with a grin.

"You wouldn't dare," Taylor laughed.

Dr. Rothlisberger cleared his throat, walking into the room with the big, black cloud that followed him around. "Excuse me, I don't mean to break up your little friendly chatfest, but we do have to close up, if you don't mind."

Kendall bit her tongue before she could say something too snarky. "No problem, Paul."

They began to lock up, putting away files, shutting blinds, making sure each room was properly disinfected.

"Where did he go?" Taylor asked, holding a bottle of cleaner in their gloved hand as they looked around.

Kendall checked the exam rooms, the lab, the kennel area… Paul was gone.

"That's weird," she said. When had Paul ever just completely bailed on helping before?

"Maybe he got tired of our chatfest," Taylor said with a wink. "Anyway, I'm going to need you to scrub the anal gland liquid off the blinds in three."

"The blinds?"

"And the ceiling."

Kendall smirked. "Paper rock scissors you for it."

———

She looked up at the building in front of her and then back down at her phone, making sure the address was correct. She was in the heart of Cap Hill, where all the buildings were plentiful and parking was non-existent. She was spoiled by her home in West Highlands with a garage where she never had to even consider parallel parking.

She sent a text to Joey.

Kendall: I think I'm here.

Joey: Okay, it can be a little confusing. Be down in a sec.

She waited on the front porch until Joey opened the front door. Joey's hair was pulled up in a messy bun and she wore the same casual leggings and top she had earlier. Kendall was suddenly grateful that she had taken a moment to change out of her scrubs, but she felt a little overdressed in a pair of loose-fitting jeans and a blazer over a plain t-shirt.

Kendall held out the laundry hamper to her. "I brought your thongs," she said with a smile.

Joey's mouth dropped in shock for a moment.

Kendall backpedaled as quickly as she could. "I mean things. *Things*!" She pointed down to the dog crate leaning against her leg. "And this."

Joey laughed, holding open the door. "I'll grab the crate if you can take the laundry?"

Kendall lugged the laundry up the three sets of stairs — walk-ups were a young woman's game. She was completely out of breath when she got to the top.

"I know, right?" Joey said, opening her apartment door. "You should see me try to get an entire load of groceries up those things. Not pretty."

Kendall laughed, walking into the apartment. It was... almost completely bare. It was a tiny shoebox of a place, sure, but she couldn't fault Joey for that. It was the lack of anything personal inside. Not even a couch. Who didn't have a couch? There was a single camping chair set up near the window.

"You're sure you live here?" She said without thinking.

Joey laughed, taking the laundry basket out of her arms. "I just moved in last week. Don't judge me too harshly," she said.

"How old are you?" Kendall said, eyeing her. Was she straight out of college?

Was she still *in* college?

Joey raised an eyebrow. "I'm twenty-eight," she said flatly.

Kendall dug down deep in order to keep a straight face. Wow, twenty-eight. She was such a baby.

"How old are you?" Joey asked.

Kendall pretended to clutch at pearls around her throat. "A lady would never," she joked.

Joey rolled her eyes, but she could see that she was amused.

"Want to see my setup for Ozzy so far?"

"Sure," Kendall said, grabbing the dog crate.

Joey led her over to a section of the empty space she imagined would pass as a living room near the bed. "Okay, so I was thinking of setting his crate up here, so that he's near the bed, but also in the middle of things because he likes to keep an eye on me," she said, pointing.

Kendall nodded. "Smart. Wait, I brought one more thing," she said, setting the crate down to walk back over to the laundry. On the top was a set of bright pink dog pajamas with hearts all over them. "This will keep him from messing with his stitches." She held it up to judge Joey's reaction.

Joey's eyes lit up and from this close, Kendall could see that they were the color of a forest at golden hour, all yellows and deep greens.

"He's going to look like a pink nightmare in those, and I can't wait," Joey said.

Kendall laughed. "Good movie reference."

Joey winked, her cheeks rounding in a smile.

"Do you want a beer or anything?" Joey asked, walking into the kitchen.

What Kendall really wanted was the bottle of Pinot Noir sitting on her kitchen counter, waiting for her, but she could hardly expect a woman without a couch to have a wine selection. She should have said no. She should have left and kept the relationship strictly professional. But instead, she heard herself say, "Sure."

Kendall tried to surreptitiously glance at the label of the beer Joey offered. It had honey in it. She fidgeted with it in her hands as Joey explained her pet cam situation so she could keep an eye on Ozzy while she was out.

Should she just... set it down somewhere and hope Joey didn't notice?

Joey glanced down at her hands. "You don't like that kind?" She asked.

"It has honey in it," Kendall said, shrugging. She felt guilty, suddenly. "So."

"Oh, fuck, honey. Bees. You're like, *really* vegan," Joey said, her forehead wrinkling as she frowned, looking embarrassed. "Don't worry, I have an Easy Street in the fridge. I'll check the label."

Kendall opened the dog crate and set up some bedding inside of it so that Ozzy would be cozy.

Joey handed her a beer, which she graciously took. She wasn't a huge beer fan, but it was practically a state law that Coloradans had to at least *appreciate* beer before being allowed to live there.

She sat on the ground, checking Ozzy's incision. It looked good so far. Still red and angry, but no sign of infection. His eyes were focusing, even though he still seemed a bit dopey. He had low energy, of course, but that wasn't alarming.

"Do you have any pets?" Joey asked. "Silly question to ask a vet, though. I bet you have like fourteen dogs."

"I'm very good at self-restraint," Kendall laughed. "I have two cats. Bacon and Eggs." She smiled, thinking of their furry little faces.

"Bacon and Eggs?" Joey said, laughing. "Big breakfast fan?"

"I was really into Parks and Rec," Kendall admitted, feeling a little silly.

"Oh, like Ron Swanson," Joey said, her eyes lighting up as she got the reference. "Wait. Wait. Hold up. You're a vegan and you named your cats Bacon and Eggs."

Kendall laughed, shrugging her shoulders. "Yeah, I can see how that might get a little confusing."

"A little. What did you name the kittens, Veal and Lamb Shank?" Joey joked.

Kendall laughed even harder, surprising herself. "I didn't name them, but I'm not against that idea," she said.

"Did you smuggle them in your purse this time?" Joey said, glancing back towards the door.

"No, I left them at home, safely in their Kitten Jail," Kendall assured her.

They drank their beers in companionable silence. It was only slightly awkward.

"So, what made you move here? I'm guessing from out of town, given the furniture situation," Kendall asked.

Joey raised her eyebrows, taking a long sip of her beer. "Well, just uh, wanted a change, I guess," she said, shrugging. A long pause stretched out between them as Joey picked at the label of her beer bottle. "I mean, to tell you the truth, my fiancée broke my heart, so I left town. Not too far, though. I'm from Fort Collins." She pointed in the direction that Kendall vaguely recognized must have been north. She had been to the town a few times — they had an amazing veterinary program and hospital where she had done some continuing education courses. "My work is remote, so I thought a change would do me good."

Suddenly the bare apartment made more sense.

"Ah, the ol' heartbroken move. I've done it myself," Kendall said, tipping her beer in an air-cheers.

Joey nodded, frowning. "Yeah, it... sucks. It really sucks," she said.

Kendall could see that Joey was trying not to get too emotional about it. "It'll get better. It'll fade. And one day you'll wake up and they won't be the first thing you think about, or even the second."

She took a long drink of her beer, remembering how dark that time in her life had been. It had taken her years to recover fully, to feel like things could be normal again, to go through an entire day without thinking of her ex.

It dawned on her that Joey might have been referring to the person who had called her that morning, the person she said was Ozzy's other mom. That explained the panicked look on her face and her sudden change in demeanor.

"So, you moved to Denver to be closer to friends?" Kendall suggested.

"Uh," Joey said, laughing just slightly, but without a smile. "No. Further from friends, I think. I just didn't want all the pitying looks anymore, you know? The people who were afraid to ask me questions for fear that I might somehow burst into a thousand pieces at any given moment."

Kendall nodded. She knew that feeling so well. "What do you do?"

"I'm a translator," Joey said. "So, I get to work from home, at least."

Kendall raised her eyebrows in surprise. "What do you translate? What language?"

"French, and mainly manuals. Right now my agency has me on a bunch of hair dye instructions. Last week I wrote some shampoo bottles. Really thrilling stuff," she said with a smirk.

"Why French?" Kendall asked.

"I started taking French in 8th grade and just never… stopped. It felt like a secret language and I loved it. I lived in France for study abroad in college, in this tiny town no one has ever heard of, and I was miserable being so far away from home, but I made some good connections, and I've been translating ever since," she said with a shrug.

Kendall nodded. "That's very impressive."

"If you like shampoo," Joey said with a sardonic smile.

She looked around the room again, feeling a bit sorry for Joey. It was hard to be young and alone and even harder to be young and alone and heartbroken.

She cleared her throat, unsure if she should even ask. "Hey, I'm having this get together next Friday, do you want to come? No big deal if not, of course. It's like a few boring older queers, so I can see how that might not—"

"Yeah," Joey said, nodding quickly. "That sounds fun."

"I mean, lower your standards for fun," Kendall said, laughing. "We're old and maybe not your typical idea of fun."

"Like, how old? Do y'all play bridge?" Joey teased. "Should I bring some prunes? Or is it more of a jello salad crowd?"

"Wow, it's not some potluck in a church basement, give me a break," Kendall said, pretending to scoff. "I'm just saying it's not going to be a… rager or anything."

Joey smiled, shrugging. "I'll be there."

Why was she so nervous? She was just having her friends Gertie, Imogen, Edward, and Roger over. And Joey might show up. She might have just been polite, though. She seemed polite. And young. Way too young for her. Out of the question young. Twenty-eight? She had been a freshman in high school when Joey was born.

Not to mention Joey was a bit of... well, damaged goods at the moment, though that was a harsh judgment. She knew what it was like to be heartbroken and never want to date anyone again. She also knew what it was like to be heart-broken and need a rebound. She wasn't against sex, per se, but she was against the idea of becoming someone's partner. Ever again. That chapter had closed in the book of her life, and good riddance to it.

It would be nice not to be the fifth wheel for once, though. She loved her friends, but they were all in happily married couples. That could get exhausting. She needed another jaded friend to liven things up again. Joey seemed like the perfect addition.

At the time.

But now?

What the hell had she been thinking?

She shook her head, trying to clear the thought. Joey was friendly and kind and funny, and she enjoyed her company. She'd leave it at that. New friends. No need to complicate things.

Besides, Imogen knew her better than anyone, and if she sensed something was up, Kendall would never hear the end of it.

The doorbell rang just as Kendall was tidying up the kitchen.

She threw the kitchen towel over her shoulder and opened the door, finding Gertie and Imogen standing on the step holding a casserole dish, with Edward and Roger walking up the front path behind them. Edward was waving... salad

fingers in the air? She grinned as she glanced down the road
— Joey wasn't there yet.

She let the group in with lots of hugs and cheek kisses,
thankful that they were the type of friends who knew to make
themselves at home. Roger opened a bottle of wine as Imogen
hunted down the cats. Gertie and Edward hopped in the
kitchen to see if she needed any help finishing up.

Imogen and Gertie were the kind of couple she would
have aspired to be if she were the type who wanted to get
married and have kids. She loved their life, but she loved it
for them, not for her. They had been married for fifteen years
and had been trying for a baby for the last five. Now that
Imogen was in her third trimester, they had started getting
more openly excited about the new addition.

Edward and Roger were another nice couple she had
befriended from the neighborhood. They had cornered her at
the mailboxes — read her as gay from a mile away. They were
easy-going and quick to laugh, but also quick to call her on
her bullshit.

Imogen hugged a squirming Bacon to her chest as she sat
down on the couch.

The house wasn't massive, but she had always thought it
was roomy before tonight. Now, it felt a bit like maybe she
had made a mistake by adding another person.

"I invited a friend," she said to Imogen, who tilted her
head.

"You have friends besides us?" Imogen teased.

"She's a new friend. And I don't want anyone terrifying
her," Kendall said, pointing to Imogen and Edward.

Imogen let Bacon run away as she held her hands up in a very
innocent representation of *I have no idea what you're talking about.*

Edward was ignoring her, loudly questioning the lack of
vodka and Gertie was opening the oven, murmuring about a
sauce reduction, when the doorbell rang.

"Wait, so who is coming?" Imogen asked, giving her a skeptical look.

Okay, so she hadn't been exactly forthcoming with the information regarding the new friend invited to the dinner party.

"Just a friend," Kendall attempted to sound casual as she opened the door. She could feel four sets of curious eyes on her, but tried to act as nonchalant as she could.

"Hey," Joey said, smiling. She held up a bottle of wine. "I brought you a thong." She joked.

Imogen nearly choked from somewhere behind her.

Kendall opened the door wider and let Joey on in, taking her jacket. Joey was wearing a sundress with a pair of heels that made her legs look incredible. One could platonically fantasize about a friend, right? Right. Especially if those fantasies involved skimming her hands over those smooth calves, thighs...

"Hello," Edward said, his voice startling Kendall out of her completely platonic and normal fantasy. He reached out to shake Joey's hand. "And who might this adorable little creature be?"

Oh God, subjecting Joey to this fate was the wrong choice, wasn't it?

Joey laughed, shaking his hand good-naturedly. "This little creature is Joey, so nice to meet you all," she said, holding her own.

Kendall glared at Edward from behind Joey.

"Don't mind them, they're harmless," Kendall assured Joey. "This is Imogen and Gertie and Edward and Roger. Edward and Roger live down the street and Imogen and I go way back. Gertie is her wife and my favorite wine tasting partner," Kendall explained. She turned back to the group, forcing a confident smile. "Joey and I met... recently."

"She stole my laundry," Joey said with a wide grin.

Imogen's eyes widened as she looked from Joey to Kendall.

"Ooh, I want to hear this," Roger said, taking Joey's arm and leading her into the living room.

Imogen nodded her head toward the kitchen, gesturing for Kendall to join her.

Kendall rolled her eyes, but did as Imogen suggested.

"How ya doing?" Imogen said, her eyes positively twinkling with the kind of delight one can only hold when they're watching their friend make questionable decisions.

"She's new to the city, and she's all alone. She doesn't even have a couch," Kendall whispered, fidgeting by opening another bottle of wine. She took her time slowly twirling the corkscrew in to avoid Imogen's pointed stare.

"So, is this a stray puppy situation?" Imogen asked.

"No," Kendall glared, tugging on the cork of the bottle. It was cemented in. It was sealed with cement. It had to be.

"Then what is it?" Imogen asked, her eyes widening.

"Oh, leave her alone, darling," Gertie said quietly from behind Imogen. She was hunched over the oven, watching the vegan mac and cheese broil.

"I don't know," Kendall said, shrugging. "A new friend."

Imogen smirked, snorting. "What happened to *my* friend, Kendall *Single-Forever* O'Hara?"

"Can I help with anything?" Joey said from somewhere behind her.

Kendall jumped in surprise, glaring at Imogen before turning around. "Yeah, this wine?" She asked, shoving the bottle into Joey's arms.

"Oh, sure," Joey said, tugging on the corkscrew.

"Here, let a *man* do it," Edward said, waltzing into the kitchen with a twirl and pose.

Thank god for Edward, always willing to lighten the mood and put the spotlight on himself instead.

Joey handed the bottle to Edward, who easily pulled the cork out.

"You must've loosened it for me, sweetheart," Edward said with a wink.

Joey laughed, her cheeks reddening.

Edward poured her a glass of wine, which she took with a playful bow of thanks.

"Let's eat!" Kendall said, clapping her hands.

Imogen grabbed her arm, giving her an intense stare. "You're so not done talking about this with me, Kenny," she whispered.

Kendall rolled her eyes and walked into the dining room.

"You have such a lovely home," Joey said, taking a large gulp of her wine.

"Thank you," Kendall said with a smile.

"I'll give you the tour after dinner," Edward said, beaming with interest. "Here, sit next to me."

Joey laughed and did as he requested.

This was fine. It was fine. Everything was going fine.

"So, tell me more about how Kendall stole your laundry?" Roger asked as he sat on the other side of Joey.

Joey grinned at Kendall. "Well, let me paint the picture. It's a Saturday night. It's deserted. And Kendall was sitting in the corner talking to her bag."

Five sets of eyes turned to look at Kendall.

"That's only half the story," she said quickly as everyone at the table laughed.

Kendall sat at the head of the table so that Imogen and Gertie could sit next to one another. She smiled to herself as she watched Gertie help Imogen dish food, as if Imogen's pregnant belly prevented her from being able to serve herself.

Edward and Roger had their heads bowed over Joey, talking in excited voices. Whereas Edward was the fun, loud one, Roger was sweet and took time to get to know people.

Joey's eyes were wide and she had already finished her first glass of wine.

Kendall held out the bottle towards her with raised brows, which Joey gladly accepted.

Dinner went well, despite Kendall's nerves whenever she thought that Joey was being bombarded with questions.

Joey held her own with remarkable confidence, given that Kendall hadn't prepared her for the lion's den that the party had become. Kendall watched her with interest as she answered questions with a smile, even relaying the tale of Ozzy's foreign body, although Kendall noted that she did not mention exactly what he had eaten. She hid her smile behind her wine glass as Joey showed everyone pictures, and then everyone also shared their pet photos.

After dinner, Edward announced with authority that they were going to play charades.

"It's very hip to play charades," Edward said, not budging one bit on his idea, despite all of the groans from the group.

Joey grinned at Kendall from across the table before turning to Edward. "Fantastic idea. Let's do this. But I hope you're prepared to lose, champ," she said.

"I like your attitude, old sport," Edward joked. "Now, let's all have Joey's joie de vivre!"

"That's... not at all what that means..." Gertie started, but faded out.

"To the living room!" Edward pointed with gusto.

The group began to refill their glasses and Kendall covered the dishes she worried Bacon and Eggs might attack unsupervised — they were hiding somewhere, but she wasn't exactly sure how brave they'd get when faced with the options of mashed potatoes and cornbread.

Joey helped, putting lids and cling wrap onto the dishes.

"Your friends are hilarious," she said quietly, once they were alone at the table.

"Oh yeah, they're a lot, I forgot to warn you about how *much* they can be," Kendall said.

"No, they're great. My friends back home are all stuck in college party mode. This is an actually fun party, though. I can't think of the last time I played charades," she said with a laugh.

Kendall grinned. "Simmer down there, tiger. I've never known charades to be *exciting*."

"Anything is exciting when you play to win," Joey said, raising a glass. "Wanna be on my team?"

Kendall laughed. "With that level of confidence, I'd hate to be on the opposing side," she said. "I just have to feed the kittens first and then I'll be right in."

Joey's eyes widened. "Veal and Lamb Shank? I want to help!"

Kendall looked at her skeptically. "I am *not* naming them Veal and Lamb Shank," she said, but couldn't help the grin tugging at the side of her mouth.

"Sure, whatever, we'll iron out the details later," Joey said, waving her hand in the air. "Now, show me those kittens."

"We'll be right there, I'm just going to have Joey help me feed the bottle babies," she said to the others.

"Oh, is that what the kids are calling it these days?" Edward teased.

CHAPTER SEVEN

JOEY

As Kendall led Joey down the hallway, she glanced around at the painting and photographs on the walls. Kendall opened a door and Joey followed her inside to find that they were in Kendall's bedroom.

She looked around, noticing the perfectly made bed — it looked like something out of a magazine. The furniture matched in a way that was more West Elm than cheesy, and there was even a bench at the end of the bed with a perfectly laid out throw blanket. Everything was exactly in place, like it had been professionally staged.

Two cats lay on the bed in tiny, tucked loaves. "Bacon and Eggs, so nice to meet you," she said, reaching for them.

"The orange fluffy one is Eggs," Kendall said, pointing.

Joey put Eggs, turning to Bacon, who was more marbled dark orange and white.

Ah, the names made a little more sense.

She spied a stack of books on one nightstand. She saw the Sarah Waters' novel was still at the top and smiled to herself.

"Wow, you're like a real adult," Joey joked, looking around as she scratched Bacon under the chin.

Kendall gave her a warm smile while lifting a blanket off a box at the foot of her bed.

Joey saw a medium-size gray tub at the foot of the bed, and she peeked inside to find two tiny kittens both mewing and rolling around.

"Oh my gosh, they're so tiny," she cooed, kneeling beside it.

"Yeah, that's why they're terrifying," Kendall joked, mixing up some kind of formula for bottles.

Joey pulled her phone from the pocket of her dress. "This just reminded me to peek in at Ozzy," she said, by way of explanation. Ozzy was lying down in his crate with his cone still on, like a good boy. "Aw, he's still sleeping."

"Yeah, he's still healing," Kendall said with a smile. "He'll probably still be low energy for a couple days."

She gently took one kitten out of the tub and handed it to Joey, then took the other kitten in her arms.

Joey cooed to the kitten, cuddling her close. She sat on the floor, and Kendall sat beside her.

Kendall smiled. "So cute, right? That's the only reason we let them live. They're such a pain," she joked. "Now, keep her on her belly, and tell me how her temperature feels. Too cold, too warm?"

Joey paused for a moment, considering. "No, feels pretty... normal, I think?" She felt the kitten's tiny forehead as though she was checking for a fever.

Kendall grinned. "Perfect. You'll know it if they're not stable, don't worry. They aren't quiet about their needs, shall we say?"

Kendall explained how to hold the bottle, how to gently rub the kitten's throat to make sure she was drinking.

Joey watched as the kitten reached for her, kneading her

hand that held the bottle. It was so cute that Joey thought she might cry just from seeing it up close.

"Did you always want to be a vet?" She asked.

"No, I wanted to be a doctor," Kendall said lightly. "And then in my first year of med school, I realized I hated it. I just liked the science behind it, and the problem-solving. I just don't like... the people aspect." She had her lips pressed together in a tight line as she stared down at the kitten.

Joey nodded, sort of understanding what Kendall meant, but thinking that she was probably better with people than she realized. After all, Joey liked her.

"I've always loved animals, though. So, I dropped out of med school and got into vet school, and the rest is... sort of history," Kendall said.

"That sounds like a pretty stressful time," Joey said, repositioning the kitten to have a better grasp on her.

Kendall raised her eyebrows and nodded with a shrug. "You could say that," she said.

Joey stopped herself short from asking about what she had heard in the kitchen earlier. Kendall *Single-Forever* O'Hara? What was that all about? And why did Imogen seem cold to her? She had never been one for subtlety or patience, but she felt that asking Kendall about it just yet would be a little too forward.

Regardless, Edward and Roger were lovely, and Gertie had been kind, laughing at a few of her jokes.

But it seemed like she was missing something with the Imogen side of things.

"Alright, I think that's probably good," Kendall said, nodding her head towards the kitten Joey was holding.

Kendall's light blue eyes locked onto hers, and Joey felt something unsaid pass between them. Surely, she had to be imagining it all, right? There was no way this woman truly felt anything for her. Her stomach disagreed, flip-flopping in excitement.

Joey looked down to see that the kitten was nearly asleep in her hand. "Aw, I want to cuddle her forever," she said, but followed Kendall's lead, placing the kitten back in the tub. "Sleep tight, Lamb Shank."

"Oh, *that* one's Lamb Shank?" Kendall said with a grin.

"Yep," Joey said with a nod. "Now, let's go kick some ass at charades."

Kendall laughed, and they walked out of the bedroom to find the group already in a heated round.

Joey climbed out of the rideshare car, thankful that she hadn't thought to drive to Kendall's given the amount of wine she had consumed.

She walked inside the building and trudged up the apartment, smiling to herself as she remembered Kendall trying to act out the word "tittynope." Kendall was comically bad at charades — all she did was mime "breast" and "no," but even then Joey had never even *heard* of the word before, so the odds were definitely not in their favor. Their team had lost by around ten thousand points, although Edward was the one keeping score, so she couldn't be too sure on the exactness of that number.

It was fun to see Kendall like that, though. She had never acted too buttoned-up around Joey, but this was truly different. She was laughing and smiling and light, even though she still held herself in what Joey was growing to think of as a classic-Kendall way: Confident and tall.

Her phone rang in her pocket as she was letting herself into her apartment.

She glanced at the caller ID to see that it was Sunny. She answered it, holding it between her ear and shoulder as she pushed open the door.

"Hey," she said.

"Hello there, dear sister," Sunny said, bright and bubbly as ever. "How's the Wizard of Oz?"

"The wizard is doing fine, I think he's sleeping?" Joey said, setting her keys down on the kitchen counter.

"You think?" Sunny asked. "Aren't you like three feet from him at any given point in your apartment?"

"It's not that small," Joey said, rolling her eyes. "And for your information, I just got home from a party."

"A party?" Sunny repeated, as if she couldn't believe the fact that Joey had friends.

"Yeah, I'm extremely popular and well-liked in Denver," Joey joked. "It was a dinner party with new friends. The vet, actually."

"Wait, your vet invited you to a party? That's kind of weird, right?" Sunny said.

Joey could hear Elliott babbling in the background. "What's Ellie doing up?" She asked.

"I see your deflection, Madame Populaire," Sunny said, laughing. "We're in the middle of bedtime battles. Last night, he took three hours to fall asleep. Three hours, dude."

Joey cringed. "That's awful. Maybe just lock him in his room?" She joked.

"Oh, I've tried. The doorknob is broken, though. I need to buy a new one," she said. Then, softer, as if she was holding the phone further away, she added, "Mister Baby, you better get back in your bedroom right this instant. Ugh, hold on, Jojo."

Joey laughed, kneeling beside Ozzy to open his crate door and pet him. He stretched, seemingly too tired to do much else. At least he looked adorable in the pajamas Kendall had so kindly let her borrow. The pajamas even had legs. He looked like Elliott in footie jammies.

"Okay, so, let me pretend to care about adult things for a moment. The vet is your new friend?" Sunny asked.

"Yeah, I think so," Joey said, considering. "She's queer and

I'm queer and all lesbians are friends, didn't you know that?" She laughed.

"It's like you're the last unicorns and you found each other," Sunny joked.

"Except there were *more* lesbians at the party tonight. A pregnant one, even," Joey said.

"God help her," Sunny said with a sigh.

Joey could hear banging in the background, as if someone was opening and slamming a door.

"They're cute for a little while," Joey laughed. "Until they can talk back."

"Until they gain the knowledge of independence," Sunny groaned. "Okay, wait, we keep getting sidetracked. Are you interested in this vet?"

Joey paused, considering it. "Well, she's extremely attractive, funny, and smart. So, she's way out of my league," she joked. "But no, seriously, I can't fathom being interested in someone."

"Not even just for the sex?" Sunny asked. "Although I realize I'm not exactly the poster child for casual sex."

Joey rolled her eyes, affixing a new puppy pee pad to the setup she had arranged on Kendall's suggestion when Ozzy had gotten home from his surgery. The stairs were still a bit much for Ozzy's tender belly. "We got Elliott out of it, so it's not all bad," she said.

"Yeah, I guess," Sunny said. "Anyway, you don't have to worry about that. So, the vet. Tell me more."

Joey grinned and gossiped with Sunny as she walked around the apartment cleaning up. Kendall's place had been immaculate, what must she have thought of Joey's apartment?

"She's a doppelbanger," Joey explained.

"Sorry, I don't know the lesbian lingo, babe. Explain," Sunny said.

"You know, like a doppelganger. Except I can't tell if I want to be *with* her or *be* her."

"Ah, a uniquely gay conundrum."

"Exactly," Joey said with a giggle.

They chatted a bit more and Joey explained how weird Imogen seemed, how Edward made her feel like translation was extremely exciting and special, and how Gertie had complimented her ability to pantomime the TV show title, "Killing Eve."

Overall, the people were fun, the food was delicious, the wine went down smoothly, and she had a great time.

She said goodbye and hung up the phone after Elliott tried to slap Sunny — the poor woman had her hands full. Being a single mother sounded like the most exhausting thing in the world. Of course she missed her sister, but more than that, she felt guilty for moving away and not being around more to help with Elliott. Their parents helped, but Joey had always been the one to randomly show up and make Sunny either go take a nap, a shower, or run errands in peace and quiet for once.

She resolved to travel back up to Fort Collins as soon as Ozzy was on the mend in a few weeks.

The next day, she woke up with a headache. Ugh, wine headaches were the worst.

She rolled over in bed and grabbed her phone.

Kendall: Thanks for coming last night. I know that the crew can be intense but you did great.

She smiled at the text and sat up to check on Ozzy. He was snoozing in this crate, his snoring extra loud with the mega-phone-like cone around his neck.

She made a cup of coffee and took out her phone to read Kendall's text again.

Joey: Thanks for inviting me! It was nice getting out of my comfort zone.
Joey: If that makes sense. Haha.

Kendall's typing dots appeared and disappeared several times.

Joey set the phone down, afraid that staring at it would make the text never come through. Watching a pot boil and all that.

She wished she had a good excuse to text her again. Maybe if she asked her a vet question?

Joey: Hey, quick vet question: When should I be letting Ozzy exercise more?

She was suddenly a ball of nerves. Had she overstepped the line by asking a vet question?

She set down her phone and walked into the kitchen, pacing.

Finally, her phone buzzed.

Kendall: When we take out his sutures next week. He doing okay?
Joey: Yeah, just cooped up.

Joey stared back down at her phone, trying to figure out how to extend the conversation.

Joey: Do you know any good brunch spots?

She watched the screen, waiting. Then, to her surprise, Kendall was calling her. She stood up, clearing her throat.

"Uh, hey, good morning," she said.

"Hey, you busy? Thought this might be easier than sending a million texts," Kendall said.

Joey could hear the kittens mewing in the background. "No, not busy. Just hungry," Joey said, forcing a laugh.

"Want to grab food together?" Kendall asked casually.

Joey's eyes widened and even though no one could see her, she hid a smile behind her hand. She shook out the tension in her shoulders.

"Sure," she said, as nonchalantly as she could possibly muster.

"Oh, I also wanted to ask," Kendall started. "This might sound weird but Edward and Roger just bought a new couch and were wondering if you want theirs."

"You don't need to go like, sourcing furniture for me or anything," Joey said, laughing awkwardly.

"Oh, I know. Yeah. They mentioned they were getting a new set this week and it just... anyway, no pressure to say yes," Kendall said.

She sounded adorably unsure of herself.

Joey turned in a circle. "Uh, yeah, I'll definitely take it though. I'm not picky," she said.

"Okay, good, because it's hideous," Kendall laughed. "But it's very comfortable, I promise."

"So, then brunch. Any ideas on a spot?" Joey asked.

"Yep. I'll send you the address. See you there in an hour?" Kendall said.

"Sure," she said, as though going out to brunch with a new friend was an everyday occurrence.

Honestly, she hated this awkward stage of friendship, when you weren't sure exactly where the other person stood in terms of wanting to spend time together or being polite.

The address Kendall sent was in the Lower Highlands neighborhood. Joey got ready, then gave Ozzy breakfast and his pills. She waited until he peed on his pad, then changed it to give him a fresh one. She considered carrying him down the steps so he could appreciate grass, but the idea of holding his tender belly in her arms made her grimace with how painful it could be.

She sat on the floor for a while, petting his chin and ears. "My poor baby," she said, and she could have sworn the cooing made his expression turn even *more* pathetic, if that was possible.

She drove to the brunch spot and drove around a few blocks until she found parking. Her neighborhood and this one seemed notorious for having terrible parking, but she only had to drive two blocks away before she found a spot to squeeze into. Thank goodness her car was on the smaller side.

She was double-checking her hair in her visor when a tap on her window startled her. She looked up to see Kendall standing beside the car wearing slacks and a button-up with the sleeves rolled to her elbows. Her hair was casually mussed and she wore aviator sunglasses that made her look way cooler than anyone wearing aviators had a right to look.

It was as if she had heard Joey talking about the doppel-banger conundrum and had decided to lean into the confusion.

They walked together to the restaurant and talked to the hostess, who told them the wait would be an hour and a half.

Kendall sighed, pulling off her sunglasses. "That's outrageous," she said, once they were a few feet away.

"What else is good around here?" Joey asked as they stood on the sidewalk with the dozens of other people who also thought the restaurant was a good brunch choice.

"I don't really know," Kendall said, looking up and down the street.

Joey spotted a taco truck with a small crowd around it. "I bet they have breakfast burritos," she said, pointing.

"I don't know if they'll have anything vegan, though," Kendall said, looking resigned.

"Let's check it out," Joey said.

Kendall didn't budge.

Joey grinned. "Come on, it'll be an adventure," she said with a laugh.

Kendall regarded her, then sighed, raising her eyebrows. "Alright, an adventure," she said with a small grin.

They walked down the block towards the taco truck and Joey eyed the menu, then went up to the window to talk to the cashier. "My friend is vegan, what can she eat?"

The cashier did not look impressed with her question. "Corn tortilla, beans, onions..."

"Do you cook your potatoes in butter or oil?" Joey asked.

"Oil," the man said.

Joey ordered a pair of taco concoctions made of everything vegan she could find on the menu, including a side of green chili, then got a basic breakfast burrito for herself.

The cashier handed her the food and Joey and Kendall sat on the curb nearby, squinting in the bright sun.

"It will either be delicious or terrible, but it's an adventure either way," Joey said with a laugh as Kendall turned the taco over in her hands, eyeing it.

"You keep saying adventure like it's a good thing," Kendall said, taking a petite bite of the taco.

"Adventures are good things. Even when they go badly," Joey said with a laugh. "My sister gave me this poem recently by Frank O'Hara — hey, O'Hara, O'Hara, I just made that connection — and I'm going to paraphrase this badly, but there's this line about how every time his heart is broken, it makes him feel more adventurous, and I want to embody that."

Kendall looked wistful. "That's awfully romantic," she said.

Joey got the sense that she was not using the word romantic in a positive way.

Translation: You're naive.

Joey shrugged.

Kendall chewed slowly, then blinked. "Okay, yeah, it's delicious. Good adventure."

They ate in companionable silence as Kendall used no less than three hundred napkins and Joey dripped hot sauce all over her shoes.

"What's one adventure you always wanted to do but haven't yet?" Joey asked after swallowing a large bite.

"Big adventure or taco truck adventure?" Kendall asked, wiping her mouth.

"Both. One big, one taco truck," Joey said.

"Taco truck adventure... I guess I've always wanted to cut my hair short, just to see if I'd like it. I've always been too afraid to try it," she said, using one hand to hold a strand of hair as though she was considering it.

Joey leaned back, looking at her. "You should definitely try it. That'd look really good," she said, nodding. "Big adventure?"

"I've never been camping," Kendall said. "I want to do a backpacking trip, but I've never done one before."

Joey gasped in surprise. "You've never gone backpacking? It's so fun! We should go this summer," she said, growing excited.

"Easy there, tiger," Kendall joked. "I need to work my way into it. Maybe try car camping first."

"You've never even gone car camping?" Joey asked, shocked. "Not even with your family as a kid?"

"No," Kendall shrugged. "My parents aren't the camping type. We would stay in cabins when we went into the mountains, but never a tent on the ground or anything."

Joey laughed. "Let's go car camping, then. It's really fun. We can eat vegan s'mores," she said, grinning.

Kendall nodded, grinning. "Alright, what's a big adventure you've always wanted to try, then?" She asked.

Joey considered. "Okay, taco truck adventure... I've never ridden a horse," she said.

Kendall's eyes widened in surprise. "Miss Of-Course-I've-Gone-Camping has never tried horseback riding?"

"Nope, I've always been a bit afraid of them," Joey confessed, blushing.

Kendall laughed, nodding. "I got kicked in the leg by a horse once. Had the biggest bruise. They're jerks when they want to be."

Joey laughed, taking a bite of her burrito to give herself a moment to think.

"Big adventure, I've always wanted to go to Hawaii," Joey said. "Hike to a waterfall and lie on the beach..."

"My parents own a place in Hawaii," Kendall said with a shrug. "But I've never been."

Joey's eyes widened. "Are your parents super-rich? Are you secretly an heiress?"

Kendall laughed, shaking her head. "No, it was always my dad's dream, so they worked hard and made it happen," she said.

"Then, why haven't you been?" Joey asked.

"I don't really talk to my dad anymore," Kendall said, and Joey could tell by the forced shrug and lack of eye contact that there was way more to that story than she was letting on.

"Oh, I'm sorry to hear that," Joey offered, feeling awkward. She wanted to ask more, but she wasn't sure they were on that level of friendship yet.

They ate in companionable silence again for a few moments.

Kendall turned, wiping her mouth again. "What do you think it will take to make your adventure happen?"

Joey considered the question for a moment. "Do you want to be my adventure buddy?" She asked.

Kendall looked surprised by the question. "In what sense?"

Joey sat up straight, holding out her hands as if they might keep Kendall's judgment at bay long enough to explain. "Look, I know this is a big ask, so feel free to say no. But what if we tried these adventures? You can take me camping, I can take you horseback riding, yadda yadda. We'll try it together."

Kendall tilted her head to the side, and although the aviators hid most of her expression, Joey could see a hint of a grin at the edge of her mouth. "I don't know," she started. "How would we decide?"

"Okay, just hear me out. What if we each wrote down five adventures, taco truck-small or Hawaii-big, and put them in a jar, and then drew one whenever we needed an adventure?" Joey asked, growing excited about the idea.

Kendall smiled. "That could be fun," she said, shrugging. "Why the hell not?"

CHAPTER EIGHT

KENDALL

Kendall recorded the kitten's weight in her notebook, pleasantly surprised that the little water balloons were gaining weight on exactly the right track.

They still needed formula every two to three hours and they still needed to be stimulated to go to the bathroom, but overall, her hard work was proving to be worth it.

She checked the teeth of the female — LS... that was the closest she was getting to naming the kitten Lamb Shank — ensuring that her incisors were still coming in properly.

Since she had a few minutes until her next appointment, she took a toothbrush out of her Kitten Kit and started gently pretending to groom the kitten, petting her in long strokes with the brush. LS mewed, stretching out one tiny arm full of needle-sharp claws.

"They're just so cute," Taylor said, walking past where she was sitting over their tub.

Kendall groaned. "They're cute until it's their third feeding of the night and you're so tired you try to shove the syringe of formula up their–"

"Okay, that's a pretty vivid picture already," Taylor said, laughing.

"For a tech, you're awfully squeamish," Kendall said, raising her brow.

Taylor let their expression fall flat as they deadpanned, "I've seen some things, Kendall."

Kendall laughed, putting LS back into the tub. She checked the heated pad she kept in there with them to make sure it was adequately warm and snuggly.

"You're so cute," Kendall said to the kittens. "Open those eyes, come see the world."

"You're in a good mood today," Taylor said, twirling around in their chair.

"Am I?" Kendall said, but even she couldn't stop the grin spreading on her face. "Just had a good day yesterday, that's all."

"Oh yeah? Is this a lesbian thing?" Taylor smirked. "Listen, I used to identify as a lesbian. So, you can talk to me."

"Very comforting," Kendall said, snorting. "You're lucky Paul isn't here to tell us this is an inappropriate work conversation."

"Kendall, your 4 p.m. is here and I've got the history," Kat said, leaning her head into the back room. "You have a moment to go over it?"

"Yep," Kendall said, motioning to the chair in front of her.

"Well, first, I'd recommend you put a muzzle on him," Kat said.

"Okay," Kendall said, raising a brow as she waited for more information.

"Second, he had diarrhea all over the front rug, so I'm going to need the clinic to buy us pizza if I'm expected to clean that up," Kat said, crossing her arms but smiling.

Kendall laughed. "Taylor told you I was in a good mood?"

Kat grinned, glancing over to Taylor. "Something like that," she said.

It had been four days since they had agreed to the adventures, but Kendall was already reconsidering her acceptance.

She sat at her dining table with a notebook and her favorite pen, ready to write down her adventures.

Camping.

Haircut.

Buy a bespoke, tailored suit.

...But what else? She still had two to add, and Joey was going to be over at any moment.

Could she steal Joey's Hawaii idea? She stared down at the blank page before her, racking her brain to think of her bucket list items.

Ugh, it was no use. She rubbed her eyes and held her face in her hands for a moment, but she was startled when the doorbell rang.

She glanced at the clock. Joey was a bit early...

More than a bit early. An hour?

She opened the door to find Imogen standing on her front step.

"What's wrong?" Kendall asked, opening her door a little wider. "What's up? Did I miss your call or something?"

"Nothing's wrong. I just feel like an asshole," Imogen said, flipping her dark hair over her shoulder as she walked in and headed for the kitchen. "Do you have maraschino cherries?"

"Uh, not that I know of?" What the hell had gotten into Imogen? Kendall followed her into the kitchen, watching her hold a jar of peanut butter while still apparently searching in the fridge for something else.

"Damn, okay," Imogen said, unscrewing the lid of the jar of peanut butter while opening the silverware drawer. She dipped the spoon in the peanut butter, then shoved the spoon in her mouth as she turned, opening up the pantry cupboard.

"There's cookies in there if you want," Kendall said,

leaning over the kitchen island. "Why are you an asshole, though?"

"Because I got jealous of your new friend," Imogen said in a huff, as though it annoyed her to say it. "Gertie made me come over and apologize. There, I've done it."

"That wasn't an apology, babe. You said neither 'Sorry' nor 'I apologize,'" Kendall smirked.

"I'm your best friend, right?" Imogen asked. She looked like the answer she needed to hear was yes.

Kendall nodded slowly, trying not to laugh or even grin at the utter absurdity of it all.

"And if you think things are going to change once the baby gets here, then you're probably correct," Imogen continued, waving around a jar of sprinkles in her hand.

Kendall nodded, watching curiously.

"But I will not be replaced by some twenty-three-year-old," Imogen said.

"She's twenty-eight, actually, but that's beside the point," Kendall said, waving her hand in the air.

"What could you possibly have in common?" Imogen asked, looking exasperated.

"Time? The shared experience of being single?" Kendall said, shrugging.

"But you're friends with her because you're interested in her?" Imogen asked.

"I don't know. I like her, but I also have begun to really value our friendship, so I'd rather be her friend than a casual hookup," Kendall explained.

"Why are those mutually exclusive? Why isn't there a plan C?" Imogen asked, tilting her head quizzically.

"What, like... dating?" Kendall asked, cringing at the thought.

"You could at least *try* dating," Imogen said.

"I don't want to," Kendall said firmly. "And you, of all people, should understand why."

It was true that they had a complicated history together, but they had worked hard to get past that. She thought they had been on the same page. After all that Imogen had seen after Fiona left...

Imogen narrowed her eyes. "You're seriously blaming *me* for the fact that you're..." She let her words trail off.

"That I'm what?" Kendall asked, feeling defensive.

Imogen shook her head. "I don't want to go there. I'm just mad. I'm mad and I'm sad and I'm hungry and I'm upset all the time," she said.

"Well, take your weird anger out on someone else," Kendall said, rolling her eyes.

"Listen, I love you and I want you to be happy and if banging a pre-teen is going to help you get through a midlife crisis, then be my guest," Imogen said in a huff.

There was the line. The imaginary boundary of how much Imogen could push until Kendall shoved her back. Kendall knew that boundary well. Imogen had been testing it for the entirety of their friendship, nearly twenty-five years.

Kendall hardened her expression. "You can blame this on the hormones if you'd like, but you're being a real asshole, and I think you should go home," she said.

"I was just leaving," Imogen scoffed, then she popped a cookie into her mouth and stomped out the front door, slamming it in her wake.

Kendall felt as though she had just been slapped across the face. Had that conversation even happened or was she imagining it?

She pulled her phone out of her pocket to text Gertie.

Kendall: Hurricane Imogen on her way home. Good luck.

Gertie: 10-4. Thanks for the heads up. Take it the apology went great?

Kendall sent a thumbs-up emoji and walked into the kitchen to fill the kettle with hot water. It was irresponsible to start a bottle of wine at 3 p.m. just to drown her feelings, right? Tension Tamer tea would have to do for now.

She eyed the cookie packet, but before she could change her mind, she sealed it, putting it away in the pantry.

She poured herself a cup of tea to soothe her hurt feelings. Was Imogen being paranoid? And if she was just being hormonal and intense, then, why did her words sting so bad?

Joey showed up around fifteen minutes later — just enough time for the tea to make her feel slightly calmer.

Kendall opened the door to see her standing with Ozzy in his pretty pink pajamas. The dog started wiggling as soon as he saw her. She had, of course, invited Joey to bring Ozzy, but it was good to see him again. She knelt down to pet his ears and neck as he excitedly tried to lick her face.

"I see the Prince is feeling better," Kendall joked, taking a step back to let Joey and Ozzy in.

Joey grinned. "He's lived with a cat before, just in case the breakfast duo decides to make an appearance.

"Noted," Kendall said, nodding. "Did your ex have a cat?"

"Oh, no," Joey laughed. "Just an old roommate. I never lived with my ex."

"Ah, maybe a good idea," Kendall said, nodding. She picked up her mug to take another sip of tea.

Joey's brow furrowed as she watched Kendall. "What's wrong?" She asked.

Kendall frowned in surprise. "Uh, nothing," she said. Then, she sighed, waving her hand in the air. "Just had a weird thing with Imogen, but it'll be fine."

"Weird how?" Joey asked. "Because she was a little… cold the other night, too."

Kendall sat down at the table, shrugging. "She was, wasn't she?" She said. She was afraid to tell Joey anything more, worried that she'd freak her out or hurt her feelings.

"She said something that was really strange about you

being single forever," Joey said as casually as possible, watching Ozzy walk around the room to sniff things.

"Oh," Kendall said, forcing a laugh. "That was nothing important."

Joey raised a brow. "Well, you've been friends for a billion years, right?" she asked, sliding out a chair from the table.

Kendall laughed, shaking her head. "Something like that," she said.

Joey raised a brow, and Kendall realized that sounded kind of cryptic.

She inhaled deeply, as if preparing for a long monologue. "Imogen was my first girlfriend." There. Now it was out in the open. That's all she needed to say. Right?

Joey paused and turned to fully face her as though a record had just scratched to a full stop. "How does *that* work?"

Kendall shrugged. "We were young. We dated all through college and for a little while after. When we broke up, we didn't talk for a year or two, but we reconnected when... when I was leaving a bad relationship." Well, that was the very bland version of it, at least.

Joey's eyes stayed wide for a moment. "You two are so normal together, though. I think I'd punch Raina in the face if I saw her right now," she said.

"Hence the time apart. Helped to heal the wounds," Kendall said.

"Why'd you break up?" Joey asked. "I mean, if that's not too personal." She added the last part quickly.

"A lot of different reasons. Mostly, we were young and didn't know what we wanted for our futures," she said. "When I dropped out of med school, the stress of the entire thing took a huge toll on our relationship. I think by the end of it, we were more roommates than partners, you know?"

Joey nodded. "You sound like you've thought about this a lot," she said.

"Oh, tons of money poured into therapy helped me get to this point, don't worry," Kendall said with a laugh and a wink.

Joey didn't seem too bothered after the initial surprise, at least.

"I don't think I'll ever forgive Raina for what she did. I don't think we'll ever be like you and Imogen," she said, her expression growing more solemn.

Kendall reached across the table and touched Joey's arm. "And that's okay," she said.

Joey glanced from the place where Kendall touched her, and Kendall realized it might have been the first physical contact between them. She sat up, clearing her throat, and looked around for Ozzy.

She found him lying on the floor under the table, his head resting on Joey's foot.

"Aw, a little Mama's boy," Kendall teased. "I'll check his incision later, but from what I can tell, he seems to be in good spirits."

Joey seemed to beam with pride at the comment. "I've been working hard to make sure he's okay. Don't want my vet thinking I'm a bad dog mom."

Kendall smiled at Joey's comment. She couldn't help but think that Joey's light mood was contagious — she was feeling better than she had all day, just from the fact that Joey was sitting at her table.

"I've brought my adventures," Joey said, reaching into her purse to produce a mason jar with slips of paper inside. "But, I have a confession."

Kendall watched her skeptically. "What is it?"

"I could only think of four," Joey said, laughing. Her cheeks turned slightly more pink.

"Better than me, I could only think of three," Kendall said with a laugh.

"Okay, put them in here," Joey said, unscrewing the lid of the jar. "Do you have any tape?"

"Uh, yeah, I think so," Kendall said, getting up to go search the junk drawer in the kitchen. "Will painter's tape work?"

"Sure," Joey said, and Kendall brought the roll with her back to the table. Joey wrote *Adventure Jar* on a piece of paper in scribbled handwriting and tore off two pieces of blue tape, sticking it to the side of the jar. "Ta-da!" She smiled, holding up her masterpiece.

"Beautiful work," Kendall teased, giving her a thumbs up.

"Why, thank you," Joey said, giggling. She looked at the jar for a moment, a line appearing on her forehead as though she was in deep concentration. "What if we save our last three adventures and decide on them after we finish all of these? I'm sure ideas will come to us."

"We have to finish all of these? I thought it was like a revolving bucket list," Kendall said.

"Oh no, we're definitely doing all of them," Joey said. "No matter how scary or dumb they may be. If it's a one-sided adventure, like getting a hair cut, then the other person has to go for moral support."

Kendall bit her bottom lip. "You didn't put anything in there like... pole dancing or take LSD at Burning Man, right?" She asked.

"Guess you'll just have to find out," Joey said with a grin and wiggled her eyebrows.

Kendall laughed. "Well, who knows what we're in for then," she said.

"Pinky swear you'll do them no matter what?" Joey asked. She held out her fist, her pinky extended.

"I pinky swear," Kendall said, reaching out to link her pinky with Joey's.

Joey leaned forward and kissed her own thumb.

"What was that?" Kendall asked, watching her.

"You have to seal it with a kiss," Joey said, looking exasperated. "It's the most basic rule of pinky swearing."

"I've never heard of that. Must be a new one." Kendall looked down at their linked hands and leaned forward to kiss her own thumb. Her eyes flicked up to Joey as she did so, and Joey's eyes flashed with something she didn't want to fully explore just yet. Then, just as quickly, a wide, easy smile spread across Joey's full lips.

Joey clapped her hands together. "Perfect," she said. "Now, let's draw our first adventure!"

Kendall looked at her in confusion. "Already?"

"What better time than now?" Joey said, grinning.

"Okay, you draw it," Kendall said, nodding her head toward the jar.

"Alright," Joey said with a comical amount of conviction. She shook the jar, then reached inside. She fished around for a piece of paper while making a point not to look, and then drew one out.

Her cheeks turned bright red. "Well, I wasn't expecting this one to be our first. It's mine, so I can pick again," she said.

"Nope, rules are rules," Kendall said, as though there were any rules besides what they had pinky-sweared about.

"Buy a..." She paused, swallowing as though her mouth had become dry.

"What is it?" Kendall said, leaning forward.

Joey set the piece of paper down on the table. It read, "Buy a sex toy in a shop."

Kendall laughed. "You've never been to a sex toy shop? Wait, you do own... well, of course, you do, because you had a harness. But, wait. I'm confused."

"No, I've always just bought them online. And not like, *many*. Just the... you know, the basics," Joey said, looking around the room as though making eye contact in that moment would have been devastating to her pride.

"The basics? Like, what?" Kendall asked, crossing her arms

to watch Joey struggle. It was too funny not to find joy in her prudish discomfort.

"Like... the..." Joey said, moving her hands in vague gestures.

"I'm assuming if you had a harness, you have a dildo. But when you're single, those are less fun. So, most importantly, do you have a vibrator?" Kendall asked, trying her best to keep her expression as still as possible in order not to embarrass Joey even further — but she could feel a grin or laugh creeping up on her.

Joey nodded. "Um, I have a little bullet thing?"

Kendall's eyes widened. "Why? How? No. Those things are clitoral jackhammers," she said before she could help herself.

Joey flushed an even deeper shade of red, and Kendall would have bet money on the fact that she was considering climbing under the table.

"We're going to get you a nice vibrator," Kendall said confidently. "Everything else is just icing on the cake. We have to get the foundations."

"Well, oh wise and noble guide, glad I have you to help me on this journey," Joey said, shaking her head.

CHAPTER NINE

JOEY

Why the hell had she written down "Buy a sex toy in a shop?"

She had been mentally kicking herself for the few days since she had pulled that slip out of the jar. They had waited a few days to coordinate when they were both off on the same evening. Saturday was the lucky day.

She had arrived a few minutes early to make sure that she had the right place, but she hadn't realized that having a few extra moments would also give her time to start chickening out.

Nerves swirled in her belly and her hands were clammy. She wiped them on the skirt of her dress.

What if she went inside and they started judging her? Or judging her choices? What if she looked like she knew nothing about sex in front of Kendall?

She didn't know if she'd ever be able to recover from that one.

She knew *plenty* about sex. Specifically, how to have it without purchasing items where another person has to look you in the eye.

She looked down at the map on her phone, which showed that she was at the right place. Kendall had sent the address earlier that day.

She lingered down the block, waiting for Kendall to show up. There was no way she was going in there alone.

Even if going in there with a woman she had a crush on seemed… somehow both worse and better?

"You okay?" Kendall asked from behind her.

Joey spun around, startled.

Kendall, of course, looked effortlessly good. She was wearing a denim jacket and black jeans, like some kind of off-duty rock star. Seeing her instantly made Joey feel much more nervous.

Joey shoved her hands in the pockets of her skirt. "Yep," she said. "Yep. Great. Can't wait."

Kendall grinned. "It's going to be fine. This is a female-owned sex shop, so it's not skeezy. No edible panties in here." She paused. "I think."

Joey nodded. "Cool. Cool cool cool." She couldn't stop words from coming out of her mouth. Why couldn't she stop saying the word cool? She rocked back on her heels, trying to calm the fuck down.

Kendall reached out to take Joey by the upper arms. "It's going to be fine. You're going to be so happy you did this," she said, winking.

Joey nodded, trying not to focus on the fact that Kendall's face was mere inches away, staring deep into her eyes. Kendall's bright blue eyes were stunning from so close up, especially in the late afternoon light.

"Now, come on," Kendall said, hooking one of Joey's arms through hers.

She might have meant it in a sign of solidarity, but it also worked to keep Joey from bolting down the street.

Still, having her arm through Kendall's made Joey's stomach swirl in a whole new way.

Ugh, her friend was doing something kind for her. She had to stop trying to make it something it wasn't.

Bells jingled over the door as they entered, announcing their presence for all to see.

She took a deep cleansing breath through her nose, expecting the worst.

The shop was painted dark green and there were plants tucked into nearly every corner and on every surface. A velvet wingback chair sat in one of the corners, and an entire wall was lined with books. Feist was playing over the speakers. It was as familiar and cozy as walking into a friend's home.

Okay, so it wasn't quite the sticky den of perversion she had been envisioning. Maybe she wouldn't need the hand sanitizer in her bag after all.

"Hello," a woman with dyed blue hair standing behind the counter said. "Let me know if you'd like any help or if you have any questions."

Alright, so her idea of a pushy salesperson talking to her about nipple clamps or questioning her interest about anal beads was also not a reality.

Kendall unhooked their arms and reached to hold up a book to show her. It was titled *How To Date Men When You Hate Men.* "Resounding evidence to just date anyone but men," she whispered conspiratorially.

Joey burst out in giggles.

She let her shoulders relax, stepping around a few tables piled with books, trinkets, and smooth crystal wands, the latter of which made her wonder where those... went, exactly. She noted an entire table covered in dildos of all shapes and sizes, set up as a tiny army of silicone soldiers. She walked towards a bookshelf lined with trinkets, books, plants, and surprisingly, vibrators.

They were so damn aesthetically-pleasing for being vibrators. Like tiny, pleasurable works of art. She took one box off the shelf to look at the back of it, turning it over in her hands to see what its features were. That's how vibrators worked, right?

"I liked that one, but it needed constant recharging," Kendall said, rolling her eyes.

"You have this one?" Joey said, feeling slightly scandalized. She tried her hardest not to imagine Kendall with the vibrator in her hand...

Kendall nodded. "Yeah, not worth it."

Joey grabbed another box off the shelf. It was a tiny metal piece without much information on the package.

"Butt plugs?" Kendall asked, raising her eyebrows.

"What? No," Joey said, quickly putting the box back down.

"Don't knock it 'til you try it," Kendall said with a wink.

Joey's mouth dropped open slightly. Wow, Kendall contained multitudes.

Kendall cleared her throat. "Okay, so the whole fun part of coming to the adult toy shop is to see the size of things, maybe even test whatever they have open, and get a feel for what calls to you."

"You can *test* them?" Joey whispered, feeling horrified and looking suspiciously at all of the merchandise on the walls. She was overcome with the urge to wash her hands and run.

Kendall laughed, shaking her head. "No, no, you test them by turning them on and holding them in your hand, not... like, using them." She shook her head again, wiping at the corner of her eye. "God, no, this isn't some play party... no."

Joey took a side step away from the shelving unit, just to be on the safe side.

"You can also ask questions, because the staff here are super knowledgeable and awesome," Kendall said, glancing at the blue-haired woman with a smile.

Blue Hair smiled at them both. "Thanks, we try," she said. She had tattoos covering both her arms and Joey could even see another peeking out from the low V-cut of her shirt. —

good tattoos were normally Joey's kryptonite, but was Blue Hair Kendall's type?

Joey looked between them, watching the cashier check out Kendall right in front of her. Did they really give off friend vibes so strong that Blue Hair felt fine checking out the woman with her so blatantly?

And why did that bother her *so* much?

Her immature jealous feelings were interrupted as Kendall reached for a vibrator out of the box. It had a gold inlay and a beautiful, sleek look. "This is my favorite one," she said.

She turned it on and handed it to Joey. Joey held it in both hands.

"Now, see how it's more rumbly than buzzy? Hold it on that fleshy part of your palm," Kendall said, her voice lowering.

Joey wondered briefly if the palm was an erogenous zone. The way Kendall was standing so close, talking quietly... even if it wasn't, it was for her now.

"What's this part for?" She asked, pointing to the part of the vibrator that was sticking out separately.

Kendall pointed. "That goes outside, and this part goes inside," she said. "Clit. Vag."

Joey laughed, shocked. "I can't believe you just said that."

Kendall laughed again. "I can't believe you think this is so scandalous," she said.

She took another one off the shelf and handed it to Joey, turning it on just as it touched Joey's hands.

It wiggled in her hand, which startled her into nearly dropping it. Instead, she juggled it between her hands like a hot potato, and Kendall reached, catching it for the both of them.

"You doing okay?" Kendall said, dropping her voice.

"Doing great," Joey said, nodding quickly.

Kendall pointed to another vibrator, which was a massive wand that looked terrifying. "That's my second favorite."

"That looks like my mother's back massager," Joey said, looking at the device skeptically.

Kendall gave her a pointed look, then grinned.

"Oh," Joey said. "Wait, no, gross." She had full-body shivers just thinking about it.

Kendall laughed. "I'm joking... kind of," she said.

"Are you two shopping for anything in particular?" The woman at the counter asked.

Kendall nodded. "We're finally getting this girl a good vibrator. I recommended the Soraya," she said.

"Oh, a very good choice," the woman said, looking her up and down.

Joey bristled slightly, even though she had begun to realize she had no right to. Kendall had definitely been clear about Joey being only a friend. She would have made a move by now otherwise, right?

And maybe that was good for Joey. She was probably still too heartbroken anyway to deal with anything but a rebound, and she liked Kendall far too much to make her a rebound. She'd just jump into something way too fast and get heart-broken all over again once they'd inevitably break up. They were way better off as friends. Way better.

Still though, the confidence Kendall had about sex and toys made Joey feel a little... curious. Sure, curious was the word for that. Not intensely turned on or anything. Apprecia-tive of her knowledge. Yes. *Appreciative*, that was the right word.

Kendall turned back to her and Joey stole another look at the woman at the counter, who was definitely checking out Kendall's ass.

She resisted the urge to put her arm around Kendall, which she imagined was the equivalent of peeing on her terri-torially. Besides, she couldn't *claim* Kendall. Kendall could definitely sleep with that woman, and Joey would just have to be happy for her. She would.

She flipped over the vibrator in her hand to check the price. Holy shit. That was like a car payment. She couldn't justify spending $200 just on her own pleasure. She set it back down on the shelf, shoving her hands back in her pockets.

"You don't like it?" Kendall asked, her eyebrows raising.

"Uh, no, it's very pretty and... rumbly, but," Joey began, shrugging. She was too embarrassed to admit there was no way she could justify that expense after Ozzy's vet bill.

Her translation job paid well, but it did not pay $200 for a vibrator well.

"Would it be weird if I bought this for you?" Kendall said, taking the box from the shelf, turning it over in her hands, and also apparently reading her mind. "Like as an adventure kind of gift. And as a Please-Stop-Using-A-Bullet gift."

Joey blinked. "No way," she said.

"I just refuse to let you not have mind-blowing orgasms anymore," Kendall said, and was Joey just imagining it or was Kendall making intense eye contact with her? Had she taken a step closer? Had the space between them just become static charged?

Joey's stomach flipped again and she cleared her throat. She licked her lips, and Kendall's eyes slipped down to her mouth.

Was it all in her head or was there the chance that Kendall returned the feelings? No, she couldn't possibly.

Right?

Kendall's features relaxed as she turned away.

Right.

"You seriously do not need to do that," Joey said, reaching for the box, but Kendall held it out of her reach.

Kendall shrugged lightly. "Ooh, what about this? Or is this a little too on the nose?" She gestured to a mannequin modeling a harness.

"Mine was nicer," Joey joked. Then, raising her voice

slightly to be overheard by a certain cashier near them, she said, "But you should know that, you saw it, right?"

Kendall smirked, then glanced at her phone, swiping the screen with her thumb. "Hey, are you free tonight, like all night?"

Joey inhaled quickly, which caused her to choke, which kicked off an entire coughing fit.

Kendall looked concerned. "Are you okay?"

Joey nodded, covering her mouth and turning away. "Yeah, sorry, just... wrong tube," she said. She took a step backward to avoid coughing in Kendall's face, bumping right into the table with dildos set up in an aesthetically-pleasing arrangement.

The next part happened in slow motion: The table teetered under the sudden force as she lost her balance, falling back to the floor with a yelp, as the table tipped towards her. She managed to roll away from the tipping table, but not the dozen or so dildos that launched sideways off of the surface to pelt her like tiny, rubbery torpedoes.

The icing on the cake was the massive rainbow dildo that smacked her right in the face.

"Jesus," Kendall said, falling onto her knees beside Joey, eyebrows drawn with concern. "Are you okay?"

"Oh my goodness," the cashier said, rushing over to help.

Joey considered pretending to be dead, just in case that might make them leave her alone to wallow in self-pity. Or maybe she'd get amnesia from hitting her head and forget this happened? Maybe she'd be lucky and it would all be a terrible, terrible nightmare.

Instead, she opened her eyes to find Kendall inches from her face, staring at her with a panicked expression.

Kendall was kneeling beside her, looking into each of her eyes. "Are you okay? Don't move just yet."

Joey immediately neglected the instruction and pushed

herself up on her elbow, reached to feel the back of her head where she had smacked it on the ground.

Kendall reached for her, feeling the back of her neck, then around on her scalp. "Anything hurt?"

"Just my pride," Joey said. She sat all the way up and looked down at her lap, where a giant blue dildo lay. "Did I break any of them? Am I going to have to buy, like, twenty dildos right now? I really only came here to buy one."

Kendall glanced down, then back up to Joey. Joey could tell she was holding back a laugh.

"Don't you dare," Joey scolded, but as she said the words, laughter bubbled up inside of her. A mix of intense embarrassment and adrenaline just added to the moment, making her start laughing so hard she could barely breathe.

Kendall began to laugh, too, picking up a neon pink dildo and pointing it at her. "You were attacked," she said. "Or did *you* attack them?"

Joey held up a veiny blue dildo as it jiggled in her hands and apologized to it, which made them both laugh harder.

The cashier stood over them with wide eyes.

Kendall pulled Joey up with her, checking her over again.

Joey wiped the hysterical tears from her eyes, trying her best to take a deep breath and stop giggling. "I think that's enough adventure for me," she said.

This was why she bought toys online. Nothing bad ever happened to her in a virtual sex toy shop.

The cashier began straightening the display and Kendall knelt to help her, still grinning.

"I'm going to go wait outside," Joey announced, ready to run from the premises and never return. Maybe just leave town. Change her name, dye her hair. The whole thing. She was never recovering from the Great Dildo Attack.

Kendall nodded. "I'll be out in a second," she said.

She walked as carefully and quickly as she could out of

the store and stood on the sidewalk, looking around for holes she could crawl into and die.

When she glanced back in the window, she saw Kendall leaning on her elbow on the cash register. Great. She had brought them together through the adversity of straightening a dildo display.

She busied herself by texting Sunny, still giggling when she pictured what had just happened.

Joey: You're never going to believe what I just did to a table of dildos.

Sunny texted back immediately.

Sunny: Did you mean to text this to me?

Kendall left the store, holding a bag in her hand. "You okay?" She asked.

Joey shrugged. "Can't wait to tell the grandkids about that someday," she said, trying to play off her humiliation. She avoided looking at Kendall and opted for staring at the ground instead.

"Well, I got your dignity a Get Well Soon present," Kendall said, holding out the bag.

"You didn't seriously buy me anything, did you?" Joey said, looking in the bag. It was the $200 vibrator. "I can't... you shouldn't have done that. I can't repay you."

Kendall leaned in. "Next adventure is on you," she said.

Joey couldn't help herself. She leapt forward, wrapping both arms around Kendall in a tight hug. Kendall laughed, but returned the hug. Kendall was only slightly taller than Joey, but she felt strong and protective in that moment.

"Thank you," she whispered against Kendall's shoulder.

"Of course," Kendall whispered back.

"I'm sorry if I embarrassed you," Joey said.

"Are you kidding? That was one of the best things to ever happen to me in a sex toy shop," Kendall said, pulling away to give her a smile.

Joey felt the loss of her as soon as she pulled away.

She really had to stop fantasizing about Kendall if she wanted this friendship to last.

"Thank you, even though this is absurd," Joey said.

"I hope it's not awkward that I bought that, I know you're... less than open about this kind of thing, so I don't want you to have weird feelings around it," Kendall said. "And I wanted our first adventure to end on a positive note."

Joey smiled and nodded. "You're a good egg, O'Hara," she said.

Kendall grinned. "Thanks, pal."

Translation: Pal.

Hmm, a cognate.

"Hey, why did you ask me if I was free?" Joey asked, remembering what triggered her coughing fit in the first place.

"Edward and Roger were asking if they could bring the couch over to your place," Kendall said, grabbing her phone out of her pocket.

"Sure, I don't have concrete plans," Joey said, shrugging.

"Okay. I have to get back to the kittens, so I might leave you to fend with them on your own, if that's okay," Kendall said. "I'll send them your contact info."

Joey nodded. "I think the three of us can manage just fine," she said.

Three hours later, she was maneuvering a couch up three flights of stairs, singing a different tune.

"I can't believe we thought doing an act of kindness was a good idea," Edward yelled up the stairs to Roger, who had taken the front of the couch.

Roger groaned from somewhere on the other end of the couch.

"Not sure why you guys had a couch built from the heaviest material known to humankind," Joey said, her entire body aching as she and Edward tried to lift the bottom end of the couch again.

"It wasn't heavy until it came into this building. I think gravity is a little more intense here, for some reason. It's like Mercury or something," he said, panting.

"You mean like Mars? You'd be lighter on Mercury," Joey corrected.

"Don't you science me, young lady," Edward said.

They somehow made it to the third floor and through the studio, setting down the couch in her living room.

"And that's where it lives, because we'll never move it ever again, not even across the room," Edward said, falling onto the couch dramatically.

Ozzy's tail beat against the sides of his crate in the excitement of visitors.

"Y'all want a beer or something?" Joey asked, wiping sweat from her forehead.

"You got vodka?" Roger asked, leaning on the couch, catching his breath.

"I think so," Joey said, walking into the kitchen to find a bottle in the cupboard. "What do you want to mix it with?"

"You got seltzer?" He asked.

She grabbed one of the off-brand seltzer waters her mother had bought her from Costco during one of her first weeks in the apartment. She had brought seltzer water, frozen waffles, and coffee. The woman sure knew how to keep a kid alive.

She handed both to Roger, then pointed at Edward. "You want the same?" She asked.

"Beer is fine, sweet cheeks," he said with a cheesy smile.

Joey laughed, finding two beers in the fridge. She handed one to Edward and opened the other.

"Thank you so much for this favor. I will never underestimate the need for a couch ever again," she said, reaching to open Ozzy's crate. He wiggled over to Edward, licking his hand, before dashing to Roger, sniffing his pants intensely. Then, he gingerly hopped onto the couch, curling into a small ball.

"Any friend of Kendall's is a friend of ours," Roger said with a smile, raising his seltzer can in a cheers.

Edward gave him a skeptical look. "Since when?"

"Since now," Roger said.

Joey laughed. "It's weird that Kendall decided she'd be my friend, but here we are," she said.

"Why? You're adorable and if I were even remotely bisexual, I'd be all about it," Edward said.

Joey raised an eyebrow, sipping her beer. "Uh, thanks? I think?"

Roger rolled his eyes. "No, but seriously, I can't wait until you and Kendall get over your hangups and just get together already."

"I don't have hangups," Joey said, furrowing her brow.

"Everybody has hangups," Edward said. "Plus, we know you're freshly out of a relationship, and probably a little nervous, but our girl Kendall is a catch."

Joey wasn't sure how to proceed. She didn't want to tell Roger and Edward she was interested in Kendall if it would get back to her and jeopardize their friendship. Instead, she laughed. "She *is* fantastic. I'm just not ready for anything."

"God, what is it with people when it's always nothing or marriage? You can hit it and still be friends," Edward said, rolling his eyes.

"Tell me how that worked out for you, baby," Roger said, a snarky smile on his face.

"You're the exception," Edward said, reaching out to squeeze Roger's cheek.

Joey giggled. "How long have you been together?"

"Together for six, married for two," Roger said, nearly beaming as he said it.

That's what Joey wanted. True, lasting love. Eventually. In ten years or so, when she could fathom trying to date anyone ever again.

"I was engaged like two months ago, so I'm just trying to... you know, do me," Joey said, remembering her new vibrator. She almost laughed, but didn't want to have to explain herself.

Edward's eyes widened. "Oh my giddy aunt, tell me *everything*," he said.

Roger leaned further over the back of the couch, his eyes wide. "What happened?"

She told them the story, including the details of The Worst Pizza Party Ever, and ended with Raina calling her at the vet's office. She had avoided giving anyone else so many details about the event, but Edward and Roger made it easy by being vocally Team Joey throughout the story.

Edward gasped. "You deleted her number?"

Roger reached out to high-five her.

"But, wait, you totally have it memorized, don't you?" Edward said, winking.

"That's beside the point," Joey said, holding a finger in the air as if to stand her ground. "It was very freeing."

"Fuck that girl. You're so cute and wonderful and she's crazy," Edward said, and Roger nodded.

Joey nearly teared up. "Thank you," she said. "It's been... it sucks." She admitted, petting Ozzy.

"We should go out sometime," Edward said, growing excited. "Have you been to the gay bars here yet?"

"I've been to Charlie's, I think? That's the half-country bar with line dancing, half-hip hop bar with normal dancing?"

"We have so much to teach you," Edward said, reaching forward to place his hand over hers. "And I can't wait."

An hour later, after Edward and Roger left, Joey curled up on the couch with Ozzy.

She pet his favorite spot, right behind his ears, and tried to stop replaying the day's earlier Dildo Whack-A-Mole Experience over again in her head.

She shook her head, frustrated and ashamed all over again.

She FaceTimed Sunny, hoping to distract herself.

Sunny answered, except it was Elliott's adorable face in the picture instead.

"Well hello there, Mister Baby," she said. Even though Elliott was a toddler now, he was still the baby of the family. Poor guy would probably always be referred to as a baby as long as she was around. Happy Graduation, Mister Baby.

"Guess who went pee-pee in the potty?" Sunny said excitedly from somewhere behind the oversized forehead that was now taking up the entire screen.

The thought made Joey slightly sad that she was missing a major milestone, even if it was literally just toddler potty training.

"Wow, good job, Ellie," she said, giving him an excited thumbs up.

Sunny's face came into view. "Okay, tell me everything," she said.

Joey groaned, recounting the experience.

"*No*, it hit you in the face?" Sunny said, already laughing so hard she could barely breathe.

"In the face," Joey confirmed, nodding solemnly. "Who knew a six-inch dildo would be the death of my ego? What if I just have an obviously shaped bruise on my face tomorrow?"

"I mean, you wouldn't be the first," Sunny quipped.

Joey giggled. "Gross."

"Okay, so wait, let me get this straight. You went to a sex shop with a friend as part of an agreed-upon adventure?" Sunny asked.

"Yeah, it's the vet I was telling you about. Kendall," Joey said.

"Wait, the hot vet saw you get pounded in the face by a dildo?" Sunny asked.

"You sure paint a picture when you say it like that," Joey said, rolling her eyes. "I wouldn't say pounded is the right verb. Smack? Slap?"

"You're not doing yourself any favors," Sunny said, giggling.

"Pretty much sealed the deal on us never becoming a thing," Joey said, rolling her eyes.

"Why? Because one embarrassing thing happened to you?" Sunny asked. "Embarrassing things happen to you all of the time, Jojo."

Joey narrowed her eyes at the screen. "They do not."

Sunny gave her a skeptical look.

Joey stood up, flipping around her camera. "Look, I got a couch."

"Ooh, that's a nice couch. Hi Ozzy! Are those... bright pink pajamas?" Sunny asked.

"Yeah, my dog believes in pizza rolls, not gender roles," Joey joked.

Sunny rolled her eyes. "Sure," she said. "Anyway, talk to me about the hot vet. What was her reaction to the whole Dildo Capades?"

"Oh, good one," Joey said with a grin. "No, she was very kind about it. She bought me..." She glanced toward the bag she had set down on her nightstand. Was it weird to admit that Kendall had bought her a vibrator? Out of context, it sure seemed strange, but in the moment, it was definitely only a gesture of pity, right?

"Bought you... what?"

"Oh, ice cream," Joey lied. "She bought us ice cream after the fact."

"I thought you said she was vegan." Sunny was like a Bloodhound when it came to lies.

"It was vegan ice cream. Denver has tons of vegan things. Vegan ice cream, vegan... bread," Joey said. Okay, that was really a stretch.

"Vegan bread," Sunny said, her eyebrows raised in amusement. "So, like... normal bread?"

"No, like special vegan bread. You wouldn't understand," Joey said. "Well, it looks like Ozzy has to go out, so I'm going to let you go."

Sunny snorted. "Sure, Jo. I'll talk to you later. Oh, remind me to send you the video of Elliott singing his brand new potty song. I can only make out half the words, but I think my kid's a lyrical genius."

Joey grinned. "Sounds epic."

They hung up, and Joey cringed at her vegan bread comment. She glanced down at Ozzy, who was lying across the couch snoring. "Wanna go outside?" She asked.

Ozzy didn't move. His ear didn't even twitch.

"Fine," Joey conceded, walking over to her bed. She stared at the black plastic bag, then reached to unwrap it, setting the box back down. She stared at the box for a moment, then walked away to brush her teeth. The box kept catching her eye as she washed her face and put on pajamas.

Finally, she sat on the edge of her bed and broke the seal, opening the lid of the box to a shiny teal and gold vibrator. A sticker inside the box said, "Partially charged for your convenience!"

She raised an eyebrow and took a deep breath.

Well, it would be rude to not try out her new gift, right?

CHAPTER TEN

KENDALL

"Got the couch all moved in," Roger said.

Kendall sat on the floor, feeding V. He was holding her thumb in his paws, his brand new blue eyes staring up at her as he lapped up the bottle hungrily. His gray fur stuck up around him wildly as though he had accidentally stuck his paw in an electric socket. Three-week-old kittens were the cutest animals on earth, hands down.

"Thanks," she said, relieved that Joey had a couch, at least. "What do I owe you?"

"Don't worry about it. I wasn't *really* going to charge you $200 for it," Roger said.

"The hell you weren't," Edward said, and Kendall realized she was on speakerphone.

She laughed. "Well, I seriously appreciate it."

"Why aren't you two a thing already?" Edward yelled from the background.

"Oh my God, Edward, you can't just ask people why they aren't a thing," Roger said.

Kendall rolled her eyes.

"But seriously," Roger said. "She's very cute, she's smart, and she likes us, so clearly she has wonderful taste."

"It's not like that with us," Kendall said. "I don't think. Did she say something?"

Edward cackled in the background. "I knew it," he said.

"Knew what?" Kendall asked.

"How is this like a soap opera I can't stop watching and also like a train wreck that I'm nervous about?" Edward said.

Roger laughed, murmuring something that sounded suspiciously like, "I know, right?"

"I can still hear you," Kendall said.

"He means that lovingly," he said. "Okay, we're pulling into the drive-thru for milkshakes, so I'll talk to you later. Bye!"

He hung up quickly.

Kendall looked down at her phone in confusion.

What did they mean? Had Joey said something?

It didn't matter, anyway, because nothing was going to happen between them. They were far too different to make anything serious ever work, weren't they? And nothing said This Will End Badly quite like dating a woman newly out of a relationship.

Whoa, where had the idea of dating come from?

She shook her head. None of that.

LS mewed, falling onto her back so her little water balloon of a belly was up. Kendall smiled and thought of sending a picture of her to Joey, but thought better of it.

Had she come on too strong earlier in the adult toy shop? Was it stepping over a major line to buy a friend a vibrator?

And why couldn't she stop imagining Joey using it?

She shook her head, taking a deep breath, and filled up another bottle for LS, determined to focus on anything but a silly little crush that had the potential to ruin a perfectly good friendship.

Joey playfully glared at her through the computer screen as they video chatted.

"Just draw the dang adventure already," Joey said.

It had been a week since the toy shop and they were ready for something new. Kendall got the impression that Joey was dying for any excuse to bury the memory of the first adventure.

Kendall sipped her coffee leisurely, taking pleasure in Joey's impatience. She sat on the couch, the laptop on the coffee table in front of her. "You're sure you're ready for another one?" She joked.

Honestly, watching Joey fall in the shop was simultaneously one of the funniest and scariest things that had happened to her in a long time. It was only funny because Joey was completely fine, but when she thought Joey might be hurt, panic took over her entire body.

The visual of the table display of dildos falling on top of her was hilarious, and she grinned just thinking of it.

"What's so funny?" Joey asked, her brows knitting together.

"Just thinking of the big rainbow one," Kendall admitted. "It got you right in the eye."

Joey huffed, crossing her arms. "I knew I should have ended this friendship right then and there. You're never going to let me live that down," she said.

"Nope."

"Well, I hope this next adventure levels the playing field. It better be one of yours."

"We'll see," Kendall said, reaching into the jar to grab a slip. She held it up, unfolding the paper to find that she had accidentally grabbed two. "Ah, dammit."

"That's okay, what are they? We can pick the fun one for today," Joey said with a grin.

"They're both mine. Get a haircut and buy a tailored suit," she said.

"Easy," Joey said, clapping.

"Easy for you, because they're both mine," Kendall said, staring down at the paper.

"Fact," Joey said simply. "Now, the haircut isn't a difficult one, but the suit... Any ideas?"

"If I had an idea, I think I'd have gotten it already," Kendall said matter-of-factly.

"Alright, alright, simmer down. I'll do some searching and we can figure it out once you have your sweet new haircut," Joey said.

"About that," Kendall said. This was the part she was most nervous about. "Would you help me find a style?"

Joey's eyes lit up. "Yes," she exclaimed. "I'll start a Pinterest board right away."

Kendall raised an eyebrow. "I don't know what that means," she said.

Joey laughed, and Kendall thought she could perhaps detect a hint of mischief in her tone. "Oh buddy, you're about to learn," she said. "I basically became an expert when planning for the we–" She paused, as if considering a different word. "New apartment decor. Now, what style are you going for here?"

Wow, Joey was a terrible liar. Even the thought of weddings made her cringe. Even when the thought was nearly twenty years old and buried beneath endless hours of therapy.

Kendall considered it. "I'm thinking short, but something I can still style professionally for work. Nothing like... soccer mom, you know? And nothing too..." She couldn't figure out a better word for what she was trying to say.

"Nothing too..." Joey repeated, trying to determine her meaning. "Butch?"

"I guess? I just... that's not..." Kendall tried to explain. "That's not my style. Nothing too... hard."

"You're really painting a picture."

"I know, I'm just..." Kendall sighed. "I want it to be softer."

"Soft butch," Joey said with a nod.

Kendall rolled her eyes. "More androgynous than anything else," she said. "Is any of this making sense?"

Joey tilted her head. "I'm going to send over what I'm thinking you might like and what I know would look good, and we can go from there," she said.

Twenty minutes later, Joey had invited her to join a Pinterest board of ideas. She clicked through the pictures as Joey described what she was going for with each addition.

"Okay, so here's this K-Pop dude," Joey said with a laugh. "Look past the silver and purple color."

"Too short in the back," Kendall said, clicking to the next.

"Alright, now, here's Evan Rachel Wood," Joey started.

"Too long," Kendall said, flipping past.

"Sheesh, Goldilocks."

Kendall grinned. "I'll know it when I see it," she said. She clicked through a few more, then landed on a photo of Kristen Stewart with a perfectly androgynous, edgy but also somehow soft, piecey, not outrageous haircut. "Okay, now this is something."

"I knew it," Joey said, laughing. "No one can resist the idea of looking like Kristen Stewart."

Four hours later, Kendall sat in a barber chair. Joey had talked her into asking Roger and Edward where they got their hair cut, because, and she quoted, "A barber won't be afraid to make you look less feminine." It was a good point, at least.

It also turned out that Roger and Edward's barber on Tennyson street was not only available on short notice, but a young guy by the name of Oscar who wore a snapback and a stretched out t-shirt.

Her nerves were not soothed by his appearance, and yet, Roger and Edward always looked impeccably well-kept.

She had always wanted to cut her hair, but she could only think of what her parents would say. She was a woman in her forties who was still worried about her parents' opinion. She tried to make a mental note to bring that up in her next therapy session.

Joey sat in the barber chair beside her.

"You want like, a beer or something?" Oscar asked her.

"You got any wine?" Joey asked.

"Uh, sure, white or red?" Oscar asked, looking between them.

"Does it come in a box?" Kendall asked.

Oscar's eyes met hers in the mirror. "Sure does."

Kendall nodded. "Uh, beer sounds great," she said. "Anything but an IPA."

"And it can't have honey," Joey added with a small grin. "Wow, you're such a snob." She teased once Oscar walked to the backroom to grab her a non-honeyed beer.

"I have my limits, and the haircut is already hard enough. I don't think we need to add bad wine to the ambiance," she said.

Joey reached out to put a hand on her arm, and just the single touch made her feel warm. "Hair grows back, so just try to enjoy the experience," she said with a smile.

Kendall couldn't help but look at her full lips. "Yeah," she said, distracted. "Yeah, you're right."

She tore her eyes away from Joey to look around the shop, which was decorated in a laid back cabin-style. The walls were a navy blue color and everything was fairly simply decorated.

Oscar returned with two cans of beer, handing one to Joey with a wink.

Seriously, her barber was already flirting with Joey?

Joey smiled politely. "Thanks, man," she said, cracking the top of the can opener.

"Alright, what are we going for here?"

"I brought pictures," Kendall said, worried that might sound uptight. She took out her phone, showing him a few angles of the particular haircut she liked.

"Okay," he said, and was Kendall imagining it, or did he sound a little... casual? "So, what do you like and what don't you like about this?"

Kendall was impressed by the question. "Love the bangs, how it still looks good when it's messy, but that it will be a bit tamer if I want it to. And the back is perfect being less... hard? If makes sense?"

Oscar nodded. "So, no straight razor?"

"No," Kendall said quickly, feeling like she had just avoided something horrific.

Her hair was shoulder-length, so it wasn't like she was donating the whole of it to a charity, but it was still a big step for her.

She opened the beer and took a long drink while Oscar hit the foot stand to raise the chair.

"You ready?" Joey asked.

Kendall grimaced in return, closing her eyes. "Sure," she said.

"I'm going to get the back a bit shorter with the scissors first, then we'll bust out the clippers to get it shaped up nicely," Oscar explained. "Then, we'll do the top."

"Uh, okay," Kendall said. Clippers? Like bzz-bzz clippers? This was going to be awful, wasn't it?

Oscar pinned her hair and sectioned out a piece of the back. She held her breath as the scissors sliced through the first chunk of hair, and she watched her blonde locks fall to the ground with a growing sense of dread.

Was she going to throw up? She might throw up.

"You know what would be fun and dramatic? Can you turn her around so she can't see until it's done?" Joey asked, grinning.

"Would that be fun?" Kendall asked, unable to turn her head to glare at Joey properly for such a cruel suggestion.

As Oscar turned to grab something behind her, she chugged the rest of her beer.

"Just think of the table of dildos falling on me if you need a reference of how easy this is for you."

Oscar paused for a moment, and Kendall watched as he stifled a grin.

"Yeah, definitely should turn her around. I'll let you know the length for the front," Joey said, winking at Kendall.

Kendall tipped the beer back, chugging half of it before nodding her head. She looked up at Joey and couldn't help but grin about how genuine her excitement was. "Fine, I guess you can," she said.

She thought she had grown out of making dumb decisions around cute women.

Oscar turned her around, and for a truly terrifying half-hour, she heard him shear her head without having a clue how it would look.

He used a spray bottle to dampen the top section of her hair and Joey stood in front of her, giving direction on the length. Judging by how energetic Joey was getting and how many times she had stopped to clap in excitement, this was either going to be extremely awful or pretty good.

After another exceptionally long and painful period of time, including what felt like nine hours when he spent blow-drying and adding product, Oscar spun her around.

In the mirror was the reflection of an entirely different person.

She still looked feminine, but she also had an edge of masculinity that immediately changed the way she saw her face. Her cheekbones appeared higher and her jawline looked sharper. She turned her head, studying the shape of the hair-cut, and how it flattered her long neck.

It was exactly what she wanted.

She almost felt melancholy that it had taken her so long to cut it.

Joey stood behind her, holding her hands in fists under her chin in tentative excitement. "Do you love it?"

Kendall leaned forward, running her hands through the longer top section, then turning her head to see the sides. Oscar handed her a mirror, spinning her slightly so she could see the back.

"Well?" Joey asked impatiently. She was positively beaming.

It was as though she was seeing herself for the first time. For the first time, her reflection looked exactly how she wanted it to. How could she put that into words?

"It's..." She said, not able to find the words. Or perhaps not ready to admit how good it felt. "Yeah, I like it."

Oscar nodded, releasing her cape, and she walked to the register feeling lighter than she had in... who knew how long. She paid and they walked outside. Joey turned to take her elbow, making her pause on the sidewalk.

"If you hate it, we can fix it. We can go back to get exactly what you want," she said, looking concerned.

"No, I..." Kendall said, reaching to feel it again. "I..."

An emotional lump lodged its way in her throat, and she paused, trying to swallow it down.

Joey said put her hand on Kendall's shoulder. "What's wrong?"

"I've always been too scared to have short hair, and now that I've tried it, I'm so mad at myself for waiting so long," she said in a rush of words that seemed to all garble together into something incomprehensible.

Joey paused, her expression softening. "I'm proud of you,"

she said, nodding. "And also, just letting you know as a friend, you look so damn hot."

Kendall laughed, sniffling. "Thanks," she said, shaking her head. Why did that phrase disappoint her — as a friend?

Of course, Joey was so much younger and would probably start dating one of the hot young lesbians that looked like they had just walked off The L Word set. The newer one, obviously. It would be so much less believable for Joey to be interested in a forty-something cat lady.

"Like, dayum," Joey said, grinning. "Want me to take a picture to send to the crew?"

"Sure," Kendall said. "Wait, let me get myself composed." She blinked quickly, sniffling and taking deep breaths to appear normal.

Joey pulled out her phone and contorted her stance. "Okay, take like one step to the left, and then angle your face that way," she said, pointing.

Kendall did as she was instructed.

"Put your chin up slightly," Joey said, closing one eye and sticking out her tongue in concentration.

"Wow, I wasn't aware I was in the presence of Annie Leibovitz," Kendall teased.

"Yeah, yeah, joke all you want, but these are like, Tinder-level good," Joey joked.

"Well, too bad I'm not a Tinder gal," Kendall said, tilting her head slightly.

"Don't knock it 'til you try it," Joey winked. She stood up, looking down at her phone. "Okay, sending."

Kendall smiled. "Thank you," she said, slightly embarrassed.

"Okay, next step: Suit," Joey said with confidence. "I've already found the perfect spot and we're due there in about twenty minutes..." She glanced at her phone. "Want to ride together?"

. . .

Kendall stood on a platform, getting her measurements taken. Joey had somehow found a queer-friendly suitmaker in town, specializing in bespoke suits for folks who might not feel comfortable going to a typical men's suit shop.

Joey sat on a chair, sipping an iced latte that she had insisted on stopping for on the way.

Kendall tried not to watch her in the mirror, tried not to focus on the way her long legs looked in her dress. God, why did she always wear sundresses? Didn't she know they were Kendall's weakness?

Heidi, the woman taking her measurements, paused, writing down the numbers. "Now, what type of fabric were you thinking?" She asked.

"I don't know for sure," Kendall admitted.

"Do you have samples we can look through?" Joey asked.

Heidi looked back at Joey. "Sure, let me go grab the binder," she said. She walked into a back room.

"What color are you envisioning?" Joey asked.

"I'm not sure," Kendall said.

"Okay, where do you see yourself wearing this suit?" Joey asked, tilting her head.

"Great question," Kendall said. "Um..."

Heidi walked back into the room with the binder and Joey stood, crossing the room to join them.

"Okay, do you want this suit for like, conferences? Or as a wedding guest? Or to wear on a nice night out?" Joey asked.

"Can it be all of them?" Kendall asked, looking from Heidi to Joey.

"Sure," Joey said, shrugging. "What kind of fabric says 'I like fine wine, I will dance to the YMCA unashamedly, and I can talk to you for hours about proper suturing techniques?"

Heidi grinned. "Uh, let's see," she flipped through a few pages of darker fabrics before pausing. She looked up at Kendall. "With your hair color and skin tone, I think you could pull off a cream really well."

"Ooh," Joey said, her eyes widening. She looked at Kendall with approval. "Yes, I love that," she said.

Kendall looked down at the cream color, reaching out to feel the fabric. It was sturdy but soft. Touchable, but durable. She nodded.

"Okay, now here's the really fun part," Heidi said with a smile, flipping to pages of patterned fabrics. "Interiors."

Kendall's phone rang, and she sighed, feeling like someone had let the air out of her fun. It was the ringtone she had given the clinic number.

"Hold on just a second, I'm so sorry," she said to Heidi, stepping off the platform to grab her phone out of her pocket.

Jenny at least had the decency to sound apologetic right off the bat. "Hey Kendall, I know you're not on-call, but Dr. Rothlisberger isn't feeling well and wanted you to take this rat poison patient if you can."

Kendall glanced back at Joey and Heidi, who had begun discussing fabrics without her.

She wanted to stomp her feet and yell about it not being fair. Instead, she took a deep breath. "I'll be there in thirty."

A few moments later, when she returned to Joey and Heidi, she apologized and explained the situation. "That's okay, we can reschedule," Joey said with an encouraging smile.

"You're not mad?" Kendall asked.

Joey looked as though she had grown a second head. "Don't be ridiculous. This is part of your job."

Kendall rolled her eyes. "I'll make it up to you," she said, hurrying out of the shop.

"Wait," Joey called after her. "We drove together."

CHAPTER ELEVEN

JOEY

"Pull it, pull it!" Joey chanted, clapping her hands.

Kendall smirked. "For someone whose first adventure went so awry, you sure are excited for this next one."

They had just come from the clinic after Kendall had removed the sutures from Ozzy's belly. He had healed wonderfully so far, Kendall had said, and she was celebrating the end of the puppy pee pad era.

Joey filled her wine glass, pouring out the last of the bottle. "I'm just ready for something else to take my mind off of the Great Dildo Explosion."

Kendall laughed, holding the jar out to Joey. "Why don't you take it? It's your turn to draw."

Joey shrugged, taking a large gulp of wine, before reaching into the jar. She swirled the tiny pieces of paper around with her hand, then grabbed one of the slips out, looking at it. Her cheeks reddened immediately and she regretted ever adding it. "Oh, we don't have to do this one. It was kind of a throwaway. I mean, it's something I've never done. But we don't have to do this if it will be weird."

Kendall gave her a confused look, frowning slightly. "What is it? What does it say?"

Joey stared down at the paper. It was her own handwriting, but it had been a gamble to even suggest it to herself.

Have a one night stand.

"It's just…" Joey chewed on her bottom lip, her heart suddenly pounding her chest.

Oh no, Kendall was going to think she was an idiot or, worse, desperate.

"Hand it over," Kendall held out her hand.

"Okay but just don't judge me," Joey said, passing her the slip of paper.

Kendall unfolded the piece of paper in her hands and stared down at her. Her expression remained blank, as if she was purposefully trying not to show any kind of reaction.

Joey stared at her with wide eyes until Kendall looked up.

"How is this an adventure?" Kendall asked, her tone sincere.

"What do you mean? I never… I just never…" Joey shrugged, unable to admit it out loud.

Kendall tilted her head. "You've never had a one night stand? Seriously?"

She did not want to wonder what that translated to.

Joey tried to appear casual, but her shrugged shoulders were a bit stilted and awkward. How many times could one shrug in the span of one minute? She was about to find out. "This is the longest I've ever been single."

Kendall's eyes widened in shock. "You're saying you haven't been single for more than two months… Ever? Are you one of those serial monogamists?"

Joey frowned, a noise coming out of her mouth that sounded a bit like a *guffaw*.

"Serial? I wouldn't say serial. That sounds intense. I would say lucky, or really good at staying in relationships once I'm in them?"

Kendall shook her head slowly. "I have no idea why that sounds so appealing to people," she said with a laugh taking a sip of her wine.

"Easy for you to say, Kendall *'Single Forever'* O'Hara."

Kendall slowly lifted a brow staring at her. "Not single forever. Well, maybe single forever. But by choice."

Joey tried to maintain a completely blank expression. By choice?

Translation: Not with you.

"All right," Kendall said with a smirk and a shrug. "I guess we're going dancing."

"Dancing? What?" Joey laughed out of surprise.

"Yeah, this Friday."

"Wh-what?" Joey nearly spit out her wine.

"Good. Wear something low-cut," Kendall said with a wink before chuckling.

Joey finished the wine in her glass, more nervous now that there was a plan. Especially any plan that involved meeting women in front of Kendall.

What had she agreed to?

She looked around as she followed Kendall inside the warehouse. Kendall had promised that every lesbian in Denver would be there, and so far, that promise looked to be about right.

"Okay, so this venue is set up kind of weird," Kendall yelled over the music as they walked in. "This first room is the popular music room," she said. She pointed to one side. "And through that door is the hip hop room." She pointed to the other side. "And through that hallway is the oldies side. And when I say oldies, I mean, like the 80s and 90s."

"Oh, yeah, that sounds best," Joey said, taking a step in that direction.

Kendall grabbed her arm. "Nope, that's not what we're here for. You want a one night stand? Get thee to the hip hop room."

"Why?" Joey asked, glancing toward the archway where Kendall had pointed.

"Because how do you dance to hip hop?" Kendall asked, looking at Joey as though she was slightly dense.

"Oh, yeah, that checks out," Joey said, shrugging. "Anyway, first step, alcohol."

Kendall laughed and they made their way to the bar on the opposite side of the room. Kendall leaned on the counter, her shoulders looking incredible in the tank top she had chosen, and her hair perfectly messed as though she had just gotten out of bed looking flawless.

How did she manage to look completely irresistible at any given moment?

Envisioning running her hands through Kendall's messy hair sure wasn't helping with that Friends Only thing.

Joey had, as instructed, worn a dark t-shirt that was low-cut and fitted, tight dark jeans, and heeled ankle boots. Kendall had sent her back inside her apartment to change shoes when she saw that she was wearing sneakers.

Joey looked around as they waited for the bartender to make her way down to them. It was dark — how was she supposed to meet anyone in there?

Kendall nudged her. "What about her?" She said, nodding casually to someone on Joey's other side.

Joey glanced at the woman, who was attractive, but looked a little... young.

"She doesn't look like she's even old enough to drink," Joey said out of the corner of her mouth.

Kendall rolled her eyes.

Joey looked down at the other end of the bar. So many long-haired butches in snapbacks. Who thought that wearing a hat to a club was an attractive idea?

And yet... some of them really did look good in it...

Why did she imagine none of them had bed frames, just mattresses on the floor? Maybe even posters tacked on the walls?

"Lower your standards," Kendall said, raising her eyebrows as she leveled her with a stare. "It's a one night stand for a reason. Just have good sex and then walk away."

Joey grinned and nodded in an effort not to grimace.

Kendall ordered them each a vodka soda and a shot of whiskey. Both came in plastic cups. Kendall handed her the shot and raised it in a cheers, waiting until Joey did the same.

Alright, liquid courage might help. She raised the glass and tipped it back, the liquid burning her tongue. She cringed, coughing and wiping at her mouth.

"God, I hate whiskey," Joey said, reaching for her other drink.

"Well, I don't think this place is sanitary enough for a tequila shot," Kendall said, turning away from the bar. "Now, on with our mission."

Joey nodded and they walked through the Top 40s room. She saw all levels of undress, from pasties and booty shorts to women in button-downs and baggy jeans.

She thought she saw a familiar flash of purple hair — Nikki?

"I think I just saw my friend," Joey said, taking out her phone to text her.

"You're not having a one-night stand with your friend," Kendall said, placing her hand over her phone.

Joey deliberately chose not to read into that statement.

Joey rolled her eyes. "You're on such a mission right now," she said.

"What about her?"

"I don't like her glasses."

"Well, she won't be wearing her glasses in bed."

"True, but then I won't look back on the memory fondly, because I'll only be thinking of those glasses."

"Okay, fine, what about her?"

"Nah."

"What's wrong with her?"

"Nothing. But I don't see anything right with her, either."

"You're a real judgmental asshole," Kendall laughed, sipping at her drink.

A beat-heavy remix of a Hayley Kiyoko song came over the speakers and Joey lit up. "I love this song. Let's dance a little to loosen up," she said, grabbing Kendall's arm.

They wound their way into the dance floor and Joey closed her eyes, swaying her hips. She wasn't a fantastic dancer, by any means, and she definitely had a bad case of What Do I Do With My Hands, but she could keep a beat.

She opened her eyes to find Kendall immediately in front of her, dancing awkwardly.

Joey laughed. "Oh my God, loosen up, Dr. O'Hara," she said, reaching for Kendall's arm.

Kendall sighed, letting her body loosen up just barely. "I don't... this isn't..."

"Just move your hips," Joey said, and she reached for Kendall's waist, trying to help guide her.

It was strangely delightful to see Kendall, who was good at everything, have the inability to keep a beat.

As the gap between them closed, Kendall began to mimic Joey's movements. Joey kept her free hand on Kendall's hip and Kendall put her arm on Joey's shoulder.

She had never been so close to Kendall before. Up close, she could smell the sweetness of Kendall's pomade, feel the warmth of her body through her thin tank top.

Kendall's eyes seared into her own and she smiled, biting her lower lip.

The sight did many funny things to Joey's insides, all of them swirly and jumping in anticipation.

Pressed together in a sea of bodies, it was the first time she had ever seriously contemplated if Kendall might return the crush. If her feelings weren't unrequited, what would that look like?

Her heartbeat sped up at the thought and she gripped the fabric of Kendall's shirt in her hand. Was it the whiskey giving her the courage? Or just the heat of the moment?

One tug and Kendall would be against her...

She swallowed, and someone caught her eye over Kendall's shoulder.

Perfectly coiffed dark hair, a dimple in her right cheek, piercing dark eyes... Raina.

Her heart came to a stutter-stop and she stopped dancing for a moment. She hadn't seen her since the breakup. She looked so gorgeous, so put together, so... *happy.*

Kendall looked up at her in confusion. "What's up?" She said, leaning into Joey's ear to be heard.

"It's Raina, like ten feet behind you, looking at us. Quick, look like I just said something really funny. Laugh or something," she said, forcing her own laugh.

Kendall gave her a strange look. "What?"

"I want her to think I'm having a good time, like I won the breakup," she said, as if the idea was obvious.

Kendall narrowed her eyes for only a moment before taking Joey's face in the palm of her hand and pulling her close, claiming her mouth with a heated, passionate kiss.

Joey's stomach somersaulted in surprise and delight and excitement as Kendall hungrily kissed her.

She found herself melting into the kiss, wrapping an arm around Kendall's neck to hold her close.

The world quieted around her for a moment, and all she could think of was Kendall's soft lips, the warmth of her mouth, the slight taste of whiskey on her lips... It was an intoxicating mix and she craved more.

How many times had she imagined this exact moment? It

was better than she expected. Kendall had this kissing thing down — Joey felt desired and turned on in a way that she hadn't known was possible.

Kendall slipped her tongue through Joey's parted lips, deepening the kiss.

Was it possible to completely melt in another person? Her body was alight with pleasure.

Kendall pulled away slowly, blinking as though adjusting her eyes. "Is she still looking?" She asked.

"Wh-what? Who?" Joey said, dumbly.

Kendall furrowed her brow. "Raina," she said.

She glanced over Kendall's shoulder, but didn't see Raina. "Uh, no," she said.

"Okay, perfect," Kendall said, standing up straighter to put a bit of distance between them. "Do you think she bought it?"

Joey tried to hide her disappointment. The kiss was only to make Raina jealous? She swallowed, trying to calm her racing pulse. Of course it was. "Oh, yeah, definitely, yeah," she said, chasing the straw around her cup with her mouth like a total spaz. Why did she feel like she wanted to cry?

"I'm going to go to the bathroom really quick," Joey said, clearing her throat.

"Alright," Kendall said. "I'm going to go stand over by the bar and scope out babes for you." She winked conspiratorially.

Joey tried to fake a smile. "Great, yeah, great," she said, then hurried away towards where she thought the bathrooms might be.

She pushed through the crowd, willing herself not to tear up. She felt so embarrassed and stupid, thinking that Kendall had kissed her because she wanted to.

The way Kendall had dragged her lip between her teeth… obviously Raina wouldn't have been able to see that, so couldn't it have been less of a performance than Kendall was claiming it was?

That kiss had felt so intense, surely Kendall had to have felt something, too?

Joey had to stop it with the wishful thinking. It would just make their friendship more awkward.

She stood in line for the bathroom, leaning against the wall with her arms crossed over her chest. She wanted to close her eyes and imagine herself anywhere else.

"Joey," she heard a familiar voice say. She turned to find Nikki smiling behind her, coming towards her for a hug.

"Hey," Joey said with as much enthusiasm as she could muster, trying her hardest to sound surprised and happy as she hugged back Nikki. She blinked back the tears that had been threatening to break the damn. "It's been forever. I didn't know you came to things like this. You should have called me."

"Yeah, I've just been like, so busy. Totally last-minute decision. How's Denver treating you?" Nikki asked, smiling widely.

"So great. Best decision ever," Joey said, perhaps overinflating her experience the tiniest bit. "How's Fort Collins?"

"Oh, you know, small," Nikki said with a laugh.

"Baby, you'll never–" Raina said, turning the corner to the bathroom hallway. She'd have recognized that voice anywhere.

...Baby?

Raina stopped short when she saw Joey. "Oh, hey, Jo," she said.

Joey nodded, suddenly unable to speak or think. She looked between Raina and Nikki. "Oh, you're here, like... with Raina?" She said, slowly piecing it together.

"Yeah," Nikki said, suddenly very interested in the floor.

"Fun," Joey said, her eyes wide. "How fun for you. That sounds really fun. How cool and fun." Why wouldn't her mouth stop moving?

Raina nodded. "We wanted to tell you," she said.

Nikki shot her a look.

"Wanted to tell me what?" Joey said, her voice pitching into a near-Helium level.

Raina put an arm around Nikki, who tried to shrug out of it.

Translation: Joey was an idiot.

"Oh," Joey said, staring up at Raina. "That was... quick."

Nikki was flushed red, but Raina barely reacted.

Joey's hands balled into fists at her sides and her internal monologue shifted into Primal Scream Rage.

"That's great," she lied. "So great. I'm actually here with my girlfriend." Another lie.

"I saw, yeah," Raina said, nodding. "She seems really old."

"She's a doctor," Joey said. It wasn't the entire truth, but it also wasn't entirely untrue.

Raina's eye barely twitched, which Joey knew was a sure sign that something had pressed a button.

"Anyway, she's probably waiting for me," Joey said. "This bathroom line is taking forever anyway. I'll just pee when we go home. To have tons of sex. Yep. Best sex of my life. Doctors, man."

Oh good Lord. Shut *up*, Joey.

Nikki's eyes widened and Raina nodded.

"So good seeing you, though," Joey said, waving as she stepped out of the line, hurrying back down the hallway.

She walked back into the hip hop room to see Kendall chatting with a hot woman at the bar.

She could not deal with that right now. She felt like she was suffocating, or that the walls were closing in on her.

She grabbed her phone and texted Kendall a quick, "Met a hottie in line for the bathroom. Think this is my chance. I'll let you know when I get home in the morning" text.

She watched as Kendall completely ignored her phone.

She pushed through the crowds of the club and walked outside, the cool evening breeze a salve on her wrecked heart.

The tears came in the backseat of the rideshare, much to the dismay of the mid-sixties stoner guy driving her. He kept adjusting his rearview mirror, looking increasingly concerned as she continued to sob and sniffle.

"You okay?" He asked about a block away from where she'd put the drop-off location.

"Yeah, my period," she said, knowing that he'd go back to minding his own business as soon as the fated word left her lips.

Sure enough, he didn't say another word, even as she got out of the car.

She walked the half block to her building and walked inside, trudging up the stairs.

Ozzy wiggled excitedly at the door with a sock in his mouth for her, and she smiled despite herself. His little wiggly body was too cute to be upset around. She hooked his leash onto him, trudging back down the stairs and around the block on a quick walk.

When they were safely back inside, she forced him to cuddle her on the couch as she cried herself to sleep.

"So why don't you just tell her how you're feeling?" Sunny asked, dishing another piece of pepperoni and pineapple pizza onto a plate.

Joey grimaced. "Because that's hard? And uncomfortable? And I'd rather never talk about it if that's an option?"

Sunny gave her a knowing look. "Is that an option? Because it sounds to me like you're miserable, and you're only delaying the inevitable."

"Well, that's for future Joey to worry about," Joey said, shrugging as she opened a can of orange soda.

A herd of screaming toddlers ran past them, yelling about a dinosaur attack. Ozzy ran gleefully behind them.

They stood in their parents' backyard, which had been decorated in bright primary colors for Elliott's third birthday.

"I wish the only thing I had to worry about was a dinosaur attack," Sunny said.

"Me too, I'd let a tyrannosaurus rip off my face if it meant I didn't have to feel feelings."

"But you have such a pretty face," her mother cooed as she wrapped her arms around Joey's shoulders from behind.

"You only say that because everyone says we look alike," Joey teased.

Her mother grinned knowingly. She turned to Sunny. "Speaking of Tyrannosauruses, Dad's changing into his T-Rex costume right now."

Joey chuckled, apprehensive about what kind of dinosaur her father would be. "I can't believe you bought an inflatable dinosaur costume for Dad just for this."

"Oh honey, he's been wanting to buy one forever, this was just the perfect excuse," her mother said with a wink.

Sunny gave Joey a deadpan expression. "Didn't you miss this so much?"

Joey grinned. "More than I realized."

An hour later, after the party had broken up — bless toddler parties where everyone had to go home and nap immediately after the presents were opened — she walked around the backyard, cleaning up paper plates and sneaking a few scraps of pineapple to Ozzy.

Her parents suddenly cornered her, appearing out of seemingly nowhere.

"Susannah told us about Raina," her mother started.

Wow, her sister had kept that secret for all of one hour.

"Oh, yeah it's a little awkward isn't it?" Joey said, gathering up juice boxes. "Hey, Dad, you made an amazing T-Rex, by the way. I feel like you might have finally found your calling."

Her father grinned. "Right? Although it did go slightly awry when Ozzy tried to pop me."

"He's a very good guard dog. He thought you were really going to hurt Elliott," Joey said, shrugging. "Would you rather he held Elliott still for the child-eaters of the world?"

Her mother laughed, then looked pointedly at her father.

Her dad cleared his throat and touched his thinning gray hair in his signature nervous tick.

Uh oh.

"Honey, you know that we support you no matter what," her father began.

Joey really did not like the sound where this was going. She looked between the two of them at their entirely-too-sincere expressions.

"What's wrong? Do you have cancer?" She asked.

"What? No, honey," her mom said quickly. "Just listen. Everything's fine."

"I'm not moving–" She started, but her mom cut her off.

"Josephine, I swear," she said. "Just listen."

Joey sighed and crossed her arms.

"We want you to know that we think you really dodged a bullet not marrying Raina," her mother said.

Joey raised an eyebrow. "Dodged a bullet?"

Her father sighed. "Raina sucked. We knew that you loved her, and we didn't want you to feel awkward about bringing her around. But she sucked."

Her mother nodded. "We will always try to get along with all of your partners, don't get us wrong. But we are so relieved that we never have to sit through another dinner of Raina telling us about Call of Duty."

"Or termite populations in Asia," her father added.

"Oh, remember when she went on that diatribe about Orange Julius workers?" Her mom said, laughing.

She definitely didn't need a translation to hear anything they were saying.

"Okay, yeah, I'm getting the idea" Joey said, sighing.

"That said, we didn't want your engagement present to go to waste," her father added.

Joey frowned. "Whatever it is, just use it on yourselves." The idea of her parents giving her a present to celebrate a failed engagement didn't sit right with her — even if they had liked Raina.

"No, we still want you to have something special," her mother said.

This was sounding worse and worse.

"We don't want to ruin the surprise completely," her father said. "But it's going to be in your mailbox sometime next week."

"You really don't have to do this. Seriously, we can probably just get a refund for it," Joey said, panic rising in her chest.

"Shush," her mother said, wrapping her in a hug. "You deserve to be happy again. And if we can be some small part of that, we're happy too."

Joey hugged her mom back and reached to include her father. She was startled by tiny arms wrapping around her legs and a face-planting itself firmly in her butt.

She turned to find Elliott squeezing her. She laughed and bent, picking him up and setting him on her hip. His dirty blonde hair had blue frosting in it and his sugar high was making him look delirious.

"My name's Elliott and I like warm hugs," he said in a silly voice, quoting his favorite movie. Even the inside of his mouth was dyed blue. She did not envy Sunny's job of cleaning him up or trying to get him to settle down in the next day or two.

Joey grinned as she tickled his belly reveling in his high-pitched laugh, feeling comforted by the warmth and familiarity of unconditional love.

CHAPTER TWELVE

KENDALL

Joey stood beside the car as Kendall repositioned the last of the necessities in the trunk.

Cooler, sleeping bag, tent...

It had been a week since they'd gone dancing, and Joey had been a little more distant.

Kendall tried not to think about how Joey had gone home with some random person that night. She tried not to think about how Joey going home with someone else made her feel like she was wearing a lead x-ray vest.

She'd gone to the bathroom and then she never came back.

Correction: She'd nearly sprinted to the bathroom after Kendall had kissed her.

And of course the kiss was just to make her ex-fiancée jealous. That's all it was. Kendall was being a good friend.

She'd kissed her, and she'd opened Pandora's Box.

Before the kiss, she couldn't quite imagine what Joey's lips felt like, what she tasted like, if she was the type of kisser whose lips were too hard or if she used too much tongue...

And now? Now, she knew that Joey kissed her the way

she wanted to be kissed. The kind of kiss that dulled the world around them, to the point where she wasn't sure if she was hearing bass or Joey's heartbeat.

Then, Joey had bolted.

"The party has arrived," Imogen said, walking up the driveway. She was wearing a flowing, long dress and a large sunhat.

"Thanks again for watching the kittens for me," Kendall said. "We'll be back tomorrow afternoon, but I've left instructions on the kitchen counter. We could have brought them to you, you know."

"And miss out on a night's sleep without Gert's snoring? Not a chance. This is a vacation for me," Imogen joked.

Joey grinned.

"Now, you girls be safe. Don't let the bears eat you," Imogen said.

Joey laughed. "I've chosen a site with bear boxes, don't worry."

Kendall looked between them both. "You're kidding, right? We're going to a place with bears?"

"We live in a place with bears, Dr. O'Hara," Joey said, furrowing her brow together.

Imogen clapped her hands. "This is going to be so fun for you. And a tent! On the ground! How quaint."

Joey laughed. "It's the only way to camp," she said. "Kendall is now the proud owner of a brand new tent of her own."

Kendall shut the back of the car. "Alright, that's everything. We might not have service up there, apparently, so call the number I left for you if you have any questions with the kittens. Taylor is my favorite tech, so they'll be able to help." She had shown Imogen how to care for the kittens earlier in the week when she and Joey had decided to purposefully make camping their next adventure instead of waiting to draw it out of the jar. Luckily, the kittens were eating canned food now, and didn't need the bottles anymore, so it should be an easy night for Imogen.

Joey opened the back door to clip a seatbelt holder to Ozzy's harness, then climbed into the passenger seat.

Kendall took a deep breath and opened the navigation on her phone as she slid into the driver's seat. They'd chosen a campground about two hour's drive into the mountains.

Kendall put on music and they spent the drive in near-silence.

A song about a stolen kiss by The Shrikes came on the playlist and Joey reached to skip the song almost immediately.

"Can we talk about the elephant in the car?" Kendall asked, exiting the interstate and turning onto a side road toward the campground.

"Ozzy's a dog, not an elephant," Joey joked, and Kendall got the impression that she was deflecting whatever Kendall was trying to say.

She remained undeterred. "Dancing the other night... it was kind of weird when you saw Raina, right?"

Joey groaned, tipping her head back. "Yeah, that was..." Her voice trailed off as she paused. "That was weird. Weird is a good word for it."

"I want to apologize for just, uh, kissing you like that," Kendall said, concentrating hard on the road in front of her.

"You don't have to apologize." Joey laughed, shaking her head.

Kendall stole a glance at her. Was she not upset about it?

"It was not cool for me to do that without your permission," Kendall said.

Joey shook her head. "I'm not mad or anything. It definitely worked. Until I found out she's dating one of my friends from back home now," she said.

Kendall pulled into the campground, unsure what to say.

"That's awful," she said. "You know, I know a bit about euthanasia if you ever decide to go the mercenary route."

"A bit?" Joey grinned.

"I've done it once or twice."

"On a person?"

Kendall lifted a brow. "You second-guessing camping with me now?"

"This really escalated quickly." Joey laughed again.

"Speaking of quick escalations, you never told me about the woman you took home," Kendall said, finding the spot they'd reserved. She backed the car in like the sign told her to.

Joey shrugged. "Not much to tell. Oh look, we're right on the river," she said, clapping her hands and jumping from the car the moment it was in park.

They unloaded the trunk and Joey tied up Ozzy on a long lead so that he could sniff around and explore without running off.

Kendall set up the chairs around the fire. Joey had borrowed her family's camping gear, but they hadn't been able to find a tent. Joey had one, but upon her advice though, Kendall had purchased a tent that week. Joey's was a small backpacking tent and she'd barely be able to fit inside with Ozzy, much less Kendall and Ozzy.

Joey opened the cooler, looking inside. Her brow furrowed and she walked back to the car, opening the back again.

"What's wrong?" Kendall asked, anticipatory.

"Where's your cooler?" Joey asked.

"What do you mean? We packed it, didn't we?" Kendall asked, walking to the car. "I set it next to the car."

"Well, it didn't go *in* the car, apparently," Joey said, gesturing to the empty trunk.

Kendall set her hands on her hips, trying to think. "Well, what'd you pack?"

"Beer and s'mores fixings," Joey said, her eyes wide.

Kendall sighed, rubbing her face with her hands. "Okay.

Well, let's put up our tents while we still have plenty of light. I think the town is only thirty minutes away," she said.

"There was a gas station just down the road," Joey said.

Kendall groaned. "I set the cooler right next to you," she said, defeated.

"And?" Joey asked, as if she didn't see the point of the observation.

"Yeah, and all you brought was beer and candy," Kendall snapped.

Joey's eyes widened, then narrowed. "And I'll be fine with beer and s'mores for one night. And you're being weird, so, I'm going to go set up my tent, and you can set up yours. And if you need food, go wherever you need to go, and Ozzy and I will be fine here," she said.

Kendall immediately regretted snapping at Joey. Their entire dynamic had been off since the kiss. It had obviously been a mistake to kiss her, and she wished she could take it back.

Kendall rubbed her hands over her face as Joey walked over to a flat patch of ground with her tent.

Ozzy whined at her, and she reached down to pet his chin. "It's okay, buddy. Your mom is fine," she assured him.

They set up their tents on opposite sides of the campsite, and Kendall was pretty proud of herself for figuring out how to put a brand new tent together despite having never done it before. She had glanced at the directions, and had even put the footprint down beneath the tent as she set it up. She was feeling rather pleased herself for even recognizing what a tent footprint was.

Joey glanced up to the sky, scowling. "I think it's going to rain," she said, pointing up at the dark clouds above them.

Kendall shook her head. "No, I checked the forecast, and it said it would miss us," she said.

Joey shrugged. "Well, I think the forecast lied," she said.

"It didn't–" She stopped herself short from continuing to

argue about the weather. "Do you want to come with me to get food?"

Joey shook her head, pulling on a hoodie and sitting down in front of the fire ring as she began to fuss with twigs and kindling she had gathered. "I'll stay here," she said, trying to keep her tone light, but Kendall could see that she was obviously still irritated.

Kendall eyed her warily, but thought that a short trip to the gas station would at least give them something to eat. Surely, the gas station had sandwiches or something? Plus, thirty minutes away from an irritated Joey might do her some good to calm down, too.

"Okay, I'll be right back," she said, climbing in the car.

"Drive safe," Joey said, glancing back up to the sky.

Whatever. Thirty minutes was enough time to reset her attitude.

She was about five minutes away when the rain began. Not a light drizzle, either. The sky opened up, pouring down on her. She could barely make out the road in front of her as her windshield wipers worked as fast as they could.

Perfect. Ideal. Fantastic.

She pulled into the gas station parking lot, parking under the cover, then ran inside.

She looked around at the pitiful little store. No sandwiches. Not even a hot dog. She had bought veggie dogs, foil-wrapped potatoes, prepared pancake batter... Her stomach gurgled with hunger.

Fuck it, they'd just have to subsist on junk food until tomorrow. She grabbed any vegan snack she could find — cookies, chips, candy... The real find was a box of granola bars that didn't contain honey.

The rain hadn't let up once she got back outside, making the drive back painfully slow.

She ached to apologize to Joey. The cooler had been her

responsibility, so why had she blamed Joey for it? That wasn't fair.

The idea of Joey sitting in the rain back at the campground made her drive a bit faster, anxious to get back and at least offer for them to sit in the car.

She pulled into the campground and found their site, not bothering to back the car in yet, given she could barely see five feet in front of her. Joey wasn't sitting in front of the fire — was she in her tent?

She grabbed the tube of Pringles as an apology gift and got out of the car, running to Joey's tent and unzipping the flap. She saw Joey sitting with her arms around her knees, hunched down in the small space. Ozzy was sprawled out at her feet, and his tail started wagging once he saw Kendall. She crawled into the tiny space and zipped the tent flap shut behind her.

"Ah, it's tight in here," Kendall said, crouching.

The tent was stifling hot and humid, and the rain pounded on the top. Ozzy sat next to Joey, panting as he anxiously glanced up at the ceiling of the tent.

Kendall looked up at the mesh roof, offering the only source of ventilation, then at the rain flap hooked above it.

She didn't remember a rain flap for her own tent... maybe hers didn't have one?

She handed the can of chips to Joey, who took them without smiling.

"I was a jerk," Kendall started.

Joey nodded.

"And I'm sorry that I got frustrated and took it out on you," she added.

Joey nodded, ripping the foil seal on the chips.

"Do you still want to be my friend?" Kendall asked, trying to look contrite.

Joey cracked at that, a smiling taking over her features.

God, she was beautiful when she smiled. It made her eyes

turn up at the edges, like the smile was touching every one of her features. Kendall's heart clenched at the sight.

"It's hot in here," Kendall said, pulling off the quarter-zip she had put on when they'd arrived.

Joey reached out, holding down her t-shirt as she pulled the sweater over her head.

"Thanks," she murmured, aware of Joey's hand being so close to her skin.

She took a deep breath and they sat in near-silence — except for Ozzy's panting — until the rain turned to a gentle patter, then a drizzle.

"We should try to get the fire going. I put all of the wood we brought in the bear box so it'd stay dry," Joey said, referencing the large green locker on the edge of their site. It had a thick lock on the front to prevent bear-related theft, apparently.

Kendall nodded, climbing back out of the tiny tent. The air was heavy with humidity and the ground was soaked and muddy. Why would anyone in their right mind choose to spend a night like this?

"Ken, look," Joey said in a whisper, standing beside her and pointing across the river.

She paused, searching. Then, she noticed a small deer, standing perfectly still near the river's edge. The doe dipped her head, drinking from the water, then casually walked back up the embankment and into the trees.

Kendall smiled.

Oh, maybe *that* was why people camped.

Joey smiled, then gasped loudly. "Oh no, what have you done?" She said.

Kendall turned, panic rising within her at Joey's tone. "What? What?" She looked around wildly.

"Your rain flap," Joey said, walking over to Kendall's tent. "Where is it?"

"Oh, I don't... I didn't think it came with one," Kendall

said, following her. She couldn't believe this was happening. The entire situation felt surreal, like maybe she could just rewind somehow?

Joey looked back at her with wide eyes, then began to laugh. She held her hand over her mouth, shaking her head. "What did you do with the large piece of tent fabric that came with your tent?" She spoke slowly, as if Kendall wasn't able to understand her.

"I read something about a footprint... That was the..." She pointed to the ground, where the tent sat.

"How did you even manage that?" Joey said, still laughing. "You're supposed to bring a tarp."

"A tarp? No, I read all about it," Kendall said. She stood with her hands on her hips, unable to come to terms with her mistake.

Joey looked at her with a pitying look. "I don't think so," she said, crouching down at the entrance of Kendall's tent and unzipping it.

"Yeah, everything's soaked," she said, reaching inside. "Your sleeping bag is soaked."

"No," Kendall said, shaking her head. Had she seriously made such a stupid mistake? Her cheeks flushed with heat. Especially after arguing with Joey and putting up her tent solo, she felt like such an idiot.

"Yeah," Joey said, pulling out a duffel bag of her things.

She handed it to Kendall, and Kendall felt that it was sopping wet. It dripped down her arms as she held it in her hands, shaking her head.

"It's all soaked," Joey said, holding a hand to her mouth to hide an obvious smile.

Joey's amusement made Kendall even more embarrassed.

"We should just go home," Kendall said. "I don't think this is an adventure we can pull through."

"No," Joey said, waving her hands in front of her as though she was stopping traffic. "No, it'll be fine. You've had two very easy adventures so far, so I think karma is just evening out."

Kendall looked at her in disbelief. "Are you kidding me? Where am I supposed to sleep? On the muddy ground? In the backseat of my sedan?"

Joey kept a hand over her mouth, trying not to laugh.

"It's not funny," Kendall said, glaring at her.

The scolding just made Joey start to laugh harder.

"Stop it," Kendall said, but even as the words came out, she felt laughter rippling through her, too.

It was beyond awful. It was so terrible that it was... well, if she didn't laugh, she'd cry.

"It's not funny," she said again, still laughing.

Joey took a few steps towards her and pulled her in for a hug. "I'm sorry, buddy. Don't worry, we'll figure it out.

Hours later, she could hear nothing but Joey's soft breathing in her ear.

She smiled to herself, keeping her arms carefully tucked against her sides in order to not touch Joey beside her. They were basically on top of each other, and keeping her arms against her sides took an intense amount of concentration.

She was exceedingly aware of how close Joey was to her, how her arm gently brushed Joey's, how she could imagine the curve of Joey's hip and shoulder in the darkness. She was so close.

Kendall fisted her hands to keep from reaching out to touch her.

Her tent was hanging from a tree to dry, her sopping wet sleeping bag on a branch next to it. Nothing was immediately salvageable. It'd all have to dry for a few days.

They'd spent the afternoon and evening sitting around the fire, drinking beer and making interesting concoctions out of the snacks she had picked up. It turned out that chips topped with dark chocolate wasn't as bad as she would have imagined, but sour gummies ruined everything they touched, which she might have predicted.

She had eaten her body weight in s'mores, and Joey bashfully admitted that she'd spent hours trying to find the best vegan marshmallows in Denver.

Why had that detail made her so... giddy?

Before they'd settled in for the night, they extinguished the fire, and Joey made her stand on the far side of the campsite near the river to look up and see all of the stars. The sky was practically glowing with so many stars, and she could vividly make out the Milky Way across the middle of it.

It made her feel small and content, and seeing Joey's awed expression, staring up at the sky, suddenly made the entire strange trip worth it.

She'd wanted so badly to reach out and take Joey's hand in hers, but she settled for staring up at the same sparkling sky, sneaking glances to see Joey's excited smile as she pointed out constellations.

In the end, they'd decided to share the tiny tent. Joey had brought extra blankets for Ozzy, who was apparently the type of dog who preferred not to sleep on the ground, and Kendall had an emergency blanket in her car.

They'd laid out the sleeping bag on the ground, then arranged the blankets as best as they could. The tent was barely four feet across, and even with both of them on the very edge of each side, their shoulders touched.

Ozzy had been side-eyeing her in the lamplight as she had snuggled under a particularly cozy sherpa blanket, but he'd cozied himself up across her legs the moment she'd laid down.

She stared at the roof of the tent, listening to the noises of the night around her. Bugs, rustling leaves, Ozzy's soft snores, and Joey's quiet and steady breathing.

She'd only just begun to drift off when she heard the banging.

Her body tensed as she listened.

There was definitely metallic banging, and then shuffling footsteps. Was someone trying to break into their car?

She reached to shake Joey awake.

"Do you hear that?" She whispered.

"Hmm?" Joey said, turning onto her side to face Kendall. "You okay?"

"What's that noise?" Kendall asked.

Joey lay beside her in silence, and Kendall thought that perhaps she was listening until she realized that Joey's breathing had returned to its slow rhythm.

"Jo, wake up," Kendall said, shaking Joey again.

Joey startled, then turned onto her back. "What?"

"I think either someone is trying to break into the car or a bear is about to attack us," Kendall whispered frantically. Her heart was pounding. What could she use as a weapon against a bear? Joey had told her they didn't need bear spray, but what if the bear came ripping through the tent? Or worse, if it was a crazed human murderer, ready to attack?

They were sitting ducks.

Joey yawned, shifting noisily on top of the sleeping bag. "It's just a bear, babe. He's not even close," she said. "It'd be much louder if he was trying to get into our bear bin. That's why we locked all the food away. No food in here."

"*We're* the food," Kendall whispered, her voice rising higher in pitch, and even she realized she was sounding a bit... unhinged.

Ozzy lifted his head off her leg, seemingly to glare at her until she shut up and fell back asleep.

"These bears know what they're about. They're not going to attack two humans and a dog just for kicks. They want snacks," Joey said.

"I don't... I don't know," Kendall said, straining to hear where the bear intruder was going to approach from.

"If Ozzy's not growling, there's nothing to be afraid of," Joey said. She turned onto her side again and wrapped an arm around Kendall, pulling her closer. "We'll protect you, don't worry."

She sleepily nuzzled into Kendall's side, her cheek pressed against Kendall's shoulder.

Kendall tensed, afraid to enjoy the moment too much. Afraid of letting herself get used to the feeling.

"But–" Kendall started.

"Shh. Go the fuck to sleep," Joey said groggily, squeezing her again.

Kendall relaxed into Joey's arms. It was hard to trust someone who could fall asleep during a crisis — but then again, if Joey could fall asleep in the face of imminent danger, shouldn't that mean Kendall was overreacting?

Having Joey snuggled against her side was the ultimate distraction, though. Joey was warm and soft, and Kendall felt oddly comforted by her. How was she expected to sleep when every nerve on her body was electric with Joey's presence so close to her? Every exhale of Joey's breath tickled her neck, making her body increasingly aroused.

She let out a long exhale and closed her eyes, trying to focus on the night sounds again, along with the metallic banging of a bear in need of a midnight snack. Focusing on anything but Joey's body stretched along her own.

She awoke in the morning in a strange, contorted position. Ozzy was behind her, acting like a big spoon, wrapped against her back. She was, in turn, wrapped like a koala around Joey, who was sprawled out like a starfish, with one arm under Kendall.

How the hell had they ended up like that?

She looked up at Joey, noticing how young she looked when her features were blank and relaxed. She reached out, brushing the hair from Joey's cheek and tucking it behind her ear. Courage welled up inside of her and she ran her fingers through Joey's golden brown hair. It was just as soft as it had always looked.

Joey's eyes blinked open and her brow furrowed in confusion for a moment before her expression softened. She smiled. "We survived," she said, blinking in the light.

Kendall tried to casually unwind herself from Joey, like it wasn't a big deal that she'd had an entire leg wrapped around her. She ran a hand through her hair, worried about what her bedhead would be. "Just barely," she said.

"Bear-ly! I see what you did there," Joey said, giggling.

Ozzy stretched at the sound of Joey's voice, pushing his paws into Kendall's back, which pushed her further into Joey.

She groaned, reaching behind her to gently tickle his belly.

"I slept like a rock," Joey said, sitting up to stretch.

"I know," Kendall said, rolling her eyes.

Joey grinned, reaching forward to unzip the tent. "I've got to pee so bad," she admitted, crawling out of the tent. slipping sandals on her feet. "Come on, Oz." She patted her leg.

Kendall sat in the tent for a moment longer, not wanting to start the day just yet, because it would mean the night of being wrapped in Joey's arms was over.

CHAPTER THIRTEEN

JOEY

Joey threw her hands up like Rocky. "Made it," she said triumphantly.

Kendall bent over, putting her hands on her knees. "Is this the part where we get to stop for snacks?"

They'd decided to go on a light hike after a morning of a quick breakfast, tearing down the campsite and packing up the car. Joey had chosen the campground because of its proximity to trails that she wanted to check out, and they had not disappointed. Of course, she'd cleared Ozzy's ability to exercise with her vet first.

Joey sat on a rock and Ozzy settled behind her. "Snack time," she said with a smile.

Kendall sat on the other side of Ozzy, doling out fruit strips.

Ozzy eyed them, smacking his lips in anticipation.

"Sorry Oz, this isn't dog food," Kendall said lightly.

A spit bubble formed on the side of Ozzy's mouth in response.

Joey giggled, cringing. "Gross," she said, shaking her head.

Kendall chuckled, talking to Ozzy about how dogs couldn't have people food because all day long she dealt with overweight dogs and didn't want Ozzy to go down a dark path.

Joey watched her, a strange feeling coming over her. It was as though Kendall's mere presence was a calming treatment for her soul. She felt safe with Kendall, like Kendall could take care of anything bad that could happen.

She didn't remember the bear conversation the night before, but she did remember waking up in Kendall's arms. How would she ever forget that feeling? She felt like some lovesick puppy — some awful combination of hopeful and agonized over Kendall's presence.

She pulled off a piece of her fruit leather, trying not to fixate on the vision she had of waking up to Kendall's face, inches away from her own, and the gentle, warm look in her eyes. Had Kendall been running her hands through Joey's hair, or had Joey dreamt that?

Joey reached for her hydration pack hose, biting down gently on the mouthpiece to release the water.

"Oh man, can I have some of that? Would that be weird?" Kendall said, watching her.

"No, of course," Joey said, unclipping the hose to extend it further.

Kendall took a long pull from the end of it, and Joey tried to look deeply interested in a bird in a nearby tree to avoid watching Kendall's mouth touch exactly where hers had been moments before.

Maybe she really should have gone home with someone last weekend — she was so turned on by something like Kendall sharing her hydration pack... it was clear that she needed to get laid before she burst into flames from sexual frustration.

She couldn't even use that incredible vibrator without

thinking of Kendall, even though she'd rather cut off her left arm than ever admit that to Kendall's face.

"I'd have never guessed you were so outdoorsy," Kendall said, looking sideways at her with a smile.

"My family likes to hike. It's a thing we've just always done, I guess. I've never considered it to be special in any way," Joey said with a smile.

"I think my mother would die on this hike," Kendall joked.

"Why?" Joey snuck a tiny pinch of the fruit leather to Ozzy.

"I saw that, and no, she's not really that bad. She just sided with my father instead of me. She isn't a bad person, per se, but she's not the supportive person I'd prefer," Kendall said, her voice trailing off.

Joey regarded her with a neutral expression. "What do you mean sided with your father?"

Kendall nodded, her brows drawn in thought.

Joey waited, not wanting to push her to open up any more than she was comfortable. Ozzy's attention shifted to a passing butterfly, and Joey reached down to hook his leash around her ankle so that he'd be able to have room to explore.

"Not good?" Joey asked.

"No, he's never... We don't..." Kendall started, trailing off again. "Sure, he wasn't thrilled that I was gay, but then I did something stupid that was kind of related, and he's never forgiven me for it."

Joey reached to cover Kendall's hand with her own. "It's his loss," she said firmly.

"What is?" Kendall asked, swallowing hard.

"Not getting to know and cherish what a fucking wonderful person you are," Joey said.

"That's really... That's very kind," Kendall said.

"Kendall, I mean it," Joey said, desperate for Kendall to believe her. "You are one of those rare people who can make another person's life better just by being in it."

Kendall looked at her, her eyes searching Joey's. There was a shift in the air between them, and Joey's heart thumped wildly in her ears. Kendall's gaze dropped to her mouth.

She knew with certainty that Kendall was going to kiss her. She just knew it.

She suddenly felt panicked, like this was the kind of eyes-wide-open leap they'd never come back from. She'd never again be able to pretend they were just friends. She'd never be able to squash down her crush, bury whatever hopes she had for them together...

Her mouth felt dry, but she found herself leaning in, as if drawn in by Kendall's magnetic field.

Kendall's phone began to beep, it's repeated piercing tone breaking the spell almost immediately.

What the...

It had been nice to spend an entire day without cell service, pretending the world was somewhere far away.

"I guess I have service up here?" Kendall said, sounding confused.

She reached into her pocket and drew out her phone.

"Whoa," she said, scrolling on her screen. "I have like fifty texts."

She scrambled to her feet.

Concerned, Joey grabbed Ozzy's leash and pulled out her own phone. She had sixteen missed calls from Roger and dozens of texts.

"Imogen's in labor," Kendall said quickly. "Something's wrong."

They rushed back down the path to the trailhead where they had parked. Kendall dropped her keys and picked them up with shaking hands.

"Hey," Joey said, putting a hand on her shoulder. "Breathe. Freaking out isn't going to help her right now. Give me the keys, and I'll drive so that you can make the phone calls."

Kendall nodded, handing her the car keys.

She drove a touch faster than the legal limit on her way back to Denver, listening to Kendall try to piece together what had happened.

Apparently the baby wasn't due for another four weeks, but Imogen's water had broken sometime the night before. They had gone to the hospital and after hours of labor, the baby's heartbeat had slowed.

They'd gone into an emergency Cesarean.

Apparently Imogen had called the only other person she could think of to help with the kittens — Kendall's mother.

Roger and Edward hadn't been allowed to see them, and Gertie had stopped answering her texts.

Kendall sat quietly in her seat, staring out the window. She held a knuckle to her lips. Joey stole a glance and saw that tears slid down her cheeks.

"Hey, it's going to be okay," Joey said, even though she had no way of knowing that.

Kendall nodded, sniffling.

"Imogen is like, the toughest person I've ever met, so she's going to get through this, and so is the baby," Joey said.

Kendall nodded again.

"Do you want me to go with you?" Joey asked as they pulled onto her block. The plan was to drop her and Ozzy off at home, then Kendall would go to the hospital and try to figure out what was going on in person.

Kendall shook her head. "No, it's okay, it might be boring until we know anything," she said. She was a terrible liar.

Joey pulled over in front of her building. "Okay, but let me know if you need..." She stopped herself from saying 'me,' and instead, said, "Anything."

Kendall gave her a quick hug and then practically tossed her things out onto the sidewalk from the back of the car. "I'll call you once I know anything," she said.

How quickly the day had gone from idyllic to terrible. She felt selfish for the thought the moment it passed through her mind, knowing that no matter what she was feeling, Kendall was feeling ten times worse, knowing that her best friend was possibly in danger.

Joey sat, clipping Ozzy's toenails to pass the time. She hadn't heard back from Kendall but she also didn't want to bother her, given that she was probably stressed out in the hospital. Should she have tried harder to go with her? The waiting felt horrible. The not knowing. Kendall had promised to keep her updated, but what would she do if the update wasn't good?

"She's probably just busy," she said to Ozzy. "She'll definitely text me soon."

She clipped Ozzy's nails, giving him about ten thousand treats to get through the task. He hated it so much and made such a production about it, it became a wonderfully distracting ten minutes for her frantic brain.

Her phone buzzed and her insides swirled in anticipation. She reached for her phone, but paused when she saw it was Nikki's name on the text, not Kendall's.

She glared at the notification, then set her phone back down without reading it.

She got up from the couch and walked into the kitchen, busying herself with putting away the items from the cooler. Kendall had forced most of the leftover snacks on her. Her stomach ached from only eating junk, but that didn't stop her from opening the top of the cookies and taking one out.

She washed a few dishes in the sink, glancing back over to the couch to where her phone sat.

What the hell could Nikki possibly be messaging her about? Curiosity wore at her self-control, and she dried her hands on a towel, walking back across the apartment.

She could just read the message and not reply back. That would help quiet the voice inside her mind, wondering if

Nikki was texting to gloat, apologize, or pretend nothing had happened.

She took a deep breath as she held her phone in her hand, then clicked the message open with her thumb.

Nikki: Hey, I'll be in town this weekend, want to grab a drink?

Oh, so Nikki had chosen the Pretend Nothing Happened path.

She turned to Ozzy. "She's gotta be fucking kidding me," she said.

Ozzy's eyebrows raised in confusion.

"I know, right?" Joey said. "Does she really expect to go back to being friends?"

Was she being childish? Raina had moved on, clearly, why couldn't she?

Plus, the dating pool in her hometown was pretty small, so it made sense that Raina would start dating someone she knew.

But, one of her closest friends?

She turned to Ozzy again. "Can I even really call her my friend? I mean, the entire time I've lived here, it's not like I've heard from her."

Ozzy scratched at his ear.

"No, I don't think I should have to message back," she said, as if Ozzy was trying to talk her into replying.

A new text from Nikki came through.

Nikki: it was never our intention to hurt you and we'd really like to make it up to you.

Joey snorted in frustrated amusement.

"We? *We*?" She said, tightening her grip on her phone.

Ozzy got up from the couch and walked over to his crate,

lying down with a sigh.

She screenshotted the texts and opened a new message to Sunny.

Sunny: Want me to go Tonya Harding on her?

Joey: No, I just want to complain, I think.

Sunny: Let me put Ellie down for his nap and then I'll call you so you can get it out of your system before you accidentally let anyone else know what a judgmental jerk you truly are.

Joey: That's love.

She leaned her head back on the couch, closing her eyes.

The phone rang and she answered it without looking. "Okay, so first of all, what the fuck," she said.

"What?" Kendall asked.

She sat up straight. "Oh, I'm so sorry, I thought you were my sister," she said quickly.

"Oh," Kendall said. She sounded exhausted. "Um, are you busy?"

"Nope," Joey said.

"I have a favor to ask." Kendall's voice sounded strained.

"Sure, what's up?" Joey said, standing. She was suddenly full of nervous energy. "Wait, how's Imogen? How's the baby?"

"Felix is in NICU with a pneumothorax and it was scary for a while there," Kendall said,

"Ken, human words, not doctor words," Joey said, pacing around her living room.

"Sorry, collapsed lung," Kendall said.

Joey gasped. "Oh my God, will he be okay?"

"His chances are good. He got his mama's fighting spirit, that's for sure," Kendall said. "Anyway, yeah, everything's fine here. But my mom just called and she needs someone to take over for the kittens for the evening. Can you please–"

"Of course," Joey cut her off. "Of course."

She fed Ozzy and put his harness back on him — he was exhausted after the hike earlier, and even though it had been an easy hike given he was still recovering, it was the most action he'd had in weeks. Kendall had given him a full check-up earlier that morning over a breakfast of unfrosted pop tarts.

She remembered to grab her mail on the way out to her car and stuffed the letters in her purse as she walked out of the building.

She made it to Kendall's and walked to the front door, not knowing if Kendall's mom was still there. If she was, it'd probably terrify her for Joey to use the spare key Kendall had told her about.

She knocked, standing on the porch with Ozzy on his leash, and after a few moments of not hearing an answer, she turned to walk to the back gate to find the specific flower pot Kendall had fitted the key inside.

As she stepped off the porch, the front door opened, and a woman who looked surprisingly nothing like Kendall smiled back at her.

"You must be Joey," she said.

Joey nodded. "And you're Kendall's mom?"

The woman smiled again. "Call me Lina."

Joey smiled politely. "Thank you," she said, walking into the house past Lina. She let Ozzy off of his leash, and then out into the backyard.

"I'm so sorry to do this. Lawrence was getting a bit testy with me being gone so long. You know how it is," Lina said, gathering a few things she had sitting on the front chair.

"Lawrence is Kendall's father?" Joey asked.

Lina nodded, smiling sadly. "It'd be one thing if he'd just stay the night here with me, but..." She shrugged, smiling again.

Joey awkwardly fidgeted with her purse strap. "Do you

want to give me a quick tutorial on how you've been feeding the kittens?"

Lina led the way to Kendall's bedroom, and Joey saw that the kittens were no longer contained to a Kitten Jail tub. At six weeks, they were big enough to run around the entire bedroom, but they'd been sectioned off to one part of the room. Still, they tried climbing the fence in a prison break, and they were much more stable on their feet than the last time she saw them.

"Hey Lamb Shanks," Joey said, reaching for the female to cuddle to her chest.

Lina gave her a sideways look but didn't say anything. She explained where the canned food was and how to mix it with water.

Lina sighed, rising to her feet. "Well, that's about it. I fed them three hours ago, so they shouldn't be needing food for another hour or two, I think," she said.

Joey set a reminder alarm on her phone and stood, setting the kittens back into their Kitten Corral.

She walked Lina to the front door, and just as Lina passed through the threshold, she turned around. "Oh, and I left Kendall a bottle of wine I thought she might like. It's on the table," she said.

Joey smiled. "That's so kind of you," she said.

"Well, I do what I can," Lina said, shifting her weight between her feet.

Joey awkwardly bit her bottom lip, unsure what to say. "Yeah," she said, awkwardly smiling.

She'd talked to Kendall about her parents just that morning, knowing that it wasn't a very good relationship. Hadn't she been out for over two decades now? Lina and Lawrence had had plenty of time to "come around." Thinking about that now empowered her.

"You know, you could just call Kendall sometime," Joey

said. Her heart pounded in her chest, like what she was doing was dangerous. And in a way, it was.

Lina paused, her face falling for only a fraction of a moment. Then, her perfectly placed smile came back.

"Have a good night, dear," Lina said, then walked off of the porch.

Joey watched her go, thankful to have the parents she did. She closed the door and pulled out her phone to dial her own parents, just to reassure herself.

"Just checking in," she said after they'd said hello.

"Did she get it?" Her father said excitedly in the background.

"Get what?" Joey asked.

"Hold on." Her mother put her on speakerphone.

"It said it was delivered yesterday," her father added.

"What?" Joey asked, confused. "I didn't get any packages." She hadn't seen any packages at her doorstep. Had someone stolen it? No, they had lockers for packages. But she had checked the mail on her way out and she'd have found a key for the locker.

"It might be in a letter," her mom suggested.

Joey walked over to her purse, pulling out the stack of letters she'd received. Most of them were junk, but then she saw a letter with no return address.

"What'd you guys do?" She asked, ripping open the top of it. She pulled out an airline gift card with $1500 written on it. She sighed. "You guys really should have spent this on yourself," she said.

"No, we want you to use it to go get your groove back," her mother said.

Joey laughed. "My groove? That's not a real thing," she said.

"It is, and you are missing it," her father said.

"Well, thank you," she said, feeling choked up. "This is incredible."

"Go give yourself the trip you deserve," her mom said. "Now, dinner's almost ready, so I've got to go, but let's have a video call tomorrow. I miss your beautiful face."

She said her love yous and goodbyes, and then sat down on the couch, holding her face in her hands. Why was she crying? Why was she feeling overwhelmed? She was grateful, but it felt so real to have an engagement present in her hands.

She had spent two years dreaming of what type of life she'd have with Raina, and what their wedding would look like, and where they'd go on their honeymoon, and what they'd name their first child...

And it was over.

Raina ripped that dream from her.

And then she'd realized that she hadn't wanted the dream, anyway. Because that's all it was. It was a dream.

Eggs, one of Kendall's cats, rubbed against her legs, but didn't hop onto the couch or come within arm's reach. Ozzy climbed onto the couch next to her, setting his head in her lap.

She cried until she heard the alarm on her phone go off, telling her it was time to feed the kittens.

She got off the couch, wiped her face on her sleeve — it was hers, after all — and went to Kendall's bedroom to find two bright-eyed and bushy-tailed whiners begging for dinner.

Her mood lifted as she fed the kittens, their tiny faces getting dirty as they face-planted themselves into the food.

She felt needed and important. And that felt good.

After the kittens were fed, she helped them into their tiny litter box until they'd used it. She gave them snuggles until they'd both fallen back asleep, and then she tucked them into their cozy bed.

She set another four-hour alarm on her phone.

She looked at her phone on the way out of the bedroom, her stomach grumbling. She hadn't eaten real food since before the camping trip, and surely Kendall would come home starving.

She prepared a simple meal using what she could find in the fridge — a bundle of kale on its last leg and a tub of tofu. She found cashews in the pantry, and toasted them as she browned the tofu and sauteed the kale. It would warm up well given that she had no idea when Kendall would be home.

She climbed onto the couch with her meal, searching on her phone for flights. Ozzy curled up on the floor beside her and she moved her foot to be able to rub his side with her toes.

The airline she had a gift card for was running a promo — the last-minute flights were comically cheap. She could purchase a round-trip ticket to Hawaii and still have enough to cover another trip for herself.

Or, she could buy two round-trip tickets to Hawaii...

Would Kendall let her do that? Would Kendall be able to get the time off work?

She was startled by a cat jumping onto the couch beside her, regarding her with skepticism.

"Well, hello to you, too, Bacon," she said.

The cat meowed and crawled onto her lap, forcing its way under her arms until she was practically forced to cuddle it.

"You don't take no for an answer, do you?" She asked, laughing.

Ozzy lifted his head and watched the cat with interest, but ultimately laid back down with a heavy sigh.

"Don't worry, I'm always going to be a dog person, I promise," she told him.

She settled back on the couch, petting Bacon as she began to purr, closing her eyes slowly.

Joey smiled, taking a deep breath, and closed her eyes, letting herself be lulled by the tranquil sound of a rumbling purr.

CHAPTER FOURTEEN

KENDALL

She came home to find Joey asleep on the couch, holding one of the cats while another curled up at her feet. She gently woke Joey to send her home, but Joey had other plans. She warmed up the tofu and kale meal while Joey drank a cup of tea at the dining table.

"I had an idea," Joey began, circling her finger around the rim of the mug. "And it's okay if you think it's crazy, because it is crazy, but I also think it'll be worth it."

Kendall had just spent the entire afternoon and evening at the hospital with Imogen and Gertie, walking back and forth as Gertie posted up at the NICU, while Imogen was trying to recover from the shock and the surgery, not to mention the intense pain killers she was on. She relayed information, held Imogen's hands while they both cried, and found Gertie copious amounts of coffee.

At the end of the night, Gertie took Kendall's hands in her own. "You've done enough. You've been here all day. Please, go home and do something for yourself."

Kendall began to protest.

"Imogen is going to be okay, and Felix is going to be okay, and that's all that matters. The rest is details. We'll be okay, I promise," Gertie asserted.

Coming home to Joey... it felt like a relief. Like everything was right where it was meant to be.

Joey floated the idea of them going to Hawaii, and Kendall had told her no immediately.

There were a thousand reasons why, including but not limited to: She wouldn't be able to get the time off work with such short notice, she wouldn't be able to afford a random trip to Hawaii, she wouldn't get care for the kittens so easily, and her best friend had just gone through a horrific ordeal and was still in the hospital.

"Let's make a deal," Joey said with a smile. "If I pull Hawaii out of the Adventure Jar, it's a sign and we have to go."

Kendall eyed the slips of paper still in the jar. The chances weren't terrible, but they weren't in Joey's favor.

Joey reached in, pulled a slip out, then passed it to Kendall without opening it.

Kendall unfolded the paper.

Go to Hawaii.

She looked back at the jar. "Did you fill the entire jar with Hawaii?"

Joey looked comically affronted. "Of course not," she said.

Kendall reached for the jar and pulled out the paper. Horseback riding. Ziplining. Camping — they'd forgotten to remove that one.

"Huh," Kendall said, looking down at the piece of paper in her hand. Hawaii.

"Although that would have been genius," Joey said, tapping her chin in thought.

Joey had called Roger and Edward to cover the kittens.

Dr. Rothlisberger had signed off on the PTO — he seemed

more flustered than usual and might not have noticed the dates properly.

Joey had explained the gift card.

Imogen had told her she was an idiot if she didn't take a few days in Hawaii.

Even her own mother had called "just to chat" — weird, but okay — and upon hearing they were thinking about going to Hawaii, excitedly given her the access code to their "bungalow."

Suddenly, she was out of excuses.

Kendall gripped the armrest as the plane shook with turbulence.

Oh God, wasn't this how Lost had started?

She glanced down to Joey, who was still asleep, her head resting on Kendall's shoulder.

"You're okay," Joey murmured, linking their arms together. "It's just a few bumps."

She took a deep breath, nodding. Sure, like sleepy Joey ever had their best interest at heart. She could sleep through a bear attack, but Kendall was meant to believe that she was now an expert aviator.

"Ma'am, do you want a drink?" The flight attendant asked, startling her.

"Yes. Wine? Tell me you have good wine. Or champagne?" Kendall asked, or practically begged, if she was being honest.

The flight attendant smiled. "Of course," she said, handing Kendall a list of the beverages on board. "And anything for your partner?"

Kendall glanced down at Joey. "Also wine," she said. She'd be drinking it anyway.

The flight attendant smiled. "Honeymoon?" She asked, her eyes twinkling.

How asleep was Joey?

Kendall smiled. "Something like that," she said with a wink. "I'll have the Chardonnay, and she'll have the Sauvignon Blanc."

The flight attendant handed her the two tiny bottles and then winked, walking away without charging her for them.

Kendall grinned. Maybe this trip would be fun, after all.

They landed soon after — or maybe the wine definitely helped pass the time a bit faster — and walked into the airport.

"Where are the people with leis?" Joey asked, looking around.

"I think that's only on commercials," Kendall said, shrugging.

"Well, that's no fun," Joey groaned.

The humidity was apparent from the very first step outside of the airport. It was hot, but not miserable. The air had a fresh smell to it, no unlike home in Colorado. Did it just smell like flowers here? Was the air magic? How many glasses of wine did she have?

She could see why her parents had saved every penny to buy a house there.

Once their luggage was safely stowed in the trunk of the taxi, they were on their way.

Joey pressed her face against the window, calling out whatever she was seeing — look at the birds! Palm trees! A fruit stand! Where's the ocean? Is it behind us?

Her parent's home was only around a half-hour from the Kahului airport, but the roads were winding and disorienting.

"Is this the address?" The taxi driver said.

Kendall craned her neck, trying to see out of the windshield.

"Yeah, this is what shows on my phone," Joey said, pointing out the window. "Is there some sort of driveway hidden around here?"

The taxi inched along before finding a break in the trees

with a road that looked like it could be some sort of driveway.

"Let's try it," Joey said.

"And if we get shot for trespassing?" Kendall asked.

Joey shrugged. "I think the people of Maui have seen their fair share of dumb tourists," she said with a grin.

The taxi driver laughed at that.

They pulled into the driveway, winding around until they were in a cleared area.

"Holy shit," Joey said, as the house came into view.

Before them was a large, sprawling home, painted sky blue with a wraparound porch.

Kendall could feel Joey watching her as they pulled in front of the garage, pausing a moment to take it all in.

"Well, if this is what they want to waste their money on, who am I to tell them no?" Kendall said.

"And who are we to deny them the chance to share it with us?" Joey said with a wink.

She got out of the car and walked to the front porch.

"Ken, you can see the ocean from the porch over here," she said, excitedly making her way around the back of the house.

Kendall shook her head, paid the driver, and grabbed their suitcases as she walked to the front door, punching in the access code.

She walked in, struck by how... normal it all seemed. It had furniture, pictures on the walls, kitchen counters... it was like a real home. She looked at the pictures lining the entryway. Her parents were fishing, snorkeling, laughing on a boat with friends.

She was simultaneously proud of them for achieving their dream and ready to strangle her parents for prioritizing a mansion in Hawaii over their own daughter.

Joey knocked on the back patio door, then turned to point.

On the patio sat a large table, and over the edge of the deck was an expansive view of forest and ocean.

It was stunning.

Seeing how excited Joey was made all of the complicated feelings swelling inside of her calm down. She was going to make it the perfect trip, no matter what.

"I can't do it," Kendall said, wanting to throw up. She clung to the pole in front of her.

"Yes, you can," Joey said, standing in front of her with a serious look. "Let go."

Why would anyone want to try ziplining? It was terrifying, and high off of the ground, and she hadn't even tried the truly awful part of flying through the rainforest with nothing but a harness and a wire keeping her from falling into certain death.

"No way," Kendall said, gripping the pole tighter. She tried not to think about how she could feel the platform swaying — that was in her head, right? Or could she really feel it?

"Ma'am, you're welcome to climb down if you need," the attendant said.

"Nope, she's good," Joey said to him firmly. "Kendall, look at me," Joey reached to hold Kendall's cheek in her palm, which made Kendall pause and look up at her. "Just stand up."

"This was *your* adventure, so why does it matter if I don't do it?"

Joey's eyes crinkled with good humor. "Because we do them together. That's the whole deal. I did not sit through your suit fitting to have you wimp out on this platform," she said firmly.

Kendall grinned, then glanced over Joey's shoulder to the canopy beyond her.

"I'm pretty sure I'll die if I do this," she said bluntly.

"And I'm confident that you won't, but if you do, then you

went out in a pretty exciting way, right?" Joey said with a grin.

"That's... that's not comforting," Kendall said.

"Take my hand," Joey said. She reached out to Kendall.

Kendall groaned. "I don't like lilies," she said.

"What?" Joey asked, lifting Kendall to stand up tall and take a step towards the edge of the platform.

"At my funeral, make sure there aren't lilies," Kendall said.

"You're a super drama queen, but I love you all the more for it," Joey said, laughing.

"Wh-what?" Kendall asked, certain that she must have misheard Joey.

"I'm going to count to three, and then I'm going to push you. So, turn around," Joey said.

"Ma'am, we can't legally push her," the attendant said.

"Well, she can sue me later," Joey quipped.

Kendall looked up at the wire hanging above her, then sank down into her harness, feeling it bear her weight. This was definitely how she was going to die. Or throw up. Ugh, throwing up while sailing through the rainforest would be awful. Worse than the Dildo Capades, for sure.

"I'm going to push you on three," Joey said. "I think you have to tell me 'yes' out loud so this nice man will let me do it.

"Ma'am, that's not–"

Kendall nodded. "Okay, on three," she said, taking a deep breath.

"One..." Joey started, her hands on Kendall's back.

Kendall's racing heart pounded in her ears, vibrating her whole body. She looked straight ahead at the horizon, trying to be brave. Her entire body was shaking.

"Two..." Joey said, and then Kendall felt Joey's hands shove her off of the platform.

She could hear Joey laughing behind her for the first terrible second, but then her mind cleared.

She was flying. Her senses kicked into high gear, and she could see every tree, hear every bird whistle, as the wind whipped her shirt against her chest. It was incredible. She'd never felt more like she was flying in her entire life.

She held her arms out, yelling in excitement. Her stomach was flipped up somewhere near her lungs, but that was okay.

The wind whipped at her face and she took a deep breath, trying not to let everything whoosh by in a blur. She wanted to remember it all.

She hit the handbrake like she was meant to once the other platform came into view and slid to a graceful stop, teetering on the edge of the platform.

The attendant reached out to grab her harness, pulling her the rest of the way.

"Oh my God, that was... That was the best," she said.

The attendant gave her a polite smile. "So glad you liked it," he said, talking into a radio. "Clear."

That must have been Joey's signal. Kendall could hear Joey's scream rip through the peaceful air. She laughed, seeing Joey come into view, all of her limbs outstretched.

Joey had a better dismount on the platform.

"You survived," she said in excitement as the attendant clipped them onto the next line.

"You pushed me on two," Kendall said, pretending to be surprised.

Joey giggled and leaped forward, wrapping her arms around Kendall. "This is the best," she said. "I'm so excited that you did it."

Kendall, actually surprised, hugged Joey back. She held Joey tight, breathing in the sweet floral scent of her hair and feeling her body against her own. "Me too." She paused for a moment. "But we've still got like three lines to go," she added.

"Yes!" Joey said, jumping in excitement.

The platform groaned under her jumps and she stopped immediately, glancing at the attendant with wide eyes.

"Okay, I get to go first this time," she said, walking to the other side of the platform.

Kendall reached for her. "Well, then I get to push."

"Uh, excuse me, ma'am–"

"On three? One–"

―――――

"It should be right through here," Kendall said, staring down at the directions on her phone.

"This looks promising," Joey said, disappearing behind a lava rock.

Kendall followed after, walking between two lava rock walls.

"Wow," Joey said, gasping in surprise and pausing as the walls opened up to the beach.

Kendall stopped beside her, taking in the sight.

Before them was a small beach, dotted with black lava rock, and flanked with palm trees.

The surf was calm and the water was an iridescent green.

"This is like a calendar beach," Joey said, walking forward. "Why is no one else here?"

Kendall looked around, then looked back over her shoulder. "Maybe because it was a hike to get in? Or maybe because it's a Thursday morning?"

Joey shrugged, walking forward. "I bet people have weddings on this beach," she said.

Kendall shook her head. "The poor suckers."

Joey raised a brow, then reached into her bag to take out a faded beach towel they had found back at the house. She laid it on the ground, then pulled her t-shirt over her head.

Kendall busied herself by looking in the bag she had grabbed labeled, "Beach Necessities." Bandaids, sunscreen, and a bottle of some liquid that smelled awfully like vinegar. She focused on literally anything other than Joey's bikini.

"Come on, let's dip our toes in," Joey said.

"Uh, okay," she said, not changing out of her shorts and sun-safe long-sleeve shirt.

She set the bag down and followed Joey, definitely not noticing how her bikini bottoms left little to the imagination... She'd never noticed before how perfect Joey's ass was — she'd, of course, accidentally glanced at it a time or two, but having it before her now...

Joey turned, looking concerned. "What's that look for?"

Kendall tried to look anywhere but at Joey's breasts, covered by the tiniest triangle of fabric.

Kendall blinked. "Do you think the water's cold?" She wanted to facepalm the moment she said it.

Joey grinned. "You're on a completely deserted beach in Hawaii and you're worried about the water being cold?"

Kendall nodded, willing to take a hit to her ego if it meant she wouldn't have to explain that she was fantasizing about Joey's body. "Yep," she said, nodding again for extra emphasis.

Joey walked to the edge of the water, turning a bit as she dipped a foot in. "It's a little cold," she conceded. "But I think you'll be okay."

The water was relatively calm in the cove, and Joey waded out until the water was up to her waist.

Kendall stood on the shore, unable to take her eyes off of her.

Maybe it was the fact that they were in a tropical paradise.

Maybe it was the fact that they were a long way away from the real world — or, at least, their real worlds.

Maybe it was the fact that she was still riding an adrenaline high from that morning's ziplining adventure.

Whatever it was, Kendall was entranced.

Body and soul — bewitched by the woman before her.

She took a deep breath, watching Joey sink down in the water, her hair flowing out around her.

"Come on in, the water's fine," Joey called out, giggling. "I've always wanted to say that."

She had no idea what exactly flipped the switch for her, but this was the moment. They'd nearly kissed a few days before on a hike, or, well, she had thought they were going to kiss.

But now, it was like she couldn't stand the thought of not kissing Joey.

She'd waited long enough. She was going to do it.

She took off her shirt and shorts, tossing them back towards the blankets. She took a step forward, the cool water wrapping around her ankles, drawing her in.

She felt full of purpose and confidence.

Joey turned, smiling back at her, and Kendall's heart clenched at the sight.

She was so captivated that it took her a moment to register what was happening when Joey started screaming, flailing around in the water as she rushed to get out, running past Kendall in a flurry of yelling and arm-waving.

...Wait, what?

"Jellyfish!" Joey screamed, grabbing her arm and dragging her out of the water.

"Were you stung?" Kendall asked, growing concerned as they hurried out of the water. "Are you hurt?"

"No," Joey said, shaking her head, visibly distressed. "No, I wasn't stung. But there's like... ten billion of them. Not an understatement. An entire army of those globby bastards."

Joey took a deep breath, pushing her wet hair out of her face.

"I saw my life flash before my eyes," she said dramatically, walking back to the towel she had laid out earlier. "Explains why this beach is deserted, though."

Kendall watched as Joey stretched out on the towel before her, holding a hand to her chest as she gasped.

Don't look at her heaving chest, don't look at her heaving chest.

"Fuck," Joey said, swinging her forearm over her face to cover her eyes. "That was..." She looked up at Kendall, squinting. "What's wrong?"

Kendall shook her head, pulling back on her long-sleeved shirt and shorts, before reaching into her bag to grab her towel. She laid it out on the beach next to Joey's, lying down beside her.

She was reminded of lying in the tent, listening to Joey's soft breathing as she slept. She was so close, and at the same time, worlds away.

Just like now.

The spell had been broken. Kendall couldn't very well kiss her now, not after her brush with death.

She reached into the beach bag and pulled out two cans of cold sparkling seltzer, handing one to Joey. "Here, this might take the edge off," she said with a grin.

"I wish it was a little harder, but this will do," Joey said, popping open the top of the can. "Do you have the sunscreen?"

Kendall nodded, handing her the tube from the bag.

Joey rubbed the lotion onto her shoulders and chest. "Will you rub it into my face so I don't have the weird white streaks?"

"Sure," Kendall said, taking the tube from her.

"Isn't this how like 90% of lesbian porn starts?" Joey asked with a giggle, leaning towards her on the towel.

"If you had asked me to rub it onto your back, then yes," Kendall joked.

Kendall put a bit of lotion on her fingers, then began to gently rub it onto Joey's lightly freckled nose and cheeks. She was close enough to see how light Joey's eyelashes were without mascara, how soft her cheeks were, how she had tiny, light hairs that curled around her hairline.

Her eyes were vividly green and yellow in the light. And they were trained so intensely on Kendall's face that it made

Kendall slightly nervous. Her stomach swirled as she continued her task.

"So, what do you want to do for the rest of the day?" Joey asked.

Stay here with you and never leave.

"I don't mind hanging here for a bit." Kendall shrugged.

"Yeah, it's gorgeous weather," Joey said, closing her eyes as Kendall wiped away the last of the white streaks.

"Yeah," Kendall agreed.

"Are you okay?" Joey asked. "You've been so quiet since we got here."

Kendall paused, swallowing. "Everything's totally fine," she lied.

"I know what's bothering you," Joey said with finality.

"Oh, do you now?" Kendall said lightly, handing her the tube of sunscreen. "Don't forget the back of your neck."

Her fingers still tingled with electric energy from touching her, and she worried she might combust if Joey asked her to rub any more sunscreen onto her body.

"Is it because we're staying at your parent's house? We can find a hotel if that would make this trip better for you," Joey said, her brows knitting in concern.

Kendall blinked in surprise, trying not to reveal just how shocked she was. "Oh," she started, rendered speechless. For one thing, how had Joey picked up on so much in such a short amount of time?

And for another, how had Joey completely misread the situation?

Was Joey so not into her that the tension and spark between them was completely one-sided? She couldn't feel any of it?

Joey reached out to touch Kendall's arm. "It's okay to feel whatever way you want," she said.

Kendall nodded, pressing her lips into a thin line as she

swallowed, trying her best to fix how dry her mouth had become.

"We don't have to change houses or anything," she said. "It does suck knowing that they have this entire life that I'm not a part of, and that my dad has been so weird since the divorce, but I seriously thought–"

"Wait, what?" Joey asked, her jaw slack with shock.

"The... what?" Kendall asked. Surely, she had mentioned the entire thing to Joey before?

"Divorce?" Joey asked, taking a long drink of her seltzer, then glancing at the label as if to question why it wasn't stronger.

"Yeah, I told you about that," Kendall said.

"Nope," Joey answered firmly. "Now, let's start back at square one. You were married? To?"

"Her name was Fiona," Kendall said.

"I can't believe you never told me about this," Joey said, blinking quickly. "When?"

"Right after the breakup with Imogen," Kendall said.

Joey stared back out at the horizon, curling her knees into her chest as Kendall fidgeted with her shirt.

"How long were you married?" Joey asked.

Kendall laughed. "Like six weeks."

"How long were you together before you got married?" Joey asked, not looking at her.

"We don't have to talk about this," Kendall said, shrugging awkwardly.

"I think we do," Joey said, turning back to look at her. "I think we very much need to talk about this." The hurt on her face was obvious and made Kendall feel guilty for keeping it a secret — because she had kept it a secret. She hadn't wanted Joey to think less of her for it.

"Why?" Kendall asked, fidgeting in nervousness, brushing sand off of hands. She felt like she was being interrogated.

"Because we're friends," Joey said firmly.

Kendall sighed, shaking her head. "Friends let things go when the other person doesn't want to talk about it," she said.

Joey's expression hardened. "Friends tell each other big things," she said.

"It wasn't a big thing," Kendall said. "It was only six weeks."

"I cannot believe you don't think marriage is a big thing," Joey said.

"Well, I'll have you know, that it wasn't even legal to get married back then. So, we had a ceremony, sure, and I wore a dress, because that's who I thought I had to be back then. And then, six weeks later, she told me she was leaving me for another woman," she said. "So, no, it wasn't a *big* thing."

Joey's glare softened and she reached out to wipe a tear off of Kendall's cheek — Kendall hadn't even realized she was crying. "That does sound big. And that woman sounds evil."

"It was my own fault. We had only been dating for a few months, and then when we got engaged, I made this big deal about how it was a serious commitment even if it wasn't legal, and then she left me anyway. My parents paid for the whole thing," she said, shaking her head. She had blocked so much of it out.

"And that's why you and your dad don't talk?" Joey asked. "I thought he wouldn't accept that you were gay?"

"Well, it is, but he had been willing to try. And then after Fiona left me, he really doubled down on the whole sanctity of marriage thing," Kendall said. Although she couldn't remember what Fiona looked like on their wedding day, she could remember every detail when she had told her father they weren't staying together.

Joey moved to sit on her knees, wrapping her arms around Kendall.

Kendall tensed for a moment, afraid to touch Joey's almost completely naked body. Afraid of how she'd ever come back from that, how she'd ever feel Joey's bare skin under her hands and ever be able to look at her like she was just a friend.

"I'm sorry I got upset about it. I understand why you wouldn't want to talk about it," Joey said.

"I should have told you," Kendall whispered. "I should have been honest about it. I just didn't want you to think…" Her voice trailed off.

"We'll get there," Joey said, and Kendall could hear her voice vibrate through her chest.

She softened, burying her face in Joey's neck, breathing in the heady coconut scent of her sunscreen. "And I haven't dated since," she said.

"Probably a good thing. Your picker is way off," Joey joked.

"My *picker*?" Kendall asked, tilting her head to look up at Joey.

"Yeah, you know, how you decide who to be attracted to," Joey said.

"You can decide who you're attracted to? It just happens to me," Kendall said.

Joey looked down at her for a long moment. "Me too," she said, though her voice was barely audible. Her forehead was wrinkled as though she was in deep concentration as she moved her hand to cradle Kendall's jaw, then ran her thumb over Kendall's lips.

Kendall's heart hammered against her ribs. She lifted herself until she was eye-level with Joey, pressing their foreheads together. Her eyes closed as she considered what she was about to do.

They'd never come back from it.

But maybe she didn't want to go back.

She tipped her mouth forward tentatively, brushing Joey's lips with her own. Just a taste, a hint.

She had kissed Joey before, and it had been mind-blowingly good, but it was bittersweet. It had been for show, not because Joey knew she was communicating how much she wanted her, craved her.

She wanted this kiss to be perfect.

She could feel Joey's warm breath on her cheeks, hear the raspiness of each exhale.

Her hands trailed over Joey's bare back, wanting to hold her, to dig her fingers in and never let go. She spread her palm flat against Joey's lower back, and moved her other hand to tangle in Joey's hair at the nape of her neck.

Joey's breathing was becoming labored, her hands twisting in the fabric of Kendall's shirt.

Joey pressed her mouth to Kendall's first, her lips soft and yielding against Kendall's, as though she was simply curious.

It was as though Joey was asking her own question, and Kendall desperately wanted to be the answer.

She held Joey firmly, convinced nothing had ever been so right.

Joey nipped at Kendall's lower lip and Kendall grinned against her mouth. She could have kissed her for hours, reveling in the taste of her, the feel of her in her arms. Finally. *Finally* in her arms.

In that moment, she was in exactly the right place, the place where she belonged. Joey let out a hum of pleasure that made Kendall smile against her lips. Her hands explored Joey's body with abandon, and as Kendall could feel Joey respond to her touch, her own body reacted ten-fold. A little too quickly, if she was being honest. She was ready to take her right then and there. She nipped Joey's bottom lip, then slowly deepened the kiss, taking more. She needed more. Any and all restraint she had saved had fled the moment Joey touched her mouth.

The sound of children's laughter rang faintly in her ears, but it wasn't until Joey shifted away from her that she realized it wasn't just her mind going to a strange, transcendental plane.

She looked sideways to find three children coming into view, a woman walking behind them. Joey pulled her shirt on, taking a hair tie off of her wrist to pull her wet hair off of her shoulders.

The woman gave a small wave and Kendall cleared her throat, waving back.

They stood, gathering their things, and Kendall worried for a moment that the spell had been broken again.

"Careful, there's jellyfish in the water," Joey called to the woman, slinging her bag over her shoulder.

The woman nodded. "Thanks for the heads up," she said, calling her kids back from the water.

Joey reached and took Kendall's hand, lacing their fingers together. Kendall stared down at their hands — how many times had she envisioned kissing Joey? How many times had she thought about taking Joey's hand?

"Want to go back to my place?" Joey winked.

CHAPTER FIFTEEN

JOEY

"Wow," she said, nearly breathless at the sight.

They sat on the porch of a fancy restaurant overlooking the ocean. The sun had begun to set, painting the sky with rich oranges and pinks and purples. The colors reflected over the water, and the golden light made the palm trees glow around them.

But that wasn't exactly what Joey was admiring.

Kendall was turned away from her, admiring the view with a glass of wine in her hand. With the sunset behind her, the golden light on her hair, and that impeccable suit, Joey had barely gotten through her meal.

It had been hard to keep her hands off of Kendall since they'd left the beach. Hell, even leaving the beach had taken extra time, since she'd pinned Kendall against a lava rock wall. She'd had a taste, and she couldn't get enough.

Kendall had pumped the brakes once they'd gotten back to the house, insisting that they go out to a nice dinner to celebrate their first full day on the island.

She'd worn an emerald green dress that hugged her

curves, and despite falling to the knee, left little to the imagination between the lower neckline and the contoured fit. She'd thought she might be slightly overdressed, but when Kendall had stepped out in her brand new cream-colored bespoke suit, she'd nearly pounced on top of her right then.

It was all she could do not to beg Kendall to skip dinner.

But, Kendall had made a reservation, so they'd gone.

The hostess who had taken the reservation ended up accidentally mishearing Kenneth, a detail that was still making Joey giggle. She reached out her foot, slipping off her heel to rub against Kendall's calf.

"Madame Moore, are you playing... footsy with me?" Kendall said, turning around from the sunset to grin at her.

"You look like a really hot, lesbian James Bond in that suit, Kenneth," Joey said, sipping her beer.

"Damn, I was going for a Cate Blanchett vibe," Kendall said, raking a hand through her perfectly mussed hair. "You do know that if I'm Kenneth, you're Joseph, right?"

Joey giggled into her beer, feeling giddy and light. "That's only fair," she said.

"Is this our first date?" Kendall asked.

Joey considered it for a moment. "I guess so? But that feels... weird," she admitted.

"It does kind of, doesn't it?" Kendall said. "Okay, so if this wasn't our first date, what was?"

Joey thought about the question. "The laundromat?" She joked.

"Romantic. Or, it could have been when Ozzy ate your harness," Kendall said with raised eyebrows and a pointed look.

Joey quickly looked around to see if anyone had heard it.

"Wait, it was definitely the sex shop," Kendall said, laughing. "Featuring the Attack of the Silicone Soldiers."

Joey glared at her. "It was not sex shop. You were flirting with that woman the whole time," she said.

Kendall leveled her with a smile. "She was very cute, but she didn't have a chance," she said.

"No?" Joey asked.

Kendall reached across the table, taking Joey's hand in hers. "No. Because I was a goner from the moment you wiped snot on the sleeve of my jacket," she said.

"Such poetry," Joey said, rolling her eyes, but she squeezed Kendall's hand back.

"When did you realize you first had feelings for me?" Kendall asked, lacing her fingers through Joey's.

Joey exhaled, taking a moment to think over a sip of her beer. "Remember when I was at your dinner party, and Imogen said that thing about you being single forever? And then we went and fed the kittens? I think it was right around there. I was so disappointed, hearing about how you didn't date, but I couldn't totally understand why. And then watching you with those kittens, and how gentle and knowledgeable you were... I think that's when I really felt it," she said. "But, I convinced myself you were just being friendly and that I was just being desperate after my breakup."

Kendall smiled, easy and slow, her eyes crinkling with amusement. "Love makes fools of us all," she said, raising her wine glass.

Joey resisted the urge to gasp. "What did you just say?"

Kendall paused. "Love makes fools of us all? It's a saying, I'm not that poetic," she said.

"No, I just mean the first word," Joey said, leaning forward.

Kendall laughed, shaking her head. "It's a saying, Joseph. Pump the brakes," she said.

Joey wiggled her eyebrows. "Damn, you really do know how to U-Haul," she joked. "I like your house, but how will I ever give up my apartment?"

Kendall smiled, but it looked like Joey might have accidentally struck a nerve. Kendall drained her wine glass in a large, comical gulp. "Want to take a walk?" She asked.

Joey nodded, and after getting their check, they exited off of the porch right onto the beach.

They linked hands, holding their shoes as they walked in the sand. She had insisted that Kendall roll up her slacks in order to not get the bottoms sandy and dirty.

The wind whipped at Joey's hair and she tilted her face so that it would stay out of her eyes.

"Listen," Kendall started in a strange tone. "I think we shouldn't... I think we should wait to have sex."

"What? Why?" Joey asked, feeling disappointed and rejected.

"Because I'm... I don't want everything to change just yet," Kendall said, and she suddenly looked pained. "I don't want whatever this is to get ahead of itself."

"Get ahead of itself?" Joey questioned, holding her hair back.

"What does this look like when we're back in our real lives?" Kendall said.

"This is our real life, Ken. This is real," Joey said, trying to stifle the urge to shake her by her shoulders. "It's just us. It doesn't have to be scary."

They walked along as an uncomfortable silence stretched between them, punctuated by the lulling rhythm of the waves on the beach.

"I will never pressure you, and I want you to know that I respect your boundaries," Joey said, trying not to take it personally. Why were people always telling her to slow down?

Kendall was quiet and paused, as if regarding her in the darkness. "I just don't want to fuck this up," she said, her voice strangled with emotion.

Joey took a step to her, reaching for Kendall's waist. "We won't."

"How do you know?" Kendall whispered.

"I don't know, but I've got a good feeling about you," Joey said with sincerity. "And I'm going to do whatever it takes to make you happy each and every day."

Kendall nodded, but didn't say anything back. They turned, walking to find a taxi with a quiet understanding before them.

Joey had spent so long pretending she didn't have feelings or repressing what she truly wanted, and now it felt strange to come to terms with exactly how much she cared for Kendall. A terrifying amount, if she was being honest.

She watched the streetlights pass as they rode back to the house, thinking that each one represented a promise to stay lit even in the darkest hour. If they could do that, so could she.

They walked inside and Joey started up the stairs towards her bedroom.

"Where are you going?" Kendall asked, tilting her head in confusion.

"I was going to change out of this," Joey said, gesturing down to her dress as she kicked off her heels.

Kendall looked her up and down. "You can lose the shoes, but not the dress just yet. I want just a tiny bit more time memorizing every detail of it," she said.

"Why?" Joey asked coyly.

Kendall only smiled, reaching out a hand. "Let's go have a nightcap on the porch," she said.

They sat, playing music and talking for hours as they sipped another wine and beer each, then eventually switched to water.

"What were you like in high school?" Joey asked.

Kendall laughed. "Different. Very different," she said. "Cheerleader. Homecoming queen."

Joey gasped in shock.

"What did you want to be when you grew up?" Kendall asked.

"The person who narrated planetarium videos."

"Really into space, huh?" Kendall asked.

"Or maybe just the sound of my own voice," Joey laughed. "Biggest regret?"

"Waiting so long to kiss you," Kendall said, looking sideways at her.

"Funny, my biggest regret is how long you waited to kiss me, too," Joey said with a grin.

"Imagine that." Kendall said. "Alright, let's hit the hay so that we can go horseback riding tomorrow."

"What?" Joey asked, suddenly feeling more awake.

"I booked a horseback riding trip tomorrow. Apparently it starts on the beach and ends at a waterfall," she said, reaching for Joey's hand.

"Well, that sounds magical," Joey said, walking back into the house.

"It's only an hour, given that you're a newbie. Anything more than that and you won't be able to sit down," Kendall said, her hand very casually grazing Joey's ass.

Joey smirked. "How thoughtful of you," she said, making her way back towards the stairs to go to bed.

"Do you... I mean..." Kendall said, rubbing the back of her neck. "Do you need help with your dress? The zipper or anything?"

Joey paused, raising her eyebrows. "This whole celibate-until-we-figure-out-otherwise thing is going to be a lot easier if you don't offer things like that," she chided.

Kendall nodded.

Joey climbed a few stairs, pausing. "It is a shame, though, considering I bought this dress with the fantasy of you taking it off," she said wistfully, then made her way to her bedroom, imagining the look on Kendall's face.

Joey shifted under the covers. They felt itchy and annoying against her skin. The humidity was strange, and she couldn't decide if she needed no covers, or a leg out of the blankets, or maybe a glass of water. She could hear the ocean waves crashing outside of her opened window if she held her breath.

Kendall had been good on her word. They'd spent the day horseback riding, then relaxing on the beach, then wandering around a tourist trap marketplace. She'd picked up a new collar for Ozzy and Kendall had found prints by a local artist that she had shipped home. She'd even gotten in a few hours of work while Kendall napped on the back porch. They'd eaten takeout at home in their sweatpants, exhausted. It felt like a surprisingly normal day with a girlfriend on vacation.

Except now, Joey had all the energy.

Her thoughts drifted to the kiss with Kendall yesterday on the beach, how she'd held Joey's body so tightly, as if desperate for her touch.

And then she remembered that strange talk on the beach... Kendall was afraid of jumping in, which made sense, but was she so afraid of relationships that things would never progress with them? Would she ever be Kendall's girlfriend? Wife?

She was getting ahead of herself. She sighed in frustration.

They'd kissed throughout the day, including a particularly intense hammock makeout in the backyard that had ended in Joey falling onto the ground and Kendall laughing until she cried.

And yet, when it came time for bed, Kendall had still gone into her own room.

Translation: Not tonight.

Joey focused on her breathing. Breathe in serenity, exhale sexual frustration.

She closed her eyes, tossing and turning and trying not to check the time on her phone every ten minutes.

She had no idea if she was asleep or awake when she heard her door open, the gentle click of the latch alerting her.

Trying to make her eyes adjust, she pushed herself up onto her palms.

She'd recognize the familiar shape of Kendall anywhere. Kendall stepped further into the room, the light of the moon through the window touching her face as she walked across the room and sat on the edge of Joey's bed.

Was she dreaming? She reached out to touch Kendall's cheek, and Kendall turned her head, pressing a kiss into Joey's palm.

"Hey, you okay?" Joey asked.

Kendall nodded, smiling in a way that felt reassuring and confused at the same time. Her eyes were wide, revealing something much deeper. Hunger, desperation… hope.

Joey scooted out of the way, holding up the edge of the covers in invitation.

Kendall settled in beside her, and Joey's entire body buzzed with anticipation as they lay facing one another.

Kendall traced the curve of her shoulder, her waist, her hip. She hooked her thumb in the waistband of Joey's pajama shorts, tugging them just slightly.

"Are you sure?" Joey asked, her question barely making a sound.

"I was being an idiot," Kendall said with a small smile.

"It's okay if you still want to wait," Joey hedged.

"I can't wait. I can't wait a moment longer."

How many times had she dreamed of this exact moment? The anticipation tingled through her entire body, making her nervous and excited and hesitant and eager all at once.

Joey reached for Kendall, her hand slipping from her neck down to her small breast through her shirt.

Kendall's breath hitched and her eyes fluttered closed. "Yes," she urged, licking her lips.

Joey's thumb circled her hardened nipple slowly and Kendall arched into her touch.

Kendall reached for Joey, gently pulling her close as she leaned in.

Joey's lips parted in anticipation, and when their mouths came together, all hesitation fell to the side. Her entire body pulsed and hummed from being turned on, just from touching Kendall through her clothes — how was it going to be when she urged Kendall's shirt over her head?

The kiss was gentle and endless, languid, as if they had all the time in the world.

Joey pulled back, taking a deep breath, trying to keep her control in check. She wanted to flip Kendall onto her back and push her clothes aside, but at the same time, she recognized what they both needed.

Slow and steady.

Which felt impossible in the moment, seeing Kendall's eyes darken as she leaned up onto her elbow to take Joey's lips in another kiss.

Kendall shifted until she was on top of Joey, their legs entwined. Her thigh fit between Joey's, rocking against her.

Their rhythm was unhurried and gentle, and Joey had to take a few deep breaths to keep her impatience from besting her.

Kendall leaned back onto her heels, pulling Joey up with her.

"This is in my way," she said, pulling at Joey's top.

"Oh, is it?" Joey teased, crossing her arms to pull her shirt over her head. She hadn't been sleeping in a bra, and she watched as Kendall took the sight of her in.

She didn't feel self-conscious… she felt worshipped.

She reached for Kendall's shirt, pushing it up until Kendall reached for the hem, tugging it off and throwing it haphazardly behind her.

Kendall's skin was creamy and smooth, and no amount of

fantasizing about her breasts could have prepared her for seeing Kendall topless for the first time.

"You're so beautiful," she said, leaning forward to place kisses along Kendall's sternum.

Kendall hummed in appreciation, tangling her hands in Joey's hair. She tipped Joey's head back, kissing her again — deeper now, as though her self-reservations were also wearing thin.

Kendall shifted them back down, moving her mouth to kiss and nip along Joey's throat, below her ear, the sensitive spot where her shoulder sloped into her neck. She took her time, teasing, nipping, kissing, sucking.

Joey squeezed her eyes closed, reveling in the feeling of Kendall's mouth already.

She rocked against Kendall's thigh, seeking release as Kendall's mouth moved to suck and tease her nipples.

Was that a whimper that just escaped her mouth?

Kendall moved lower, kissing along the softness of her stomach, then deftly removed her shorts and underwear in one swift movement.

Joey attempted to keep her breathing steady, but as Kendall settled between her thighs, opening her, her mind went completely blank. All she could do was feel. She was done overanalyzing every tiny detail. All she had to do was enjoy.

Her hands fisted in the sheets as Kendall placed gentle kisses on her inner thighs.

Joey giggled. "That tickles."

Kendall nipped the sensitive skin and Joey's hips bucked in reflex.

"Easy, tiger," Kendall whispered with a chuckle.

She brought her mouth to Joey, lightly exploring and teasing, bringing Joey close to the edge, then backing off.

Joey groaned, helpless, frustrated, and yet, wound so

tightly that she worried even making eye contact with Kendall between her legs would send her over the edge.

Kendall reached up, rolling Joey's nipple between her thumb and forefinger as she continued her assault on Joey's self-constraint.

Finally, finally, she held Joey's hips tightly, pulling her close as she pushed first one, then another finger inside of her.

One long swipe of her tongue, and Joey was arching off the bed, crying out in pleasure. Her climax tore through her, a release so long overdue that her reaction surprised even her. Kendall held her still, lingering in place until her entire body relaxed, spent.

Kendall moved back up the bed to lie down beside her. "You are endlessly sexy," she said.

"That was better than I ever imagined," Joey said, still breathless. "I can't believe I get to keep you."

Kendall looked at her for a long moment, as if considering a puzzle.

She nuzzled Joey's neck, placing a soft kiss there. "I'm glad I could live up to the fantasy," she said with a throaty chuckle.

"Did you ever fantasize about that?" Joey asked.

Kendall nodded. "More than I'd prefer to admit."

Joey's hand played across Kendall's back, over her hip. She tugged at Kendall's underwear. "Off, please," she said.

Kendall smirked, but obeyed the command.

"Are you still sure?" Joey said, moving her face to see Kendall's expression.

Kendall nodded.

"Tell me what you thought about," Kendall whispered.

Joey blushed in the darkness, hesitating.

"Tell me what you thought about when you touched your-self," Kendall urged.

Joey's hand skimmed over the hardness of Kendall's

ribcage, sliding lower. "I thought about you," she started, feeling shy about saying it aloud.

"What about me? What did you think about doing to me?" Kendall asked.

Joey shifted, her hand skimming down Kendall's long leg. "I thought about kissing you," she said.

"Where?"

"Everywhere."

"Show me."

Joey moved onto her knees, leaning over Kendall to place kisses along her chest, her breasts, where the skin was taught over her ribs, where the curve of her hip flared. She licked Kendall's hip bones, her tongue flat and wide, and felt Kendall shiver under her touch.

She leaned, kissing the soft curve of Kendall's ass cheek, the crease beneath it, the back of her knee.

Kendall moaned.

"And then what?" Kendall asked, and Joey glanced up at her to see that Kendall's eyelids were heavy and half-closed.

"I thought about using that vibrator on you," Joey confessed. "About kneeling between your legs, watching you... watching me fuck you with it."

Joey moved again until she was sitting between Kendall's legs. She reached forward, slowly sliding a finger along Kendall's folds, unable to help the guttural sound that escaped her lips when she found how very ready Kendall was.

"Yes," Kendall said, sitting up until their bodies were pressed together again.

Joey reached between them, her fingers sliding up and down through Kendall's arousal.

Kendall wrapped an arm around Joey's shoulder, as if to steady herself, as her hips found their own rhythm against Joey's hand.

Joey dipped her fingers inside Kendall, who moaned in

response. She moved her thumb over where Kendall needed it most, circling and building until Kendall crashed in waves around her, calling her name and holding her tight.

After, as they lay in the bed entwined together, Kendall placed a light kiss on Joey's lips.

"I wanted to tear that dress off of you last night," Kendall confessed.

"I wanted to tear that suit off of you, and then I remembered how much it cost," Joey teased.

Kendall laughed. "I can't believe it took us so long."

"It's okay. We've got all the time in the world," Joey murmured against Kendall's hair, and the words felt like a promise she was desperate to keep.

CHAPTER SIXTEEN

KENDALL

The sun was streaming in through the window when she awoke. She sat up in bed, looking around for Joey, who was mysteriously absent.

She got out of bed, slipping back into the t-shirt and shorts she had been wearing the night before, and walked out to the landing, glancing around.

She heard murmurs from downstairs and smiled to herself.

She walked down the stairs to see Joey sitting at the breakfast bar wearing headphones, her forehead wrinkled in concentration. "Mise en garde, ne pas utiliser sur les sourcils," she whispered to herself as she typed. Beside her on the counter was her dog camera, watching Ozzy run around the living room of her sister's house with a toddler.

Even with her hair up in a messy bun and a holey t-shirt on, the sight of her still made Kendall's insides do a bit of a skip and twirl.

She glanced up with a smile when she saw Kendall,

pushing her headphones down around her neck. "Good morning, sleeping beauty."

"Good morning, don't let me disturb your work," Kendall said, filling a coffee cup.

"Nah, the shampooing soin ultra-nourrissant can wait."

"I don't know what that means but I believe you," Kendall said, raising her eyebrows. She walked around the edge of the counter to lean in for a kiss.

Joey grinned, leaning in to kiss her with a loud smack. "I haven't brushed my teeth yet," she said.

"Me either, we're gross together." Kendall winked. "Is that my shirt?"

Joey looked down at the shirt and shrugged. "Seems like I'm wearing it, so it's my shirt now."

"Once a laundry thief, always a laundry thief."

"What do you want to do today?" Joey asked. "Oh, and before I forget, your phone has been buzzing nonstop. I think you left it down here last night."

Kendall frowned. "I don't know who would be calling unless something is wrong with the cats," she said.

She walked to where Joey had pointed and found her phone in the couch cushions. It must have fallen out when they were eating takeout the night before. She cursed herself for being so birdbrained about it. Then again, she'd had other things on her mind.

"This is weird," she said, seeing five missed calls from the clinic, then from a few numbers she didn't recognize. "Hope they realize they can't call me in today." She chuckled, listening to the first of the voicemails.

"Kendall, call us as soon as you get this," Maria, one of the daytime receptionists said, leaving it at that.

Cryptic...

None of the other voicemails were very helpful.

A text from Taylor popped up.

Taylor: I don't want to tell you this over text, but you have to get back here immediately.

Kendall: What's going on? I'm just getting messages now.

Taylor: Dr. Rothlisberger died last night.

The phone slipped from her hands, landing on the ground with a solid thud.

"What's up?" Joey asked, glancing over her shoulder. "They want you to come in to cure cancer again?"

Her hands began to shake. Then her knees. Her entire body.

Joey glanced back again, doing a double-take. "Are you okay?" She asked, standing up to hurry over to where Kendall stood near the couch. "Sit down."

Kendall sat down, staring at her shaking hands.

"What's going on?" Joey asked, reaching for her phone. She looked at the last message. "Oh, fuck."

"We've worked together for fifteen years," Kendall said, unable to fit words and emotions into the consuming feeling of shock. "And I find out in a text."

"I think you should call," Joey said, looking through the voicemails. "It looks like this number is his wife."

Kendall nodded, looking down at the phone. "Yeah, I'll call her," she said, taking the phone from Joey's hands.

She disappeared back upstairs to make the calls, first to Paul's widow, Sheena. Sheena was in hysterics. From what she could make out, Paul had died of a stroke the night before. He had gone quickly. Then, Sheena began to insist that she had to run the clinic. She hadn't read the will yet, but she was "100% sure" that's what Paul would have wanted.

Kendall felt like an elephant was sitting on her chest.

A light knock on the door interrupted her thoughts as she rehearsed what she would say to the clinic staff once she was able to talk to them. It was imperative that they could trust her, but she didn't completely trust herself.

"Come on in," she said.

"I rebooked our flights to leave at noon, so pack up your things," Joey said, glancing at her phone. "We have a little over an hour before we have to leave here."

"Thanks," Kendall said, not knowing what else to say. Now the guilt of making Joey cut her vacation short was weighing on her, adding to the pressure she felt was holding her in place.

Joey nodded. "Do you need any help packing?"

Kendall shook her head.

"Okay, I'll pick up downstairs, so make your calls and don't worry about the rest of it," Joey said.

Kendall nodded, biting back the strangled cry that was clawing at the back of her throat.

She waited for Joey to shut the door before she let the tears fall, trying her best to sob as quietly as she could.

The emotions were so complicated — she hadn't even liked Paul the majority of the time, but she respected his work. She had learned so much from him in the last fifteen years that she couldn't picture herself at the clinic without him.

She had naively planned on spending another five under his mentorship before he retired, but now? Well, she'd do the best she could.

She hastily wiped the tears from her face and took a deep breath.

"We're naming them Artemis and Apollo," Edward said, beaming as he cuddled the female kitten to his chest. Apparently they had fallen a bit in love with the kittens after they had kitten-sat during the Hawaii trip.

"I love it! So much better than Lamb Shank and Veal," Joey joked. "You guys are going to be the cutest cat dads ever. Are you going to start an Instagram for them?"

Hawaii seemed like a lifetime ago. Kendall could hardly believe it had only been a week.

"We already have," Edward admitted, looking bashful.

Joey clapped her hands together. "I'm going to follow it immediately," she said, grabbing out her phone.

Kendall spun her wine glass in her hand, her mind racing with how much she had to do at the clinic. First and foremost, she had to talk to the lawyer to get on all the bank accounts, then she had to hire another vet as soon as she could. She had been working fourteen-hour days every day since they'd returned, and although she was excited to see her friends again, she was less than enthusiastic about hosting company. Joey had cooked and prepared everything and she'd only been instructed to shower in order to attend, so it hadn't been too bad, but all she wanted to do was lie down and close her eyes.

Roger laid a hand on Kendall's arm. "You okay?"

Kendall startled. Somehow she had almost forgotten where she was. "Yeah," she said, taking a sip of the wine. "Just a busy week."

The funeral had been on Wednesday, and although she had Joey on one side and Taylor on the other, instead of feeling like a celebration of life, she had spent almost the entire ceremony making a mental list of all the things she still had to do.

"So, then Kendall was like, 'Of course I'll buy you a Tesla,'" Joey said to Edward.

Kendall turned her head to raise an eyebrow. "Oh?"

"Just checking to see if you're still here," Joey said, reaching over to squeeze her knee under the table.

"What I really want to know is, how did you both finally

get over yourselves and decide to finally get together?"
Edward said, leaning forward in his seat.

Joey giggled. "Well, we were at this secluded beach, totally
alone, and there were jellyfish in the water," she started.

Kendall's phone rang, the clinic ringtone cutting through
the story. The crushing weight of responsibility pushed on her
chest. She could hardly take a deep breath. "Sorry," she said,
excusing herself from the table to walk down the hall,
answering the phone.

"Hey Kendall, seven-year-old pom euthanasia," Jenny, the
evening receptionist said.

"Can you schedule it for the morning?" Kendall asked,
rubbing her eyes. "Seven seems a little young to be so dire."

"Seems like the dog is in really bad shape. ...Dr. Rothlisberger saw him last week, you know, before... anyway, he
diagnosed him with advanced cancer," Jenny said. "I had Kat
talk to the owner and apparently she can't wait."

Kat had good sense. She trusted the tech's opinion, so if
she said it was an emergency, it was.

"And she can't go to an emergency vet or call an at-home
euthanasia service?" Kendall snapped, then felt guilty for it.
"Sorry, Jenny, yeah, fine, I'll be there in thirty."

She walked into the bathroom, finding Bacon curled in the
sink, sleeping soundly.

She scooped the cat out of the way and splashed some
water on her face. God, she didn't want to face Joey to tell her
she had to go back to work. They'd barely spent any time
together since they'd been home. The only reason they'd
made time for Roger and Edward was to hand over the
kittens officially.

She walked back downstairs, grabbing a blazer from the
front closet.

"You have to go?" Joey turned around in her seat, her
eyebrows pressed together in concern.

"Sorry, emergency," she said by way of explanation. She

hugged Edward and Roger goodbye, reminding them that the kittens' spay and neuter appointments were already in the books, and that they could call her anytime they had questions.

She gave Joey a quick kiss and walked out the front door, nearly tripping over a snoozing Ozzy on the front rug.

She was surprised and exasperated to see Brutus and his... very interesting owner standing on the front step when she pulled into the clinic parking lot.

"You've got to help him," the owner said as soon as she stepped out of the car. "He's on death's door, I just know it."

Brutus, to his credit, wagged his tail and licked his owner's face.

Yeah, death's door. Sure.

She felt a rush of relief when she saw Taylor's car pull into the parking lot. At least she wouldn't have to deal with Brutus' owner alone.

"I'm going to do what I can," Kendall cautioned, unlocking the front door and letting Taylor in to turn on the lights. It was only 8 p.m. and still slightly light outside, but the clinic had closed all of their windows when they'd left that afternoon.

"Come on into this exam room," Taylor said to the owner. "I'm going to be right in to grab a quick history as Dr. O'Hara takes a look over your paperwork from last week." They ushered the owner into the room and closed the door, giving Kendall a pointed stare.

"What?" Kendall said, too tired to understand subtle cues.

"Let's grab the paperwork from last week," Taylor said, pulling a file from the giant bookshelf of patient files. They opened the folder and held out a sheet of bloodwork results.

Taylor dropped their voice low, gesturing for Kendall to move away from the door further. "Paul told this woman her dog had untreatable cancer."

Kendall raised a brow. "Untreatable? That's a bit dramatic."

"Well, that's what I thought, but it's not like I could say anything in the moment," Taylor said, their eyes wide. "He didn't even specify what *kind* of cancer."

She scanned the paperwork. Not a single indication of anything even remotely dangerous — no lumps, no strange symptoms. Not a single number out of the ordinary on the bloodwork.

When it came to breed-specific issues, Pomeranians weren't even that susceptible to cancer. They were much more likely to have heart disease, but Brutus didn't show any symptoms of that, either. Zero cough. Zero foam.

Even the X-rays lacked any strange details.

She flipped through the other paperwork, including the intake sheet with a description of symptoms. "Tilting his head more than usual," she murmured

"When was this?" Kendall said, pulling Taylor further from the door.

"The day before he died," Taylor said.

"You're thinking..." Kendall said, glancing up to raise an eyebrow at Taylor.

Taylor nodded. "I'm thinking some things were misfiring before that night."

Kendall groaned. "I want you to pull every patient's file that Paul saw while I was away, so that I can review the notes and diagnoses," she said.

"It's, like, forty patients, you sure?" Taylor asked.

Kendall nodded, rubbing her eyes. She had a bad feeling in the pit of her stomach. "This is bad," she said.

"Well, the good news is, you get to go tell that lady her dog doesn't have to die tonight and that we don't think he has cancer."

Kendall sighed. "Well, that's one way to look at it. But then I get to run about seventeen tests to prove it to her until she believes me, and who knows how long that will take."

"Alright, I'm going to go get info, and then I'll tap you in," Taylor said, taking a deep breath as though preparing for battle.

They opened the door to exam room one and Kendall startled, hearing loud wails. And not from a dog.

It was going to be a long night.

She returned home around 1 a.m. with two banker's boxes full of files. What else had Paul fucked up? The woman that night had seemed eternally grateful — skeptical, of course — but grateful, nonetheless. Brutus was his usual happy self. She was sure she'd see him in a week or two for abnormal amounts of tail wags or whatever else the owner could think up, but at least she'd get to check up on him.

She walked inside, lugging the boxes with her, and set them down inside of her guest bedroom that she occasionally used as an office.

She peeked in the bedroom and saw Joey sleeping in bed with Bacon on her chest and Eggs on her legs, Ozzy stretched out beside her. She grinned at the sight.

How easily Joey had fit into her life. How easily they had transitioned from friends to... more than friends.

She didn't have the mental energy to consider what they truly were.

Joey was there, and that was all that mattered.

She walked back into the kitchen and set the kettle so that she could make a cup of tea to calm down. Emergency visits always got her blood pumping, and no matter how late it was, she had a hard time getting to sleep until she allowed herself to relax.

She took her tea and sat on the couch, scrolling through her phone mindlessly.

She heard the floorboards creak behind her and glanced to see Joey standing in pajamas, rubbing her eyes with a sleepy expression on her face.

"Come to bed, baby," she said.

"I will soon, I'm just unwinding," Kendall said, holding up the mug of tea.

Joey walked to the couch and crawled on top of her, lying down with her head on Kendall's chest. "Everything okay?"

"I don't know," Kendall admitted. She was nervous about Paul's misdiagnoses, especially pretty obvious misdiagnoses — in her initial scan through the paperwork, she noticed three other possible mistakes. She kicked herself for not being there to help. He was probably stressed from having too many appointments.

"Don't do that," Joey said.

"Do what?"

"It's not your fault," Joey said.

Joey had repeated the sentiment so many times over the past week, but Kendall couldn't help but feel... responsible.

Sure, her name wasn't on the business technically, but Mountain View Vet Hospital was her clinic now.

Joey rolled off of Kendall to lean on her elbow. "I think I know what will help you unwind," she said with a grin.

Kendall sipped her tea, raising an eyebrow.

Joey moved down Kendall's body, kissing her body through her clothing. For being relatively PG, it was intensely erotic to see Joey straddling her legs, kissing her stomach, fisting her clothing in her hands.

Joey unzipped Kendall's jeans, pushing them down over her hips as she put her mouth over Kendall's underwear, exhaling warm air onto Kendall's inner thighs.

"See? I think it's working," Joey said with a wink.

In her haste, Joey simply moved aside Kendall's underwear as she dipped her face, a long, slow lick pulling a moan from Kendall.

"I think you'd better set down the tea, babe," Joey teased, looking up at her through heavy lashes.

Kendall reached, barely having time to put the mug on the coffee table before Joey continued her mission in earnest.

"What do you mean sued?" Kendall asked, trying to understand Sheena. She'd only met Sheena a handful of times at various holiday events over the years, but she'd always been under the impression that she was the type of woman who'd have been comfortable hanging out with Emily Gilmore. She'd been wearing a perfectly pressed tweed skirt suit the last time she had seen her around Memorial Day. Today, she looked... rough. Her hair was unkempt and greasy and she wore a mismatched tracksuit.

They stood in the back lab of the clinic next to Kendall's desk. She'd been eating a piece of vegan string cheese for lunch when Paul's widow had rushed in.

"I mean that this woman is suing the practice, saying that Paul caused her dog undue stress," Sheena said. "Her lawyer is a pit bull."

"Like, an actual pit bull?" Kendall deadpanned, unable to help herself.

Sheena's eyes widened.

"Okay, okay, bad joke. Plus, pit bulls are honestly my favorite patients because they're so sweet, but go on. Please," Kendall said, her nerves kicking up, increasing her ability to babble. Had she gotten that from Joey?

It'd only been four days since she'd had the emergency visit with Brutus and his owner, and now his owner was trying to sue the practice.

"I don't know what to do," Sheena said, leaning against the desk, looking terrified. "I know the business is in my name, but I don't know how to run a business. Especially not one under prosecution."

"Litigation," Kendall corrected.

"Right, whatever," Sheena said, waving her hand in the air.

"Can you sue someone who is dead?" Kendall crossed her arms as she considered the idea.

"She's suing Mountain View," Sheena said.

Kendall took a deep breath, trying to quiet the panicked voice in her mind that was screaming, *"You're getting sued! This is the end of your career! You'll never recover from this!"*

"Is my name anywhere on that paperwork?" She asked after a brief moment of clarity through the noise.

"I'm not sure," Sheena said, pausing. "I'll send it to your lawyer. You have a lawyer?"

"Of course," Kendall lied, racking her brain. Gertie was a lawyer, wasn't she? An environmental lawyer, sure, but she'd at least be able to cut through some legalese.

Joey popped her head in the back. "Hey, thought you could use a proper lunch," she said. She looked between Sheena and Kendall, reading the room. "But I can drop it off if you're busy."

Kendall nodded. "Just give me ten minutes," she said, waving to Joey.

"We don't need ten minutes. We need you to fix this," Sheena said, looking frantic all over again.

Joey's eyes widened. "Alright, I'll wait outside," she said, exiting the room as suddenly as she had appeared.

"I'll have my lawyer look it over. Until then, I'm not sure what else we can do," Kendall said, rubbing the bridge of her nose. That always calmed people down, right?

After Sheena left in a huff, Kendall laid her head down on her desk. She wanted to scream. She wanted to punch a wall. She wanted to kick something.

Instead, she went limp, too exhausted for any of it.

She opened her eyes when someone touched her back. She turned her head to find Joey and Taylor and Kat standing over her.

"You okay?" Joey asked.

She wanted to be able to tell Joey exactly what was happening, but she couldn't let Taylor and Kat know yet. In fact, it was completely inappropriate for Sheena to come to the clinic at all. She should have arranged an off-site meeting.

"Just a long day," she lied.

"You've been here since 7 a.m. Why don't we just decrease the number of hours the clinic is open?" Taylor asked.

"Or I used to work at a low-cost clinic where they'd have a vet on the premises, but the techs handled all vaccination appointments. We could change Saturdays to that, so you could catch up on work and not meet with patients?" Kat offered.

Kendall nodded. "These are ideas," she said, rubbing her eyes.

Joey's eyes narrowed, but only for a split second. "Well, I brought lunch, and it's better than vegan string cheese. That shit doesn't even pull apart," she said.

"It's all I can fit in between surgeries," Kendall said. "I don't have time for that." She pointed to the container Joey had brought for her.

Joey flinched, as though Kendall had physically hurt her, and Taylor and Kat immediately made excuses to leave the room.

"Okay, what's going on?" Joey dropped her voice. "You don't talk to me like that."

Kendall shook her head. "Nothing," she said, hardening her voice. "I'll see you at home. I'm way too busy to have this discussion here."

Joey frowned, but she nodded. "Sure. I'll... see you later, I guess," she said.

Kendall immediately regretted her tone, but didn't have

time to think about apologizing. A neurotic Doberman barked from the kennel behind her, making her jump. "Yeah, yeah, I know you need a dental. Give me a minute," she said, stuffing the container that Joey had brought into the fridge.

Taylor reached their head in through the door. "There's a news article you might want to read immediately."

CHAPTER SEVENTEEN

JOEY

She hadn't heard much from Kendall in five days. Sure, they'd exchanged quick texts, but she imagined Kendall was probably still running around, trying to keep the business in order.

She didn't envy that.

She threw herself into work, finishing three projects weeks before the deadline. She started dreaming in French, accidentally murmuring French sayings to Ozzy.

To say she had time on her hands was an understatement.

Sunny invited her to visit that weekend and stay the night. They'd get a babysitter, most likely their parents, and go out on the town — a laughable statement, considering her hometown had three blocks of good bars to peruse.

It would be good to get out and see people. It would be wonderful, in fact, to have a night out with her sister, with whom she hadn't spent time alone in months. They talked on the phone most days, but it wasn't the same.

"Be good boys," Joey said to Ozzy and Elliott as they left, waving goodbye to their parents.

Sunny had dressed in heels and a tight skirt, and somehow convinced Joey to wear something similar.

They teetered on their heels as they walked through Old Town, and Joey had never been so grateful for summer, which meant that the bars wouldn't be packed with frat boys. Maybe they could have a fun night out and not see a single popped collar.

"Have you been to the new gay bar?" Sunny asked.

Joey gasped in surprise. "There's a gay bar?"

"Yeah, it has some weird name I can never remember, it's impossible to pronounce, but it's right next door to Calzone Zone," Sunny said with an emphatic nod.

"Well, I know where we're ending our night," Joey said, linking arms with her sister.

"Calzone Zone?" Sunny asked.

"Well, obviously."

They started at their favorite bar, a quiet spot below the main square that was meant to have Speakeasy vibes. The cocktails were strong and the lighting was low and there was no dance floor, so it ticked all the boxes for Joey. Wow, she had become such a boring adult. Seating had somehow become a prerequisite for a good bar.

As they sipped on lavender lemonade cocktails, Joey caught Sunny up on everything that happened in Hawaii, and then everything that had happened in the two weeks since.

"Any idea what she was arguing with the owner's widow about?" Sunny said, her eyes wide. Sunny was one of those people who couldn't resist a true crime podcast and typically picked out the killer within the first thirty seconds of any Law & Order episode.

"No, just that she seemed really flustered after," Joey said, sipping the last of her cocktail.

"Sounds financial," Sunny said, tapping her chin as though she was solving the mystery right there.

"Maybe," Joey considered. "But wouldn't she be honest with me about that?"

"Y'all may have been friends for two months or whatever, but you're brand new to whatever it is that you are now," Sunny said.

Joey nodded. "Yeah, that's a good point. It feels so weird because it just feels like we've been dating the whole time? I'm so comfortable around her already."

Sunny gave her a pointed look.

"What?" Joey asked.

"You're doing the thing you always do," Sunny said. "You settle in too fast."

"I do not," Joey protested.

"You do. You just start every new relationship right at the same point of familiarity you had before."

Ouch. It hurt more because there was an element of truth to it. Before Raina had been Liz, before Liz had been Jess, before Jess... She really *was* a serial monogamist, when she thought about it.

"You gotta keep up the romance and the... what is it called? The mystery. You have to make her miss you."

Joey rolled her eyes. "I'm not into games," she said. And she wasn't into taking dating advice from her prolifically single sister.

Her sister had a habit of scaring men off by pulling out the baby pictures about twenty seconds into any conversation. She referred to it as 'Weeding out the bad ones right away.'

Joey ordered another cocktail, and then another for Sunny.

"I love you, and I want you to be happy," Sunny said. "And I want you to slow the fuck down for once. Just enjoy what it is for what it is."

Joey stared down at her drink. She had a point, but Joey didn't like it. She took a deep breath, wanting to shift the focus onto Sunny instead. "Alright, so tell me who you're dating."

"What makes you think I'm dating someone?" Sunny looked at her skeptically.

"Aren't you?"

Sunny gave her a mischievous grin. "Well, there might be this one guy I started seeing casually," she started.

Joey grinned, feeling excited, and more importantly, feeling grateful for anything outside of her own world. Her reality had become a little too angsty for her own liking. Sharing in Sunny's excitement sounded a whole hell of a lot more fun. "Tell me everything."

An hour later, they stepped inside the new gay bar. Joey looked around, impressed with the layout. There was a large stage area and a long bar against one wall. There was even seating and the music wasn't too loud — she felt a bit sad that it had only come to town after her departure. She'd have spent so much time there.

Maybe she could bring Kendall when work quieted down? She imagined Kendall walking around her hometown, visiting breweries, eating at her favorite pizza place... maybe even reclaiming it as a pizza place and not the site of The Worst Pizza Party Ever. She smiled, imagining Kendall hanging out with Sunny and Elliott.

It was a nice vision of the future. No walking down the aisle. Simple. Just exploring, having fun together. Adventuring, even.

She leaned against the bar counter, trying to read their beer tap handles.

"I think they have two IPAs and a Pilsner. Kind of a lame beer selection for Fort Collins," Joey said over her shoulder without taking her eyes off of the cocktail board.

"Oh fuck," Sunny said behind her.

"What?" Joey said, turning to her.

"We should go," Sunny said.

"Why? This place looks great," Joey protested. She hadn't even ordered a beer yet.

"Nope," Sunny said, moving to stand on Joey's other side, as if to block her from seeing something.

"Are you feeling sick? You sucked down like four of those lavender things." Joey tried to assess her sister's wherewithal. Sunny looked surprisingly not drunk for how much liquor was in those cocktails. Joey had two and already felt a little silly. Maybe she'd get Sunny to dance with her.

The bartender leaned over the bar and Joey turned, smiling as she leaned in. The bartender was extremely cute, but not Kendall-levels of hot. Nobody could compare.

She ordered a vodka soda for Sunny and an IPA for herself, then turned to lean against the bar and look at Sunny. "I should text Kendall," she said, pulling her phone out of her bag.

"I really don't think–" Sunny began, but she was interrupted when someone else stepped into their bubble.

Joey glanced up from her phone to see Raina and Nikki standing awkwardly in front of her.

It took her a moment to process the horror of the situation.

Of course they were there. Joey resisted the urge to outwardly groan in annoyance.

"Hey," Nikki said, smiling wide.

Neither Joey nor Sunny said a word.

"So good to see you again, Susannah." Nikki moved to hug Sunny, but Sunny held up a hand. "No, you don't deserve that," she said forcefully.

God, she loved her sister.

"Of all the gin joints," Joey said to Raina.

Translation: I hoped to never see your dumb face ever again.

"Well, we weren't exactly expecting you, either," Raina said.

Sunny glared up at her, and even as Joey handed her the

cocktail she'd ordered, Sunny didn't take her eyes off of Raina.

Had she told Sunny lately that she was the best? Because Sunny was the best.

Fort Collins was a small enough town, especially with one gay bar, but this was a whole new level of claustrophobia. She'd never been so happy to have gotten the hell out, so that she could meet new people in peace. How many other women had she dated that were in that bar? The thought made her stomach sink.

"Can we talk?" Nikki asked, looking at her meaningfully.

"You can say whatever you need to say right here," Sunny said.

Joey turned to Sunny, giving her a *What the fuck are you thinking?* look. Or at least a look that she hoped translated into something similar.

"Let's fucking hear it," Sunny said.

Joey had forgotten how feisty Sunny got when she drank. It would be annoying when Sunny was trying to convince their rideshare driver to stop at the Taco Bell drive-thru on the way home, but right now, Joey thought it was exactly what she needed.

"Look, we never meant for this to happen," Nikki said.

"How long?" Sunny snapped.

What?

Raina looked from Sunny to Joey. "No, it's not like that," she said.

"How *fucking* long?" Sunny repeated.

Joey was going to have to muzzle her sister.

"A year," Nikki said.

As if on cue, the lights dimmed and colorful laser lights illuminated the dance floor.

"Are y'all ready to make some noise?" Someone yelled into a microphone being held entirely too close to their mouth to be understood.

Who did this DJ think he was? *Where* did this DJ think he was?

Joey was momentarily distracted, but Raina grabbed her upper arm. "I wanted to tell you," she said, leaning close to Joey's face to be heard.

"What does she mean, a year? You and Nikki have been a thing for an entire year? Since one year ago?" Joey confirmed, her voice raised over the new beats, unable to wrap her head around the newfound information.

Raina looked pained.

"Why the fuck would you propose to me, then?" Joey asked. It was as though everything she had ever known about the woman before her, the woman she had once wanted to spend her entire life with, was a lie. It *was* a lie.

"Because you wanted it so badly, and I didn't know how to tell you," Raina said.

"You say, 'I'm seeing someone else' not 'Will you marry me?'" Joey felt rage flowing through her veins.

And that's when she glanced over Raina's shoulder just in time to see Sunny punch Nikki in the face. Nikki fell backward, landing on her ass on the floor.

Holy shit.

Sunny shook out her hand, and although Joey couldn't hear it over the noise, she looked as though she was repeating, "Ouch, ouch, ouch."

A bouncer grabbed Sunny by the shoulder and pushed her back towards the door.

Raina frantically grabbed Nikki, pulling her off the floor.

Nikki was holding a hand to her nose, checking for blood.

Raina turned back to Joey, as though she was going to continue the conversation.

"You know what? Don't ever talk to me again. Good luck with this hot mess," Joey said, gesturing to... well, everything around her.

She placed her untouched beer on the bar and walked

outside to see Sunny standing on the sidewalk. She stood under a streetlight, flexing and unflexing her hand.

"Are you okay?" Joey asked, still in shock about what her sister had done.

"Do you want to split a calzone or do you want your own?" Sunny asked nonchalantly, nodding across the street to the Calzone Zone.

The tension of the situation deflated almost immediately, and Joey laughed. "Whatever you want, Mike Tyson," she said, wrapping an arm around Sunny's shoulders.

"You're right, I *should* have bitten her," Sunny said.

They sat outside of the calzone shop, each holding a box in their arms as they ate the greasy goodness Joey hadn't realized she missed so much.

"Kendall can't believe you punched someone," Joey said, looking at her most recent text.

"She's clearly never met me," Sunny said with a large bite of cheese in her mouth.

Joey smirked. She wasn't wrong. That had gone from annoying to disaster-level so quickly — one minute she was trying to scream to be heard above the World's Worst DJ and the next, Nikki was going down hard.

It was an image that she wanted to keep in her brain forever.

"You didn't have to do that," Joey said.

"Yeah, I did," Sunny said, shrugging. "I would do it again."

"I don't think violence is the answer," Joey started.

"Oh, spare me. She deserved worse than what I gave her," Sunny said.

"Why?"

"Because Nikki threw The Worst Pizza Party Ever," Sunny said, her eyes wide as though it was obvious.

"So?" Joey failed to see the connection.

"Think about it. She threw an engagement party for the couple she was homewrecking," Sunny said. "She did it *on purpose*, probably to make Raina panic and realize she was in way over her head. She threw that party to push Raina into breaking up with you. And then she acted like she was trying to smooth things over, like she was still your friend while lying to your face."

Joey set her calzone down in its box, suddenly losing her appetite. "Fuck, you think so?"

Sunny nodded. "I had my suspicions, but they just confirmed them."

Joey blinked back the tears that were threatening to overflow.

She was embarrassed and ashamed, more than anything. She no longer felt heartbroken over Raina, but the fact that she'd been the butt of the joke for a year made everything feel awful all over again.

"Aw, I'm sorry if I brought up bad memories. Raina sucks, and Nikki really sucks, and you don't–"

"No," Joey cut her off, wiping her snotty nose on her arm. "I just love you so much. Thank you for always having my back."

Sunny laid her head on Joey's shoulder. "I know you'd do the same for me."

"Yeah, if Mike–"

"Mitch."

"Whatever. If Mitch ever treats you wrong, I'm going to punch him, too," Joey said.

"I'd rather you didn't."

"Why?"

"Because punching people like, really hurts," Sunny said, giggling.

Joey was so grateful for Sunny. She couldn't describe the love she felt for her sister, especially tonight.

Joey laughed. "Touche. Come on, let's go home and watch a movie on the couch and eat these in our pajamas. And we can ice your hand."

Kendall's arm snaked over her bare stomach.

Joey sighed, still mostly asleep, but aware enough to know that Kendall was touching her. Would the electric jolts through her entire body whenever Kendall even glanced at her ever stop?

She hoped not.

It was kind of fun, being so into someone that the mere gesture of cuddling made her go from asleep to ready in no time flat.

She'd spent the night before with Sunny back in her hometown, and it seemed as though absence made the heart grow fonder. Kendall had asked her to spend the night even before she'd driven back to Denver.

"You can't sleep?" Joey murmured, hugging the pillow closer.

"No," Kendall said, her breath warm on Joey's shoulder blades.

Joey rolled over to face Kendall in the darkness. "Tell me what's on your mind," she whispered. She smoothed back Kendall's hair. "Let me in."

Kendall said nothing, but her movements became more passionate, as though she was suddenly desperate to have Joey. They'd fallen asleep after having sweet, slow sex earlier in the evening, but this was something else altogether.

Kendall's fingers dug into her skin, feeling pleasurable in the pain they caused.

She kissed Joey's neck, climbing over her, and Joey tilted her head, giving Kendall all the access she needed.

"I mean, this is very convincing, but you're going to have to talk to me sometime," Joey said.

"But not right now. I've got other plans right now," Kendall said.

She took Joey's wrists in her hands, moving her hands until they were grasping the metal bars of the headboard.

"Keep them there," she commanded. She paused, staring into Joey's eyes. "Okay?"

Joey nodded, her breath hitching in excitement.

Kendall leaned toward her nightstand, pulling something out of the drawer. Then she moved back to Joey, pulling at her thighs and shifting her own leg until they were entwined.

Kendall reached down and turned on the vibrator, holding it between them as she slowly pushed her hips into Joey's.

"Oh, fuck," Joey said.

Kendall wasn't soft with her. Their hips ground together in mutual pleasure as Joey gripped the headboard so hard she worried the metal might bend.

"I'm there," Kendall said, folding over as she rode the rising waves of her own orgasm.

Just the knowledge that Kendall was close to climaxing sent Joey to the edge, and they cried out together, clutching at one another.

Kendall laid down beside her as they both gasped for breath. Joey's body was slick with sweat and she could see that Kendall was in a similar position.

"Wow, vibrators, who knew?" Joey joked, unsure what else to say.

Kendall exhaled slowly.

They lay in the darkness for a while, their breathing slowly returning to normal as they relaxed.

"Okay, so, are you ready to be honest with me?" Joey pressed.

Kendall looked at her sideways. "What do you mean?"

"What aren't you telling me?" Joey turned onto her side, resting a hand on Kendall's waist. "You can always talk to me, you know that.."

Kendall ran a hand through her short hair. "It's just work stuff. It's boring," she said.

"Don't do that," Joey said.

"I don't know what you want me to say," Kendall said. "Let's just go back to sleep."

"Don't do that. I love you," Joey said, feeling desperate. But the words were true. She *loved* Kendall. With every fiber of her being, she loved Kendall with such overwhelming force that it felt worse to not say it aloud.

Kendall ran a hand over her hair, as though comforting a panicked child. "Thank you."

Translation: I don't love you.

"Thank you?" Joey sputtered.

Kendall nodded. "That's all I can give you right now."

Joey tried to hide the hurt she felt at that statement. Kendall's sudden coldness hurt worse than all the nights she cried over Raina. She felt it so deeply, worse than any outwardly cruel thing Kendall could have said instead.

It felt as though Kendall had resurrected the walls around her heart, opened the gates, and shoved her out into the darkness.

Joey rolled onto her other side, silent tears slipping down her cheeks.

CHAPTER EIGHTEEN

KENDALL

Kendall woke up feeling awful, like she had a feelings hangover. That had to have been a thing, right? She opened her eyes, realizing Joey wasn't beside her. She turned onto her back, stared at the ceiling.

Had she dreamt what had happened the night before? She prayed that she had dreamt it — that look on Joey's face... it read like betrayal.

But how could Joey expect anything more from her?

How could she truly expect Kendall to say those words without the one thing she needed most: Time?

Joey was young, and she had a bad habit of jumping into relationships — she'd admitted as much. She should have known that would terrify Kendall. If she truly did love her already, she should have known that Kendall did nothing quickly and without a lot of thought.

That's just who she was.

When had it all become warp speed ahead? They'd kissed in Hawaii, then made love, and then she blinked and here they were, They'd met eight weeks ago, they were in Hawaii three weeks ago, and now? Well. It seemed a little too soon to be saying anything so serious.

She groaned as she climbed out of bed, her entire body feeling sore and stiff. She remembered fucking Joey, how she'd wanted something so rough that it would consume her thoughts.

It had worked until that dreaded conversation.

She pulled on a robe and shuffled out to the living room, looking around for Joey. They should talk about the night before. She'd been exhausted, but she could have been more gentle in the way she took the news of Joey's feelings.

She poured herself a cup of coffee, glancing out the back door.

Where were Joey and Ozzy?

She looked out the front door to see that Joey's car was gone.

She sighed, rubbing her eyes. It was too early for this. Joey had seriously just snuck out this morning without saying goodbye?

She pulled out her phone, her thumb hovering over Joey's name.

...Maybe Joey needed time. She'd wait. She wasn't avoiding her, of course. She was merely letting time heal the wound. That was the saying, right?

She scrolled past the last text she'd sent to Joey and landed on Imogen's name instead.

Kendall: Good morning. How's Felix today?
Imogen: We get to come home tomorrow!

Kendall smiled. Felix had been in the hospital since the delivery three weeks before. How had time folded into itself — it seemed like only yesterday that Imogen was in the hospital, clutching her hand in terror, and it also seemed a lifetime ago.

Kendall: That's amazing news. I'm so happy for you! Please let me know how I can help.

She'd just have to wait to talk to Gertie about the lawsuit. Sure, it was a selfish thought, but bothering them when they were coming home with a brand new baby seemed more selfish.

She'd received the papers late the week before and had tried her hardest to forget about them all weekend. Luckily, work was so busy that she hardly ever had a moment to think, so she'd been doing pretty well, considering.

There was a box of vegan donuts on the counter that Joey had brought home from Fort Collins the day before. A note on them read: Eat me.

Kendall smirked. She wondered if that was on purpose, some subconscious — or perhaps very deliberate — curse at Kendall for being less than warm the night before.

She took a bite of a donut and opened her phone again.

Kendall: Did you make it home okay?

Three dots appeared as though Joey was typing, then disappeared.

She stared at the screen, willing a text to come through.

Finally, the gray bubble popped up and Kendall read it in anticipation.

Joey: I fed the cats, don't let them lie to you.

Okay, she deserved that.

The cats, to their credit, were mysteriously silent. She walked through the house until she found them spooning in the bathtub. Eggs lifted his head, squeaking at her as if to rudely ask, "What do you want?"

She got dressed for work and made her way out the door

after leaving a little extra kibble in the cat's food dishes, just to remind them who their favorite person was.

The next day, she stood on Imogen's doorstep with a large wrapped present under one arm and a glass food container full of casserole in the other. She'd even put real cheese in the meal.

The door finally opened and an overwhelmed Gertie stood before her. "Come on in," she said.

Kendall hadn't had time to visit Felix in the hospital, and sure, maybe the present was slightly more expensive than she'd have normally sprung for. It was some kind of state-of-the-art monitoring system with cameras and room temperature readings.. it had an app. She had picked it out online in a blind rush the night before.

Even though she hadn't seen them in the hospital, she had done what she could with her limited time, like set up a recurring delivery of groceries and hired a weekly cleaning service, but the guilt still ran deep.

"Where's the man of the hour?" Kendall asked.

"You have to wash your hands before you touch him," Imogen called from the sunken living room off of the dining area.

Kendall handed Gertie the food, set down the gift, and walked into the powder room to wash her hands. She joined the two of them where they were sitting on the couch, falling in a chair beside them.

Imogen held a swaddled bundle in her arms. She looked more tired than Kendall had ever seen her before, but she also looked... Kendall couldn't quite put her finger on it. Content was too tame of a word. She looked satisfied, as though she had everything in the world that could possibly make her happy.

A wave of jealousy stirred inside of her, and then melancholy replaced it.

"How's being home?" Kendall asked, leaning back in the chair.

"Terrifying," Gertie admitted.

"Can you believe they just let us walk out with him? I felt like I was robbing a bank. Like, if I looked back, they'd stop us once they realized they let *us* leave with a baby," Imogen said with a smile.

"I can't believe you guys *made* a baby. And he's just *here* now," Kendall said, unable to wrap her mind around it. Seeing her best friend in this new light was so strange. Sure, she was in her forties, but she'd never been close with any parents before, much less her best friend.

"I can't imagine life without him now," Gertie said, looking down at Felix in the blankets.

"I can't remember what it was like before him, either," Imogen added.

God, would she ever be so lucky to feel so confident about anything that she couldn't remember what life was like before and what life would be like without it?

...Why did that thought bring Joey to her mind?

She shook her head.

"Do you want to hold him?" Imogen asked.

"Uh..." Kendall started. "I don't have to. He seems really breakable. Like babies can't even use their necks, and–"

Imogen stood, placing Felix in Kendall's arms. She sat on the arm of the chair beside her.

"We want you to be his Godmother," Imogen said quietly. "If you want to."

Kendall stared down at the baby in her arms. He was three-weeks-old, but his entire head could fit in her palm with room to spare. He was so tiny. He reminded her of a baby squirrel she'd stabilized a few weeks ago before finding a wildlife rescue that would take him.

Completely helpless.

"Of course," she said. "I don't know what that means outside of the Catholic sense, but..."

Imogen reached down, petting the soft peach fuzz of Felix's head. "It means we trust you with the love of our lives."

Kendall wanted to laugh, given the sheer intensity of the phrase, but she held it back. She looked up at Imogen and saw something entirely new there. Complete trust.

Kendall nodded. "Of course," she said.

Felix began to whimper, and Imogen took him back, walking back to her place on the couch to breastfeed him.

"So, can't help but notice you're without a plus one for the first time in months," Imogen said.

Gertie gave her a sharp look.

"She was busy," Kendall lied.

"What'd you do?" Imogen said.

"Babe," Gertie warned.

Kendall sighed, biting her bottom lip. Maybe it would help to let it all out. "Have any wine?"

An hour later, she had explained the entire situation to them and shared a bottle of wine with Gertie. Imogen had put Felix down in a nearby bassinet.

Gertie shook her head. "I'm not that kind of lawyer, so I can't help you," she said.

Kendall nodded. "That's what I figured."

"I'm not a lawyer, but I *can* help," Imogen began, and Kendall could see a glint in her eye.

"Go on," Kendall said. "I'm open to any and all advice."

"Just fucking admit it," Imogen said, as if it was obvious.

"Admit... what?" Kendall racked her brain for what she had to admit about the business.

"You love her and you're scared to lose her and that's why

you're pushing her away. It's classic Kendall, and it's time someone called you on your bullshit." Imogen rolled her eyes.

"Excuse me?" Kendall asked. "I know you're sleep-deprived, but that's not the truth."

Gertie looked suddenly uncomfortable and stood to take the empty glasses of wine to the kitchen.

"You're lying to yourself," Imogen said, shaking her head.

"No, I'm not," Kendall said.

"You want to lose her?"

"No, of course not."

"Then pull your head out of your ass. And I say that with love."

Kendall narrowed her eyes in frustration. "That's not what's going on here. I'm not *trying* to lose her. Women leave. Women always leave, and it's too exhausting to convince them to stay."

"Well, it's awfully easy to watch them leave when you're the one holding open the exit door," Imogen said, her voice rising.

"I'm trying not to yell at you because you have a newborn but I want to," Kendall said, standing up.

"Yeah, yeah, you're just mad because I'm right," Imogen jabbed.

"I'm mad because six weeks ago you were calling her a pre-teen and accused me of having a midlife crisis, and now you're telling me I'm fucking it up on purpose," Kendall snapped.

"I apologize for the pre-teen comment. I do like her. And I like who you've become because of her, apart from today," Imogen said.

"Make up your mind," Kendall said, running her hand through her hair, sighing in exasperation.

"You know what I think?"

"I'm sure you're about to tell me."

"You're only alone in this world because you choose to be," Imogen said.

Kendall stared at her, too angry to even think.

Gertie stood in the doorway. "You're both exhausted and saying mean things and I don't want Felix to feel this negativity, so you know what? Shut the fuck up. Imogen, you're being a dick. Kendall, she's right. Imogen, go to sleep. Kendall, go home and call Joey."

Kendall paused in confusion. She rarely heard Gertie put so many sentences together or take charge like this.

"And thank you for the casserole," Gertie said, crossing her arms over her chest.

Kendall lay awake, staring at the dark ceiling. The cats were in the bed nestled behind her knees and in front of her chest, keeping her from tossing and turning like she wanted.

She didn't want to admit that she was beginning to wonder if Imogen had been right.

She thought of the breakup with Fiona. Fiona had left her for another woman, but she hadn't even been upset about that part of it. She'd been upset about how damaged her ego had felt. She was ashamed for trusting an untrustworthy person, and how badly it reflected on her. She'd been upset about what people would say. What they'd think.

But not once had she ever been so upset about Fiona being... gone.

Not like how upset she was thinking about Joey being gone.

She sighed, throwing a forearm over her eyes, frustrated with Imogen and with herself.

But if Imogen couldn't call her on her bullshit, who could?

She was being a coward.

She'd let her broken heart and bruised ego dictate decades of her life.

Well, no more.

She climbed out of bed and put on a pair of slippers. She was in the car before she could debate the idea too much in her mind.

It was only when she was on Joey's porch in a set of pajama shorts, a tank top, and bunny slippers that she began to reconsider what she was doing.

She was... what, just going to ask Joey to forgive her? Tell Joey everything?

It had sounded stupidly simple to her just an hour ago...

She pulled out her phone and called Joey. It rang a few times, then went to her voicemail. Had Joey cleared her call?

Had she waited too long?

Her stomach turned over in nervous anticipation.

She looked around, hoping that maybe she'd get lucky and another tenant would come in or out.

She leaned on the porch railing, wrapping her arms around herself as she shivered. Why was it so cold in Denver at night, even in the summer? She wished she was in Hawaii all over again.

"Alright, come on, buddy," she heard a familiar voice behind her. Her entire body flushed with heat, knowing it was Joey. Knowing that she was about to see Joey again. Two days had felt like a lifetime.

She watched Joey walk up the front steps of the house with Ozzy.

She suddenly felt like a creepy stalker. Maybe Joey wouldn't see her, or she could hide and run back to her car and pretend it hadn't happened? How was she going to explain standing on the porch?

Joey paused, fishing her keys out of her pocket.

"Uh, hey," Kendall said, clearing her throat.

Joey jumped in surprise, taking the Lord's name in vain as

she dropped her keys to the ground. She reached into her pocket. She paused when she saw it was Kendall, but then she just looked mad and confused instead of scared and confused.

"What are you doing here?" Joey asked.

"Lurking?" Kendall tried to laugh. "Is that my jacket?"

Joey looked down at the jacket, then back up to her without answering the question.

"What's in your pocket?" Kendall asked.

"Pepper spray," Joey said, standing up straighter. "It's late and Ozzy isn't exactly the best guard dog."

As if to prove her point, Ozzy pulled toward Kendall, wagging his tail so hard that his body wiggled back and forth.

"Good," Kendall said, nodding.

Joey looked her up and down. "Sweet bunny slippers," she said.

An awkward silence stretched between them. It felt like four hours, when in reality, it was probably more like fifteen seconds.

"Can I come inside? It's freezing," Kendall said.

Joey regarded her, then nodded, and they walked in silence up the thousands of stairs to her apartment.

Joey unhooked Ozzy's leash and Kendall walked over to the couch, grabbing a throw blanket. She looked around the apartment, which was still sparsely furnished, but at least it hinted at the fact that someone lived there now. She could see touches of Joey's style throughout, like the tiny dog statue they'd found in Hawaii sitting on the desk near her computer.

"So, why are you walking Ozzy at 2 a.m.?" Kendall asked.

"He has diarrhea," Joey said, shrugging.

Kendall furrowed her eyebrows, kneeling down beside Ozzy. "Oh no, buddy, is that true? What's going on with you?" She reached to feel his stomach.

"You don't have to do that. I know you probably worked a

forty-seven-hour shift today," Joey said, standing in front of her with crossed arms.

"Of course I want to do this. I don't want him to be sick," Kendall said.

"Why are you here?" Joey asked bluntly.

Kendall tried to subtly check Ozzy's gums. They looked pink, which was a good sign that he wasn't too dehydrated. She made a mental note to have Joey pick up unflavored Pedialyte.

"Ken," Joey said.

Kendall stood, taking a deep breath. "I don't want to lose you over this." She said, holding up her palms in surrender. "I *won't* lose you. So, I'm going to tell you what's going on with the clinic."

They sat down on the couch and she relayed the facts. There was a woman suing the clinic for malpractice. She didn't have a fantastic chance of winning, but the smear campaign had just begun, starting with an OpEd about closing Mountain View Vet Hospital in the main Denver newspaper. Luckily, Kendall's name wasn't mentioned in the article, but the clinic had been personally called out several times, and her other patient's owners had begun to ask about it.

Joey listened, wide-eyed, as Kendall finished relaying the information.

She reached to take Kendall's hand. "That's intense," she said. "That's so much for you to be dealing with on your own."

Kendall hadn't let herself think about it that much, but after telling Imogen and Gertie about it, then telling Joey everything in even more detail, she felt exhausted.

"So, I don't know what to do," Kendall said, shaking her head.

"What did Gertie say?" Joey asked.

"Nothing that specifically helped. It turns out lawyers are

very weird about telling you any advice you might act on," Kendall admitted.

Joey thought for a moment, biting her lip as she stared at the far wall over her bed. Then, suddenly, it was as though she had a lightbulb idea pop over her head.

"Okay, hear me out," Joey said. "It's not what you're going to want to hear."

"Seems to be the theme recently," Kendall said. "Go on."

"Let Sheena dissolve the business. Your name isn't on it. You don't have to go down with the sinking ship. Sheena doesn't want to run it, and I'd question your judgment if you wanted to step into a literal trash fire of a situation," Joey began.

"But then I'm jobless," Kendall said.

"*And* all of your patients don't have their regular vet," Joey said, raising her eyebrows as if it was obvious.

"I see what you're getting at, but I don't want to do that," Kendall said. "I don't want to start a private practice. I don't want to start all over again from scratch."

"You're not," Joey said, shaking her head. "You're simply starting a business with a built-in client list. Your patients love you. Your staff loves you. It wouldn't be starting from scratch."

Kendall shook her head. "It's a good thought, but no," she said.

"Why?" Joey asked.

"Because it won't work," Kendall said firmly.

"Why not?"

"It just won't," Kendall said, her voice rising in frustration. "You're looking at this through rose-colored glasses and I'm trying to be realistic."

God, she was fucking this up. She expected Joey to ask her to leave.

She took a deep breath, trying to calm back down.

Joey reached for her hands. "I know change is hard for you," she began.

Kendall wanted desperately to rip her hands out of Joey's grasp and run out the door. Every muscle in her body screamed to run.

But the look in Joey's eyes made her want to stay.

Her heart pounded as adrenaline coursed through her veins, her flight versus fight instinct kicking in.

"Take your time," Joey said, her voice softening. "I know these decisions don't come easy to you, so take your time."

Kendall blinked in surprise.

No one had ever said that to her before.

Why couldn't such a big decision just be out of her hands? Why couldn't she just flip a coin and make the decision that way?

Where was an Adventure Jar when she needed one?

"Wait, I have an idea," Kendall said, standing up. She walked over to Joey's desk area, picking up a piece of paper.

"What are you doing?" Joey asked.

She tore the paper into three slips and wrote, "Start private practice" on one, "Find a job at an established clinic" on the second, and "Wait to see what happens with Mountain View" on the last.

Joey laughed, seeing the slips of paper. "Oh, I see." She held up an empty water glass. "Here, use this."

Kendall dropped the slips of paper into the glass, shaking them around to try not to notice the difference between the way they were folded.

She sat back down on the couch and looked at Joey, who was holding the glass out for her.

"Wait, before I do this, I have to confess something," Kendall said.

Joey's brows drew together in concern. "Okay..."

"I love you."

There. It was out there. There was no taking it back.

Joey's eyes widened. She had clearly not been expecting that response.

"And I need your patience in all other matters, but it's a lie to say that I don't love you. The truth is that I'm scared to love you because I'm scared of what losing you would do to me, and so it's entirely selfish for me not to tell you what I feel," Kendall admitted.

"Thank you," Joey said, repeating the same words Kendall had said to her the night before.

She leaned forward, closing the gap between them. She kissed Kendall softly and without rush, as though they had an infinite amount of kisses left between them.

When she drew back, she held out the glass again. "Now, draw the next adventure."

Kendall took a deep breath. "Okay, I'm ready."

EPILOGUE

JOEY
SIX MONTHS LATER

"The things I do for good pizza," Joey said, taking a deep breath as she turned, looking out the back window of the car at the brightly lit sign above the restaurant door. She had requested they go to her favorite pizza parlor for her birthday — it was time to rebrand the place in her mind away from The Worst Pizza Party Ever to Birthday Date Night. She had even called ahead to make sure they could make a vegan version of their famous Detroit-style pizza.

She was disappointed that Sunny was busy with a sick Elliott and her parents were out of town, but she had Kendall, and she was grateful for that. They were dressed up for a fancy date night, and she was excited to see Kendall's incredible suit again.

They'd made plans to celebrate her birthday the following weekend with Imogen, Gertie, Felix, Roger, and Edward.

"Okay, birthday girl before we go in, I want to give you your present," Kendall said.

"You didn't have to give me a present. We're going to Marseilles next month. That's my present," Joey insisted.

"That's not your birthday present. We pulled that out of the Adventure Jar fair and square. This is your *birthday* present." Kendall raised her eyebrows, giving her an assertive look.

"You don't want to bring it in with us?" Joey asked, holding her cold hands over the heater. The February cold was brutal tonight and she wanted to get inside where it was warm.

"It's not exactly appropriate for the public," Kendall said, a bashful smile on her face.

"Wow, I've never known you to be shy before." Joey giggled.

Kendall handed her a present around the size of a shoe-box. The wrapping paper had tiny dogs and cats all over it.

Joey eyed it skeptically. "And it's not safe for pizza parlor eyes why?"

"Just open it," Kendall said.

Joey tore the gift wrap, finding a nondescript box inside. She pulled at the edges, breaking the tape with a snap. The cardboard scratched as she folded open the top, pushing aside the tissue paper inside.

Her breath caught when she realized what it was. She ran her hand over the smooth leather, the burgundy color contrasted by the brass rivets and metal O-ring. It was a thousand times more gorgeous than the one that Ozzy had ripped up. She reached, lifting it out of the box, feeling its weight in her hands. She held it up, turning it over in her hands. The buckles made it adjustable, meaning that they could both wear it. The thought made her heart beat a little faster.

"Do you like it?" Kendall asked, and Joey glanced at her to find that she looked nervous.

"I love it," Joey said, looking back down at the harness.

"I know you've been wanting one ever since The Harness Debacle of last summer, but–"

Joey cut her off. "Let's skip pizza and go home."

Kendall chuckled. "Easy, tiger. There will be plenty of time when we get home later. But pizza is calling my name."

"Let's get it to go," Joey begged.

"No," Kendall said with a smile, shaking her head.

Kendall opened the door and Joey pulled her coat tighter around her body as she climbed out of the car.

She looked up at the pizza place, taking a deep breath.

Kendall's hand found hers. "Come on, you've been talking this up for so long, I can't wait."

"Maybe this was a bad idea," Joey said, her heart fluttering in her chest.

Kendall kissed the side of her head, wrapping an arm around her waist. "It's just me, you, and some pizza," she said calmly, opening the door.

As soon as Joey stepped inside, she was startled with a loud scream of "Surprise!"

Her eyes widened in shock, her stomach sinking. Was this a terrible recurring nightmare?

But then her eyes focused on the crowd of people in front of her, smiling and cheering and holding ridiculous balloons. She saw her parents, Sunny and Elliott, Imogen, Gertie, Felix, Roger, and Edward. Even Kendall's mom, Lina, was there, standing beside Mom and Dad, wearing a party hat. *A party hat.*

Kendall squeezed her hand. "Happy birthday," she said.

Joey blinked back tears, looking up at Kendall. Standing proudly beside her, holding her hand.

"I love you," she said, pushing up onto her tip-toes to give Kendall a quick kiss as Elliott ran into her arms.

She picked him up, giving him a kiss on his squishy cheek. "Hey, Mister Baby," she said.

"Happy Birthday to me," Elliott exclaimed, holding up his arms.

"Sure, buddy, we can share it," Joey said with a grin.

Sunny rolled her eyes, reaching to smooth back his hair as she gave Joey a hug. "It's Aunt Jojo's birthday, El."

"Aunt Jojo, there's a baby over there," Elliott stage whispered as he pointed to Felix, flapping his arms in a baby holder strapped to Gertie's chest.

"I know, want to go meet him?" Joey asked.

Elliott nodded.

Joey made the rounds, hugging her friends and feeling like her heart was warm and full. She couldn't believe her friends had made the drive from Denver just for her.

She turned to see Kendall joking with her mom and Joey's parents, sipping from a glass of wine. She didn't know what she had done to deserve such an incredible woman, but she'd keep trying to be deserving each and every day.

"Pizza time," Kendall announced, ushering everyone to the table.

They sat around a huge table, passing pizzas and decanters of wine and pitchers of beer as her friends and family loudly laughed and talked and celebrated, and she felt whole.

A server leaned over her, refilling a basket of breadsticks. "Way better than your last pizza party," he said, winking.

"Uh, thanks," Joey laughed, shaking her head.

She noticed Sunny watching the server with a grin.

"I'm Mitch, by the way," he said, giving her a wave before walking to the other end of the table.

She stared at Sunny. "That's *your* Mitch?" She mouthed.

Sunny nodded, giggling.

Joey looked back over the server, then gave Sunny a thumbs up.

Kendall's phone rang, and Joey's heart sank, recognizing

the on-call ring. "You're on call?" She asked, trying to hide the disappointment.

"No," Kendall said, frowning down at her phone. "I'm sorry, babe. I'll make it quick."

She stepped away from the table, talking on her phone in a far corner, then returned, sliding back into the seat beside Joey.

"Do you have to leave?" Joey asked.

"Nope," Kendall said, smiling. "The biggest perk of being the boss is that no one can tell you to be on call. Eduardo just had a question. He says happy birthday, by the way."

Joey grinned, placing her hand on Kendall's knee under the table. Eduardo was the newest vet Kendall had hired at the clinic she had opened a few months before. Things were still rocky as they had just opened, but not in the way Kendall had predicted. Her business had grown *too* fast, and she'd hired two other vets so far, and probably needed at least two more. She'd been working her ass off to make sure her patients were taken care of, but she was still booked out weeks in advance, which she complained about constantly, as if it was a terrible thing.

After dinner, she opened a few presents — a handmade wooden laptop stand from Imogen and Gertie, a set of throw pillows from Roger and Edward with Ozzy's face on one and Bacon and Eggs on the other, a fingerpainting from Elliott, a brand new set of luggage from Sunny and her parents — even Lina had given her a dainty gold necklace with an engraved O for Ozzy.

As the party wrapped up, she hugged everyone, feeling so full of gratitude and love that she thought she might burst.

Lina hugged her tightly, holding her shoulders as she pulled back. "We want to have you girls over for dinner next weekend," she said. "Will you help me convince Kendall?"

Joey nodded, feeling anticipatory, but excited. "Kendall's pretty busy with the new clinic, but we'll definitely find a time soon." Maybe this was the start of a new chapter for Kendall and her dad.

They walked out of the pizza place hand-in-hand. "That was the best birthday of my entire life," she said.

Kendall smiled warmly. "I'm so glad to hear that," she said, walking around to her side of the car.

"Thank you," Joey said, reaching for her hand to kiss her knuckles.

"You're welcome." Kendall nodded, turning on the car to get the heat started. "There's one more thing in that box that you didn't see earlier," Kendall said, nodding towards the box that sat in the backseat.

"What?" Joey asked, confused. She glanced to the box. "What is it?" The thought briefly crossed her mind: Was it an engagement ring? Was she even ready for that? They hadn't even talked about marriage, and she hadn't even thought about it. For once, she had just let herself enjoy where they were, instead of trying to push the moment forward.

"I see that look on your face," Kendall said, raising an eyebrow. "Don't get any ideas."

Joey found herself oddly relieved. She loved where they were and looked forward to their next steps: Moving in together, rescuing a second dog together... There was so much to do that felt more exciting than getting married.

Kendall handed her the box again.

Joey shifted aside the harness, looking beneath more tissue paper. There, in all its gaudy glory, was a big, veiny, rainbow dildo. The exact kind that had smacked her in the face when she had fallen in the sex shop.

"Oh, you got jokes?" Joey said, holding the dildo in her hand.

Kendall giggled, her entire face lighting up with amusement. She reached across the center console to squeeze Joey's hand. "Come on, let's go home and try out our new friend," she said.

"Our new friend, Mrs. Rainbow," Joey said.

"No."

"Roy G. Biv."

"No."

"Rainbow Brite."

"Joseph."

"Kenneth, I'm going to figure this out," Joey said, staring down at the dildo in her hand as they pulled out of the parking lot on their way home.

"I'm sure you are."

"Lady Gay-Gay. Wait, no. Lady Prism."

"No."

"Prism In My Pants."

"Jo."

"Sister Skittles."

"*Joey.*"

THANK YOU!

Thank you so much for reading The Adventurers! It truly means a lot to me that you've come along for the super silly journey that is Kendall and Joey's story.

Want to join my not-spammy newsletter and get sneak peeks of all my new books? You can sign up at: bryceoakley.com/subscribe

ACKNOWLEDGMENTS

Thank you thank you thank you to my gorgeous wife, who supports me endlessly. You are my favorite adventure. I know that's cliche. Just go with it, babe.

Big thank you to my sister who is always my biggest cheerleader and talked to me about this plot for SO long. I can't help but add sisters into all of my books because of you.

To the Dad Jobs group, you're the best people on the entire internet. Our group is the only reason this book was finished on time! I love y'all and your brilliant brains.

Infinitely indebted to my veterinarian roommate for talking me through even the tiniest details.

Maxx Steele, pleeeeeeease write your book already!

And most importantly, thank you so much to all of my readers. I read every email and I cherish your thoughts and reactions and excitement.

ABOUT THE AUTHOR

Bryce grew up in the mountains of Colorado with a taste for adventure and a head full of clouds. She never grew out of either.

She lives in Denver with her partner, two adorable rescue dogs, and a very opinionated cat.